Dream Walker

Dream Weavers, Book 2

Kimberly Dean

Published by Tiger Eye Productions, LLC

Dream Walker
Copyright © 2015 Kimberly Dean
All rights reserved.

Cover design by oliviaprodesign
Vector design by Marisha

ISBN: 0984651195
ISBN-13: 978-0-9846511-9-1

Dream Walker

Research scientist Shea Caldwell has always had a thing for security consultant, Derek Oneiros. He's smart, handsome, and built like a Greek god. As attracted as she is to him, though, she's afraid to let him into her bed – because she's dangerous when she sleeps.

Derek is known amongst his brothers as "The Machine," yet his carefully cultivated control is put to the test whenever he's around Shea. The woman is as beautiful as she is intelligent, but they've always kept things professional – until Derek learns why. Shea is sleepwalking again, but what she doesn't know is that he may be the only one who can help her. For he *is* a Greek daemon, and he's charged with protecting her dreams.

With Shea threatened, Derek makes things personal, and their nights together turn steamy and intimate. He's ready to battle against the Somnambulist that's been controlling his lover in her sleep, yet is the night creature really causing all the harm? When Shea's groundbreaking research notes are stolen, it's clear that other evil forces may be at work.

PROLOGUE

He'd found her again.

The Somnambulist sighed, his particles quivering in delight. His beloved. His She-a! He'd been looking for her for so long. Eagerly, his gaze drifted over the woman lying on the bed beneath him. She looked lovely, welcoming.

Just like home.

He hovered above her, so excited he could barely keep his amorphous form together. He couldn't wait to be one with her again. The energy he felt shimmering in her was so seductive, it made him ache. Waiting no longer, he lowered himself and eased into her from head to toe.

"Ahhhhh." Her energy, her power—he lapped it up like a cat drinking cream. He'd needed this. He'd needed her. "Why'd you try to hide from me, my lovely?"

They were so good together, a perfect match. They came together like no two ever had: she as his hostess and he as her guide. He hugged her arms around her and squeezed tight. He'd missed her so much.

Carefully, he coaxed her into a seated position. She slumped to the side, but he propped her back up by bracing her hand against the mattress. The color of her fingernails caught his attention.

"Hmm." He cocked her head, intrigued. They were a pretty rose color, just a shade lighter than blood.

1

Experimentally, he scratched them over her legs. The stinging sensation made him cry out in delight.

He pushed back the covers and did it again. Parallel lines of pink stung her thighs, and he hummed with pleasure. The sensation was heady, divine.

Just like her. His lovely. His one and only.

Feeling powerful, he swung her legs over the side of the bed and stood. She swayed, but he balanced her and took a hesitant step. One step became two, then ten. Excitement filled him when they neared the top of the stairs.

How fun! Her last home hadn't had a staircase, unless you counted the three steps that led up to the trailer's door. Then again... He frowned, his excitement dimming. The last time they'd gone down those steps, they'd fallen. But he'd had to move her so quickly then...

"We'll be careful," he promised.

She didn't respond—she never did—but they went down the steps together, one at a time. By the last step, the creature felt as if they were floating. Floating on air, dancing through clouds... Inhaling deeply, he waltzed his pretty girl into the kitchen. He could feel every beat of her heart and hear her blood rushing through her veins. Her power bled into him, strengthening him. Feeding him. Yet—

Suddenly, he sensed another presence. A hot, hard attention bored through his hostess right down to him. It was blistering with hatred. Unable to leap out of her so quickly, the creature spun toward the kitchen sink. "Dream Weaver!" he said with a hiss.

But there, framed by lacy curtains, wasn't his natural enemy. The figure wasn't even in the dream realm. It stood outside the window in the backyard, peering inside. The shape was hidden, dressed all in black, but one thing was certain.

It was human.

Human. The creature growled low in She-a's throat and took a step forward. Those hot, hatred-filled eyes blinked in surprise.

2

The next moment, they were gone.

Outraged, the creature stomped toward the window and leaned She-a over the sink. The counter bit into her waist, but he was too angry to enjoy the sensation.

Why couldn't others let them be? Why must they interfere?

Pressing her nose against the glass, he looked outside. Moonlight bathed the backyard, but he saw no figures lurking in the shadows. Still, he slapped the window with the palm of his beloved's hand. She was his. He'd just gotten her back!

The growl in her throat became a snarl. Turning on the ball of her foot, the creature surveyed her home. Windows, windows everywhere.

He lifted an eyebrow, though, when he saw the door to the basement. He opened it, wondering where it led. It swung silently on its hinges, and darkness beckoned. Ooh, more stairs. No windows down there. Excitement made him bounce his She-a up on her toes, and they nearly toppled.

Oopsie. He caught the railing, using her hand. She was so much taller now. But down there in the dark, they wouldn't be interrupted. Down there, they could be alone... and practice.

* * *

It was cold, the kind of cold that worked its way deep into a person's bones... and woke them from a dead sleep.

Groggily, Shea reached for the covers. She let out a soft grumble when she couldn't find them. Rolling onto her side, she wrapped her arms around herself and drew up her knees. They bumped into a soft, lumpy cushion. A warm cushion. Gratefully, she nuzzled closer. The well-worn fabric brushed the tip of her nose, and she settled back down.

Only something wouldn't let her sink back into the slumber from which she'd been pulled. Why was it so cold? It was summertime. But it was dark. It was always cold in the shadows.

Darkness.

With a sharp inhale, she jackknifed upward. The prickles

3

she'd felt running down her spine became something else, and the air she'd inhaled threatened to choke her.

Where was she?

It was so dark, she couldn't see a foot in front of her face. In that split second, she went from being half-awake to being so alert it hurt. She hated the dark. Hated it. And the pitch-blackness surrounding her was the worst. Trying not to panic, she jerkily felt for her surroundings.

She wasn't in her bedroom. She knew that instinctively. There was no nightlight glowing from her master bathroom. She wasn't even in a bed. There was a reason she hadn't been able to find the covers. There weren't any. Blindly, she traced the line of the cushions that had momentarily given her comfort.

"No," she whispered, her throat tight.

She was on a couch, but not the soft microfiber one in her living room. Her shivers turned to shudders. The only other sofa she owned was the old one she'd stored in the basement. The cold, dark, eerie basement.

Her feet hit the cement floor hard. Fighting against the fear, she inched along, waving her arms overhead. Where was that damn light? She was breathing so fast, her throat hurt from the dryness. She took another step forward, and something jabbed into the ball of her foot. With a hiss, she pulled back—only to let out a high-pitched yelp when something brushed her hair.

The light cord.

Spinning around, she batted at it with both hands until she got a good grip. One quick yank, and light from the naked bulb flooded the room.

A whimper escaped her. Being able to see should have comforted her, but it didn't. She stared wide-eyed at the shelves, boxes, and flower-patterned couch in front of her. She was in the basement of her condo.

Unnerved, she rubbed the goose bumps on her arms and double-checked all the corners. There were no monsters lurking, no intruders.

Except for herself.

"Please," she whispered. "Not again."

She'd thought she'd gotten past this.

Slowly, she glanced back to the staircase and followed the steps, one by one, upward. Dread filled her when she saw that the door at the top was closed tight.

"It can't be happening again."

Yet as much as the idea scared her, apparently it was. For the one thing she knew for certain was that she hadn't started out the night here. When she'd fallen asleep, she'd been in her comfy queen-sized bed, two floors up.

"God help me."

Her worst nightmare was back.

CHAPTER ONE

Oneiros Intelligence Services. The name on the door greeted Shea the moment she stepped off the elevator. As always, a shiver of excitement ran through her veins. The warm rush was pleasurable, but the dull ache in her head wasn't. Neither was the tight band of tension around her chest. Nervously, she brushed her hand along the line of her skirt.

Maybe she should have rescheduled. This meeting was important, but she wasn't feeling very well. After last night's... *incident*, she hadn't been able to get back to sleep. Oh, face it. She hadn't even tried. It had been all she could do just to keep the panic at bay. Even today, if she breathed too deeply, she'd touch upon that dark fear.

So she wasn't breathing deeply.

And she wasn't thinking about last night.

She was here to do her job and, honestly, she was glad for the distraction.

As she stared at the name on the door, though, she wondered if that was such a good idea. Whether she thought about last night or not, she was tired and out of sorts. She always felt like she had to be on top of her game whenever she came here.

Or anywhere near Derek Oneiros, for that matter...

"Going down?"

She turned so swiftly on the heel of her white slingback,

her briefcase bounced against her knee. "Excuse me?"

A balding executive had appeared from out of nowhere. He pushed the down arrow for the elevator. "Are you heading down?" he repeated.

"Oh! No." Heat rose up into her face. "Thanks anyway."

Embarrassed, she stepped forward, gripped the handle under the stenciled sign, and determinedly pushed the heavy wooden door inward. Plush carpeting silenced her footsteps as she made her way across the office suite to the receptionist's desk. "Good morning, Ellen."

"Good morning, Ms. Caldwell." The brunette rose from her chair and gestured to the office on her left. "Mr. Oneiros is expecting you. Can I get you anything? Coffee? Tea?"

"Coffee would be wonderful." Anything with caffeine. Absently, Shea swept her hand along her cheek. At least the puffiness under her eyes seemed to have gone down. Now if only she could get her sluggish brain moving. "Cream with two sugars, please."

An infusion of glucose couldn't hurt, either.

"I'll bring it to you as soon as the pot is finished brewing," the receptionist replied. "Please, go right on in."

"Thank you." Tightening her grip on her briefcase, Shea turned toward the private office. She didn't know why she was so tense about this meeting. She worked with Derek all the time. He was the best at what he did. Yet he also challenged her. The man was just an uncanny mixture of *GQ* and genius. It was why she'd hired him.

For his brain, of course. His brain.

"Get it together," she whispered softly under her breath.

She couldn't let him see her so unsettled. They had a professional relationship, but matching wits had become somewhat of a game between them. If he saw for a moment that she was weak or off-kilter, he'd have questions... or be concerned.

Her forehead rumpled. Now where had that thought come from?

Shaking her head, she gave a quick knock on the door.

7

She'd just give him the assignment and leave. Her gray matter wasn't up to much more than that today. He could get the details from the file. She was sure he'd understand.

"Come in."

She hesitated at the sound of his voice coming through the door. Surprisingly, the deep, smooth timbre was calming. Reassuring. Some of the tightness inside her unkinked, and she took the deepest breath she'd managed all day. Letting it out slowly, she opened the door. He was already halfway across the room, coming to greet her.

"Shea," he said, holding out his hand.

Automatically, she caught it in a handshake. "Derek."

His hand swallowed hers, his tough skin brushing intimately against her softer flesh. Inwardly, Shea sighed in pleasure. Genius be damned. She may have hired the man for his intelligence, but she wasn't a nun. His *GQ* appeal was why she always conducted their business in person.

Confused by the direction of her thoughts, she pulled her hand back. "I hope I'm not late."

He didn't answer. Instead, his thumb dragged across the back of her fingers as if he didn't want to let her go. Time pulsed in that instant, and she slowly looked upward. She found him staring at her.

A frown wrinkled his brow. "What's wrong?"

Her stomach took a dangerous dip, and her mouth went dry. So much for hiding anything from him. The extra concealer she'd applied under her eyes apparently hadn't worked.

His intense gaze gentled. "Headache?"

She blinked when she felt her eyes unexpectedly sting. If only that was the extent of her problems. Her panic start bubbling up, seeking escape and comfort, but she forced it back down. He was just being polite. Self-conscious, she lifted her hand to cup her cheek. "Do I look that bad?"

A derisive sound left the back of his throat. "As if you could."

He caught her by the elbow and directed her toward one

of the chairs in front of his desk. "Sit down. Can I get you anything? Aspirin? A cold compress?"

Suddenly, sitting didn't sound like such a bad idea. Shea followed along and sank into the oversized leather chair. It was a relief to remove the stress from her unsteady knees. "I'm fine," she said as she set her briefcase on the floor beside her.

Her tension level shot back up, though, when she came upright and found him way too close. Instead of taking his own chair, he'd settled his hips back against the sturdy oak desk.

"Don't lie." His impeccable gray suit creased as he folded his arms across his chest. "I can see the pain in your eyes."

She licked her tongue across the back of her dry lips. She'd always found Derek an incredibly attractive man, but the way he was hovering over her made him seem bigger. Stronger. With her emotions so close to the surface, all this fussing was making her downright... aware.

"It's not that bad," she insisted.

"I can pull the shades if it's too bright."

"No need." She rubbed her palms against the smooth leather covering the arms of the chair. "Your receptionist is bringing me coffee. That should do the trick."

The lines on his forehead only deepened. "Are you sure?"

Shea crossed her legs. On the job, Derek's tenacity was a distinct plus. Personally, though, it was disconcerting to be on the receiving end of that laser-like focus. "It was just a long night. I didn't sleep well."

Silence fell upon the room.

"Insomnia?" he finally asked, his voice almost gritty.

The reason for his concern became clear, and Shea suddenly wished the ground would open right up and swallow her. "Oh, no. *Not that.*"

Could she be any more inconsiderate? The entire city had recently endured an epidemic of sorts. For reasons unknown, people had gone through weeks with disturbed or non-existent REM sleep. Unable to experience the recuperative power of the dream state, the victims had suffered terribly. Derek's family, in particular, hadn't escaped the aftermath. His brother had nearly been killed by a dream-deprived woman.

"It was just one bad night," she said.

His fingers were wrapped around the beveled edge of the desk so tightly, they'd gone white. One bad night or not, he was concerned. Impulsively, she laid her hand atop of his.

"I promise."

"Are you sure?"

"I'm fine." She gave his fingers a soft squeeze. "I've been dreaming. Lots and lots of dreams."

That seemed to settle him somewhat. He looked down to where she touched him. Even so, she was surprised when he turned his hand and caught hers. The contact sent a thrill through her. When she searched his eyes, though, his dark brown gaze looked haunted and uneasy.

"How is your brother?" she asked softly.

The question seemed to hang in midair. For a moment, Shea thought she'd crossed the line. As much as they'd worked together, she really didn't know him all that well. She had no right to be asking questions about his family, but he was worrying her.

A muscle ticked along his jaw. "Cael's better."

"Is he out of the hospital?"

"He's staying with his girlfriend." Derek looked down at her hand in his. With a soft touch, he aligned their palms more fully. "He's getting stir-crazy, though. Devon's going to have a fight on her hands if she tries to keep him away from the newspaper much longer."

"That sounds good," Shea said, trying to find her voice. The way he was holding her hand was doing funny things inside her chest. "Isn't it?"

"Yeah, it's good."

"So why aren't you more relieved?"

He moved their clenched hands to settle on his thigh. It was the look he gave her, though, that stopped her inclination to squirm in her seat. One look, and she was pinned.

"Why couldn't you sleep?"

The question caught her off guard and, for a split second, threw her right back into the middle of last night. Into her locked basement... Into the dark... Cold fear knotted her gut, and the panic collided with the breath in her throat. His hold on her hand tightened, though, and pulled her back into the present. Into the daylight and into the professional workplace...

Embarrassment hit her hard. Childish nighttime fears had no place here. She slammed a lid on top of her emotions and smoothed her face. "It was just one of those things."

His dark eyes sparked. "Which one?"

She forced a smile onto her lips, but she gave a firm tug on her hand. "I'm happy to hear that your brother is doing so well. I know that your family has been through a lot."

"Shea," he said, refusing to let her go.

"Derek." She wasn't going to wrestle with him, but she wanted her hand back. A knock on the door saved her, and she looked at him pointedly. "That must be my coffee."

Forget the coffee.

Something was wrong. Derek could see it. He could feel it.

"Mr. Oneiros?"

Hell.

"Come in, Ellen," he called. As much as he didn't want to, he dropped his client's hand. He circled his desk before his assistant could get ideas.

"Here's your coffee, Ms. Caldwell," Ellen said as she swept into the room.

"Thank you," Shea replied.

Funny how he knew she wasn't referring to the hot drink.

His receptionist placed the cup and saucer onto the desk. "Can I get either of you anything else?"

"Thank you," Derek said. "I think we're good."

But were they?

He leaned his shoulders back against the filing cabinet and watched Shea. He'd been looking forward to this meeting all morning, but that had been before he'd seen fear in her eyes. Raw, unfiltered fear.

He knew he was touchy about the sleep issue—especially after what had happened to Cael—but the idea that she had somehow been affected? Well, that bothered him a little too much.

He watched as she picked up the coffee cup. He knew he was staring, but that was inevitable whenever she got within sight. The woman was just... perfect. There was no other way to describe her. With that blonde hair and tight, sleek body, nobody could deny she was gorgeous. That world-class brain of hers was a major turn-on, too.

But something was different today.

He watched the way she held the delicate china as if it were a lifeline. Her hands looked dainty and fine. When they shook and the cup tinkled against the saucer, he pinpointed the difference.

Vulnerable. Today, she seemed vulnerable.

He raked a hand through his hair. He'd never seen her in anything but top form. What had happened last night?

"Ah, that tastes wonderful."

She settled back into her chair, and he made himself sit down, too. "I hope it helps. How are things at Biodermatics?" he asked, trying to find a safe, non-threatening topic.

"Very well, thank you. We're quite busy these days."

Busy enough that she was losing sleep?

"I see that you've landed Audrey Lowe as a spokesperson. That's quite the accomplishment."

"It doesn't hurt to have a celebrity endorse your skin care products. We're already seeing an increase in sales."

And, obviously, an increase in headaches. He didn't think she realized it when she reached up to rub her temple, but he did.

He let out a calming breath. There was the possibility that he was overreacting. He had a tendency to do that whenever she came around—*react*. One sleepless night didn't necessarily mean that something was wrong. A neighbor's dog could have yapped all night. Maybe the summer heat had bothered her. Unfortunately, neither of those explanations accounted for the stiff set of her shoulders or the lines of tension around her mouth. That soft, pink, kissable mouth...

"How's the intelligence business?" she asked.

He flicked the notepad in the center of his desk with his forefinger. She wanted to keep things between them businesslike, he knew. Hell, she usually avoided anything personal with him like the plague. Sleep problems, though... You couldn't get much more personal for him.

"You really don't want to know." Opening the top desk drawer, he pulled out a pen. His company specialized in corporate intelligence, data mining, and information security. These days, it was difficult to keep up with the hackers, white-collar criminals, and scam artists.

Too bad he couldn't just get online and figure out what was bothering her.

"You mentioned on the phone that you wanted a background check done," he said gruffly. "Are you hiring a new research scientist?"

"Actually, no." She seemed relieved now that they were talking about business. Putting her coffee aside, she reached for her briefcase.

The movement pulled at her white suit jacket, and his gaze fell on the vee neckline in a decidedly unbusinesslike manner. She was wearing one of those close-fitting, tailored suits that brought to mind questions of what might lie underneath. On edge, he waited for a peek of something more. A bra strap... something lacy... skin?

Skin.

His body started to hum. The tiny diamond pendant of her necklace swung to the side, though, and glinted at him in warning. Letting out a quick breath, he shifted in his chair.

"Phillip and I decided that we need another administrative assistant."

Phillip. Even with the warning, Derek wasn't prepared for the cold dash of water that was thrown over his libido. His pen poked a hole in the paper, and he grimaced. Ripping it off the tablet, he crumpled it and threw it in the trash.

"Tamika is great, but there's just too much work for one person," Shea continued. "We really need someone to assist each of us."

Us. As in the two of them. Together. Derek's hand fisted around his pen. Whatever had spooked her last night, good old Phillip had certainly been there to take care of her.

She settled the briefcase on her lap, popped the latches, and thumbed through files. She handed one to him and looked at him expectantly.

The feel of her gaze on him made Derek tear his thoughts away from the unwanted visions in his head. Visions of Shea and her too-good-looking partner. He looked at the manila folder and tried to think.

"An administrative assistant," he said.

"Yes." She glanced up as she put her briefcase back on the floor. "Why?"

He let one eyebrow lift. Saying nothing, he opened the file. The applicant's résumé sat on top, and he gave it a quick once-over. The facts entered his head on autopilot, though, for his mind was already churning over other things. Like maybe he'd been onto something with his original work stress idea...

Tapping his finger on the corner of the file, he shot a look at Shea. As long as it was good work stress, he supposed that was okay. Short-term, that was.

"Congratulations," he said.

"Congratulations? For what?"

He smiled at her. "You've made a breakthrough."

He had to give her credit. Other than a slight widening of her eyes, she didn't give anything away. It piqued his interest even more.

"Things are going a bit better with my research." She smoothed the edge of her skirt over her knee. "But what makes you say that?"

She was always so careful when she talked about her work.

Part of it was humility, but there was something else... Sometimes he almost got the feeling she didn't want to jinx anything.

He understood why. The implications of her research could be so far-reaching.

Skin care products were Biodermatics' primary market, but Shea's personal efforts were focused on the medical dermatological market. Specifically, she was working toward better treatment for burn victims. Very few people knew that, and she paid him good money to keep it that way. Even under a confidentiality agreement, she'd only given him enough information so he could do his job.

Yet the pressure had to be there. The stress could be getting to her, and stress could do bad things to sleep patterns...

He leaned forward onto his elbows. "You've never had me do this thorough of a background check for a lower-level employee before."

"I think we need to change that."

"Okay," he said slowly. "I'll get on it."

A shy smile of appreciation pulled at her lips. "And our wrinkle cream is doing quite well, thank you."

Her blue eyes twinkled, and Derek felt his body harden. Oh, yeah. Major breakthrough. The woman was smart, classy, and devastatingly sexy.

No wonder she was taken.

Fuck.

Rubbing the back of his neck, he glanced down to the résumé. "So... Lynette Fromm. What do you think of her?"

Shea played with her necklace as she gave his question some thought. "She seems bright and enthusiastic. She's called several times expressing interest in the position."

"But?" His attention was suddenly drawn to the soft skin behind that pendant.

"But she's called several times expressing interest in the position." She shrugged and dropped her hand to the arm of the chair. "I just want to be sure."

"Because of the wrinkle cream."

She grinned. "Precisely."

Derek's pen skidded and poked another hole in the paper. Damn. If she smiled at him like that one more time, he was going to close the shades. There was a sofa just across the room. He'd make sure her sleep was safe and sound.

He raked a hand through his hair. *Focus, man. Focus.* "Got it."

He skimmed through the information. "She has strong computer skills."

"And a degree in chemistry, so she should pick up pretty quickly on the technical lingo we throw around."

"There's a two-year break in her work history," he said, latching on to the discrepancy.

Shea reached for her coffee again. "She claimed she was taking care of an ill parent."

He flipped to the page of notes she'd taken. As expected, they were meticulous. "I'll reach out to her references."

"But applicants always list people that will give them good recommendations. You taught me that."

And she'd been a quick study. Giving up, he closed the file and set his pen atop it. Everything seemed straightforward enough—except for this little dance they were doing. She had his brain scattered all over the place.

"This shouldn't take long. Is there anything else you want me to check into?"

Anything at all?

"That's it."

It wasn't much for the trip over here. "All right. Do you want me to call you with what I find, or should I drop by your office?"

She blinked as if he'd said something that surprised her. He became even more curious when she blushed.

"You can stop by the lab," she said after a moment's hesitation. "That's where I'm spending most of my time these days."

He nodded. Whatever she was working on, it was big. He

16

just wished she'd let him in a little more—on this and anything else she needed to share.

"How's the headache?" he asked softly.

Her lips parted in surprise. "Better."

Reflexively, his gaze dropped to her mouth. "Good, I'm glad."

He hated the idea of her hurting, especially if it had anything to do with sleep. "Shea, if there's ever anything else you need help with, you can always turn to me."

She hesitated. "That's very kind of you."

Kindness had nothing to do with it.

"It doesn't have to be work. You can trust me, whatever it is." He paused, suddenly unsure. He was venturing into uncharted territory, that land between professional acquaintances and friends. "You know that, don't you?"

The air was suddenly charged with electricity. He felt it, and apparently, so did she.

Quickly, she put down her coffee and reached for her briefcase.

"Well, thank you," she said, uncrossing her legs. "I should get back to work."

He was on his feet before she could stand. Damn, he'd pushed too far. "Why don't you go home for the rest of the day? Take it easy and get some rest?"

The suggestion was out before he could stop it. The uncharacteristic impulsiveness surprised even him. He had no right to be telling her what to do. No outward right to be concerned.

Yet he was.

She paled, but covered it with a smile. "If only I could. You know how it is when you own your own company."

There it was again, the fear. *She was afraid to sleep.*

His concern sharpened, and he leaned towards her.

Showing less grace than normal, she turned on her heel. "Thank you for your time, Derek."

He caught up with her quickly. "I'll drop by as soon as I've got the information you need."

"Informa… Oh, yes. The background search. Right."

"And Shea?" He stopped her halfway out the door.

She paused and glanced over her shoulder. "Yes?"

"Have sweet dreams tonight."

Her pretty blue eyes widened. "I… I will. I'm sure last night was a one-time thing. At least I hope it was…"

He'd make sure of it. It was, after all, his night job.

He watched her walk out of the office.

She didn't know it—and never would—but he had a vested interest in her dreams. *In everyone's dreams*, he quickly chastised himself. They were his family's domain—their responsibility and very reason for being.

For he was one of the Oneiroi, modern-day Dream Weavers.

Descended from Greek gods, it was their job to bestow dreams upon sleeping humans. At night, while others slept, his kind slipped into the dream realm to do their work.

Yet they'd failed recently.

And failed miserably.

The incident with Cael and his girlfriend, Devon, had opened a door that should have remained closed. He and his brothers were still cleaning up the mess, but the idea—even the slimmest possibility—that Shea was somehow feeling the repercussions?

It made him ill.

So whether it had been insomnia, heat, or yapping dogs, he was going to figure out what had disturbed her. Because one restless night for her was one too many for him to allow.

CHAPTER TWO

Sweet dreams.

Shea rubbed her fingers absently up and down her breastbone as she stared at the bed. She'd just taken a nice, long, relaxing bath. Sleep pulled at her, but she didn't want to close her eyes. She didn't want to give up control—not after what had happened last night—but Derek Oneiros had told her to have sweet dreams.

Warmth rushed through her. Did he know what his words would do to her? Did he know what pictures they would put into her head? Her fingertips brushed against the swell of her breasts. Probably not.

Sighing, she rubbed her hands together to get rid of the remaining lotion. He'd just been concerned for her well-being. She'd seen it in the way he'd looked at her. She'd felt it in the way he'd held her hand.

To be honest, she was concerned for herself, too.

After leaving his office, she'd thrown herself into her work, but no matter how much she'd tried to avoid thinking about it, she couldn't forget waking up in the basement this morning. In the darkness... With the chill pressing down on her... A shudder ran through her. Unfortunately, as scared as she was to put her head on that pillow again, she knew she had to do it. Being overly tired only made things worse.

She knew from experience.

She shut off the overhead light in the bathroom, but the momentary lack of vision startled her. She hadn't realized how dark it had gotten outside. Reflexively, she swatted at the nightlight over the counter. The dim bulb illuminated the room gently, softening all the hard edges.

Softening the fear.

Before doubts could creep back in, she hurried to the bed. She pulled the covers over herself and reached to set her radio alarm. It was then that she saw that one of the drawers in her dresser wasn't fully closed.

"Damn it," she whispered, unable to look away. As much as she wanted to believe it wouldn't happen again, that a bath had melted away her stress, she knew better than to risk it. The battle within herself lasted all of ten seconds. Giving in, she got up to close the drawer. She looked around for other dangers.

The chair. She sighed.

She hadn't had to do this since she was young, yet out of long-ingrained habit, she slid the potential obstacle under the vanity. That was a side effect of sleepwalking that most people never thought about—she ran into things when she wandered about in the night. As a child, bruises had just been a fact of life. Where they'd come from, she'd never known.

She put her hairbrush in a drawer, and the wastebasket caught her attention next. She tucked it up against the wall. She worried her lower lip with her teeth as she looked across the room. She really shouldn't have to… She walked over and locked her bedroom door anyway.

She evaluated the room one more time. The bedrail could cause a problem. So could the sharp edges of the bedside table. There just wasn't anything she could do about them.

"Have sweet dreams tonight."

She heard the words in her head just as the tension was starting to return. They sent warmth through her, calming her. She remembered the look in Derek's dark eyes, and her shoulders relaxed. If she just concentrated on him, how could she have anything else?

She returned to the bed and tried to find a comfortable place on her pillow.

The man saw too much. He'd picked up on her research breakthrough without her saying a word. And her other secret!

She rolled onto her back. When he'd asked if he should call or deliver the findings of his background check in person, she could have sworn he knew how she felt about him.

Discomfited, she ground the back of her hand against her forehead.

Sweet dreams...

Why had he had to say that?

Sweet dreams...

He'd held her hand.

Sweet dreams...

"Come in."

Shea hesitated at the sound of the voice coming through the door. Surprisingly, the deep, smooth timbre was calming. Reassuring. She opened the door and found Derek already halfway across the room, coming to greet her.

"Shea," he said, holding out his hand.

Automatically, she caught it in a handshake. "Derek."

His hand swallowed hers, his tough skin brushing intimately against her softer flesh. Inwardly, she sighed in pleasure. The man was just so gorgeous. She took in his dark hair, handsome face, and mesmeric eyes.

Not to mention his rock-hard body.

Surreptitiously, she let her gaze slide down. What she wouldn't give to see what lay under those business clothes. Some men could hide under a suit. On him, it just seemed to accentuate all those muscles.

Confused by the direction of her thoughts, she pulled her hand back. "I hope I'm not late."

He didn't answer. Instead, his thumb dragged across the back of her fingers as if he didn't want to let her go. Time pulsed in that instant, and she slowly looked upward. She found him staring at her.

"What's wrong?" he asked.

Her stomach took a dangerous dip. So much for verbal sparring. She hadn't had to say a word for him to notice she was hurting.

His intense gaze gentled. "Headache?"

She blinked when she felt her eyes unexpectedly sting. "Do I look that bad?"

A derisive sound left the back of his throat. "As if you could."

Her heart jumped. What?

"Come over here. Let me take care of you." Instead of leading her to his desk, he caught her by the elbow and directed her across his office to the sofa that sat in front of the picture windows. The vantage point offered a breathtaking view of the city of Solstice. The sunny skies made the skyline look crisp and bright.

"Sit down," he said. "Can I get you anything? Aspirin? A neck rub?"

Her stomach took another unexpected dip, and her body heated. "A neck rub?"

"Of course." His hands circled her waist and urged her down. For a moment, she resisted. They were professional colleagues. A neck rub seemed out of place...inappropriate... or did it? Just the thought of his hands on her made her nipples stiffen beneath her prim and proper suit. Her unsteady knees gave way, and she sank sideways onto the luxurious leather sofa. It felt warm and supple under the sunshine. "I'm fine," she said as she set her briefcase on the floor beside her. "Really."

"You don't always have to be so strong."

His lips were right against her ear when she sat back up. He'd settled onto the sofa beside her with one knee hooked onto the seat. His shin pressed tight against her buttocks, and it was all Shea could do not to wiggle against him. She'd always found him incredibly attractive, but this close he seemed bigger. Stronger. Like someone she could lean on.

Uneasiness swept over her. She needed to be responsible for herself.

"Maybe I'll move over here," she murmured.

She shifted toward the oak coffee table, but he hooked his arm around her waist. "Is it too bright? I'll pull the shades."

Her fingers bit into the cushions when he leaned across her to catch the drop cord. She could sense everything about him. His muscled arm brushing her shoulder... His hot breaths against her neck... With a twist of his fingers, he turned the blinds and muted the harsh sunlight.

"Is that better?"

If anything, it was too dim and intimate. Too cozy.

She straightened to nearly military attention when his hands settled on her shoulders. "You're tense."

"I had trouble sleeping," she confessed.

"Why?"

His voice was suddenly serious, his touch firm and protective. For a split second, it made her wonder if he knew of the dark creatures that roamed the night. But no. He couldn't know. He was a smart, levelheaded man. He wouldn't venture into the mythical world of children's horror stories that had ruled her life.

Still, his fingers bit into her skin. One bad night or not, he was concerned. Impulsively, she reached up and laid her hand across the back of his knuckles. She gave them a soft squeeze. "It was just a one-night thing, Derek. I promise."

"You can turn to me if you need help, Shea."

"I... I know."

"It doesn't have to be just business."

She melted a little. They'd crossed over the "just business" line practically the moment she'd walked in the door. Still, this was new territory for them.

His hands began moving again. His thumb found a stubborn knot on the side of her neck, and her eyelids drooped. It felt good. The massage... Him being so close... Her body slackened, and she started to lean into the strength she felt behind her.

"That's better." His voice had dropped lower and so had his hands. His thumbs were exploring deeper and deeper under her collar, discovering sensitive spots. "Just relax."

Her suit jacket was in the way, so he tugged the collar down to get better access. The movement pulled the material tighter against her breasts, outlining their shape and form. Shea bit her lip to keep from moaning as the material rubbed against her nipples.

"Do you mind?" he asked, his hands suddenly sliding around to the three covered buttons that kept her jacket together...

She took a deep breath as she stared at his hands. There was a reason why she kept things business-like between them, but she couldn't remember it. And what he was doing felt so good...

"Please," she found herself saying. She watched with fascination as he

deftly undid the top button. Then the second. And the last.

"Do you know how long I've wondered what you wear under these sexy business suits?"

His mouth was against her ear, and his chest was pressed against her shoulders. A different kind of tension entered her when he caught the lapels of her jacket and began to peel if off her.

She found herself helping, shrugging out of the confining material. Both his hands settled onto her stomach then. The contact was intimate and sexy. Slowly, his touch slid upward.

"You need to let go of the stress," he said. Her back arched as his palms slid over her breasts, caressing the soft fabric of her bra.

"Derek," she sighed.

She shifted as his hands continued to skim over her. His touch was driving her crazy. When his strong fingers settled on her shoulders again, though, she almost felt disappointed until he began to massage her for real. Skin to skin. Heat to heat.

She groaned and let her head drop back against his shoulder. She felt his gaze move over her. If she'd thought him intense before, it didn't compare to how he looked at her naked. Her breaths quickened. Even so, she was surprised when his fingers glided across her chest to the front clasp of her bra. He turned it loose, and anticipation shot through her as the cups drooped to the side.

On edge, she waited. When she glanced over her shoulder, though, his dark brown gaze looked haunted. Uneasy.

"What kept you up last night?"

The question threw her. "Excuse me?"

"Why couldn't you sleep? Why are you afraid of the dark?"

Suddenly, everything changed. The office disappeared, and Shea found herself in her locked basement... in the dim light, with only one weak bulb holding back the darkness... She was sitting on her old, flower-patterned sofa, and she smelled something. A hot, acrid odor hung in the air.

It was a terrible scent, one she recognized. Cold fear knotted her gut, and the panic bubbled up, choking her.

Abruptly, she realized she wasn't alone. Soft breaths sounded behind her.

There was a presence in the basement with her.

"No," she moaned. It was here with her! She couldn't bear it. She couldn't look.

"Hey, now," a deep voice murmured into her ear. "Easy."

She twisted sharply. "Derek!"

He was there with her. Wrapping an arm about her waist, he pulled her onto his lap. His warmth hit her back, and his strength enveloped her. She could feel his arousal pressing against her bottom.

Terrified, she glanced about the room. The smell was seeping into her very pores. She could practically taste it. "You can't be here," she said, clutching at his wrist.

"I won't leave you." His fingers spread wide over her bare belly in a protective gesture, but his other hand went to her breast. He began toying with her taut nipple, and the clash between fear and desire was sharp. It caught Shea right where she was most vulnerable, deep between her legs. She pressed her thighs together tightly and caught at his muscled leg.

"We have to get out of here!"

"But how did we get here, Shea?"

"I... I don't know."

His hot breath brushed against her neck and goosebumps popped up on her skin. "I think you do."

She heard a sound. A crackle?

"No," she whispered. "It can't be happening again."

"What can't be happening again?"

"You have to leave. I don't want you hurt. Ah, Derek!"

The hand at her belly had become bolder, the fingers sliding under the waistband of her skirt.

"Tell me," he said. "Tell me why you couldn't sleep last night."

Her gaze flicked around the basement, trying to track the source of the smell. Where was the noise? It was getting louder, the popping and the hissing. "I thought I'd outgrown it."

"Outgrown what? You can trust me. I've got you."

"No," she said, shaking her head. "It's got me. It's found me again."

Her breaths became choppy, her inhalations too short. Her lungs ached as they struggled to get the oxygen they needed. Her gaze went up the staircase, and she let out a cry when she finally found it. A flickering orange glow filled the space at the bottom of the door. Smoke was pouring *in, and the crackle was coming from the wood itself.*

Derek's embrace tightened, and he tucked her up against him more closely. "What's found you, Shea? What's gotten hold of you?"

Gotten hold of. Taken over. Assumed control.

Possessed her.

Oh, God. Not again. Fire! Fire! It had made her do it again!

Shea came awake with a jolt. Air rasped in her throat, making it burn as she gobbled up deep breaths. Her chest ached, and her entire body shook.

She nearly knocked her bedside lamp onto the floor when she grabbed for it. She finally got the knob twisted. Light popped in her eyes, causing spots to appear in her vision, but she didn't care. She just needed to keep the shadows at bay.

Quickly, she searched the room. The space under the door was empty. No flames leapt. Smoke didn't unfurl. Her home was safe and silent, except for her harsh breathing and racing heart. She could hear it pounding in her ears.

Yet none of that mattered.

A nightmare. This time, it had all been a nightmare.

She made the conscious effort to calm herself. She forced her breaths to slow, but there wasn't much she could do about her heart. With a groan, she flung off the covers. Her legs were unsteady as she made her way to the bathroom.

She found her nightlight glowing faithfully, and she patted it like a beloved pet.

She turned on the faucet, but she came to a dead halt when she glanced up at the mirror. Her eyes were wide, and her skin was pale, but that wasn't what surprised her. Mixed with the lingering fear was something else entirely. Lifting her hand, she touched a strand of blonde hair. It was tousled about her shoulders, and her eyes looked smoky.

She looked aroused.

Her cheeks turned a rosy red in the mirror. She *was* aroused.

She braced her hands on the vanity. Water rushed into the sink as she stared at her reflection. Now that the panic was tapering off, she could tune in to other things, and her body was aflame. Her nipples were hard as little pebbles, and her belly was fluttering.

"Oh, damn."

She splashed water onto her face. It was cold and bracing, but it did nothing to change the way she felt. Blindly, she grabbed the hand towel she kept next to the sink and buried her face in the soft terrycloth. She hadn't known it was possible to feel so good and so bad at the same time.

"Sweet dreams," she whispered.

More like hot dreams. Wet dreams.

With a nightmare to cap it all off.

With a harsh twist, she turned off the faucet and tossed the towel back onto the rack. Derek Oneiros. Derek Dream. She shook her head at the coincidence. She wondered if he knew the Greek origins of his name. "Oh, who am I kidding? The man knows everything."

Knew everything. Saw everything.

Pinpricks hit the back of her neck as she stopped in the doorway and faced the bed. Her meeting with him today had been different. More intimate and distracting.

Obviously, he'd gotten into her head.

She let out a sigh. It was already such a crowded place.

Turning her back on the bed, she headed to the dresser. There was no way she was going to be able to fall asleep again anytime soon, and sitting around here wasn't the answer. Not with the way her body was aching... Not with the way her brain was standing on guard...

It was late, but there was only one place she could go and totally forget herself. One place where she always felt safe and in control.

She was going to her lab.

CHAPTER THREE

The room felt cool in the post-midnight hours. Cool and still, yet alive. Breath wisped into quiet air. Hearts beat inside chests. Warm skin brushed against soft sheets. A breeze filtered in through the open windows as Derek stood looking down at the woman's bed. She was sound asleep, utterly relaxed with the covers thrown aside.

Then again, she always slept well. She was one of his best sleepers. She could sleep anytime and anywhere.

Only tonight, it looked as if she'd had help.

He took a step closer and felt the heat that radiated from the entangled bodies. Sex still lingered in the air, but he didn't worry about waking the lovers. They couldn't see him, they couldn't hear him, and he wasn't here to harm them.

He was here to help them dream.

By day, he was like anyone else, running his own business and trying to keep up with the rat race. By night, he was part of something bigger, an inheritance passed down since ancient times. The Oneiroi were responsible for maintaining the balance in the nighttime world. Dreams allowed humans to work through their issues, to explore their wants and needs.

So, while he was in the room with the couple, he remained in the dream realm, a parallel universe where only creatures of the night dwelt. It was here that Dream Weavers' spirits traveled as they went from sleeper to sleeper, bestowing dreams.

As tightly as she was being held, the woman was his—one of his charges, a sleeper assigned to his care. And right now, her brain waves were calling to him, needing him to lead her into REM sleep.

He shook his head at the scene splayed out before him. This might be the only sleep she got tonight. "Let's get you dreaming before you're wakened for more."

This relationship was new and, honestly, surprising.

Yet he wasn't here to judge. He was here to do his duty.

Concentrating on the task at hand, he reached over a man's sleeping form and touched his charge's forehead. Her skin was warm and supple. As if sensing him somehow, she murmured and lifted her hand so it lay palm up on the pillow next to her head. The gesture was open. Trusting.

A Dream Weaver's power lay in his ability to manipulate brain waves, and through his fingertips Derek sensed large, slow delta waves. The woman was in stage three of the sleep cycle. Hormones were coursing through her body, restoring the breakdown that had occurred in her cells over the course of the day. He needed to switch that restoration work to her brain.

Humans needed to dream. It was important both psychologically and physically. If he and his brothers hadn't known that before, it had been driven home by what had happened with Devon and Cael.

The man between them shifted, and Derek paused. He wasn't one of his. He'd never even seen him before, yet the way the guy's hand was wrapped around his charge's backside, he was sure he'd see him again. And soon.

Finally, the man settled down, and Derek tuned in more fully with his charge's brain wave patterns. He waited for the K-complexes to come, natural spikes in her brain waves that would signal she was ready to move into the dream state.

"There you go," he said, catching one of the spindles as they passed by.

Gently, he started to lead the woman up into REM sleep. Her breaths quickened along with her pulse rate. Her eyes began moving back and forth under her eyelids in the characteristic rapid movement that gave the stage its name. The other muscles in her body went rigid, though, as a natural protective mechanism.

"Good girl."

He waited for the movie to start to unfold in her head. He'd led her this far, but it was time for her to take over. He rarely intervened in his charges' dreams. Unlike some of his brothers who liked to play, he let his dreamers choose their own paths. They needed to sort out their own fears and desires, not play puppet to his.

Although sometimes it was tempting...

He finally let his gaze drift over the erotic scene. As far as assignments went, this one wasn't tough. His charge was an attractive woman. She was short but curvy, pleasant without being cloying. Her blonde hair spread across the pillow under her head, a bright contrast against the navy-blue pillowcase, and his gaze stuck on the soft tresses.

Her hair was darker than Shea's, more like warm honey. Shea's was softer, sunlit. His charge's curves were more opulent than his client's. Shea's breasts were firmer, her waist trimmer, and her legs... He let out a long breath. She had great legs. Long, sleek legs that put dangerous, distracting thoughts into his head.

A tingle suddenly caught the back of his neck, and his concentration jerked back to the here and now.

Something else was entering the room, something non-human.

"Damn it." He'd let his thoughts be diverted.

Leaving his hand cupped over the woman's brow, he turned and braced himself. Dream Weavers tried to remain neutral in the night world. They didn't seek out confrontation, but when their charges were threatened, they fought to protect them. Right now, his charge was vulnerable as she slipped into the dream state.

A form appeared in front of him, faint at first, then becoming more solid and visible. Derek lifted his free hand, ready to do battle. The thing was big. His muscles tensed. Night creatures tended to avoid his kind, but when they were hungry enough, *needy enough*, they could be unpredictable.

Like this one obviously was.

"Whoa!" the thing said when it materialized. Only it wasn't an *it*. It was a man who flinched and ducked when he realized another presence was in the room. "Ease up, Derek. It's me."

Derek rolled his eyes. "Don't sneak up on me like that, Tony."

"Hey, I wasn't sneaking. Your head was somewhere else— probably for the first time in recorded history." His brother looked to the bed, and his eyebrows shot up. "Now I see why. That's *hot*."

"Is this your charge?" Derek nodded toward the man in his way.

"No, but that one is."

Derek's jaw hardened as he looked across the woman to the third person occupying the bed. "That one" concerned him. Scarred and tattooed, he didn't look like the kind of man his charge would let inside her home, much less into her bed. Yet the way the tough guy nuzzled his face into her hair and cupped her breast possessively told Derek he'd had her. Repeatedly.

"I don't like him," Derek said.

"Ah, he's not that bad. He's an ultimate fighter, but he's got a good heart."

Derek slowly lifted his palm from the woman's forehead. She was dreaming feverishly, but not about the men. She was racing an Indy car going around the track faster and faster, out of control.

Tony grinned. "She must be a wild one."

Derek planted his hands on his hips. "She teaches first grade. This isn't like her."

"Oh, give her a break. Most people need to cut loose every now and then."

Derek stiffened at the not-so-subtle jab. He knew his brothers considered him the unyielding one, The Machine, but he took his responsibilities seriously. Someone had to. In this case, his concerns had nothing to do with his charge's dreams or her sleep patterns. He didn't like the idea of her taking on more than she could handle. He didn't want her getting hurt.

She reminded him too much of Shea.

Not in terms of looks or even personality. It was the softness, the femininity, the vulnerability…

Shit.

He glanced at the clock on the bedside table. Was she sleeping soundly tonight? Had whatever scared her been taken care of? He inhaled deeply and smelled the candle on the dresser. The char reminded him of her fear. He could practically taste the metallic bitterness on his tongue, and it made his gut tighten.

Troubled, he glanced out the open window at the clear night sky. He could still go to her, could still check on her…

The knot in his gut twisted.

Or not.

He wasn't her Dream Weaver.

Tony cleared his throat. "Uh, are you going to handle that other poor boy? He looks pretty wiped out from here."

Derek looked at the threesome, ready to be gone, yet Tony was busy leading his charge into what was, no doubt, a bawdy dream. It would be a waste of time for another Oneiros to visit the house. Impatience tugged at him, but he slid his hand over the remaining sleeper's forehead.

Tony's eyebrows drew together. "What's up with you tonight? You seem preoccupied."

"Long day." Derek glanced again at his charge. He'd been trying to get hold of Zane ever since his morning meeting with Shea. Gods help him, but his younger brother was the one responsible for her dreams. At the very least, Zane should know if she'd been having sleep problems.

Or if he was the source of them.

Derek's fingers curled against the man's forehead. If there was anyone in the family more unlike him, it had to be Zane. Zane, the irresponsible slacker. Zane, the irrepressible flirt. If his brother had put some of his patented erotic dreams in Shea's head, he'd have him by the throat.

Although she hadn't acted like her problem was erotic dreams...

"Ah, hell," Tony said.

Derek's gaze flashed to the fighter and then up to his brother. "What is it? Is he not dreaming?"

Tony's attention was on the woman. "You look like you want to punch something. Do you have a thing for her?"

"For *her*? No."

"Well, the way you were looking at her..." Tony's head snapped up. "Not her, but someone else?"

Derek rolled his shoulders. It had been worse than just a long day; it was becoming a very long night. "It's a work thing."

"I've never seen you get this knotted up over work." The look on Tony's face turned curious. "Did you get into it with someone? Because that's not like you."

"No, it's nothing like—" The man underneath Derek's touch suddenly dove into the dream state, and Derek was assailed by vivid pictures of him going down on his blonde charge. Derek jerked his hand away, but it was too late. The real reason he couldn't go check in on Shea came into his head with startling, unsettling clarity.

He didn't want to see her that way with Phillip.

Yet even as he tried to push the pictures away, they kept coming at him. Shea easing into Phillip's arms, snuggling against him, kissing him, and climbing astride.

Turning away from the bed, Derek raked a hand through his hair.

As much as he wanted to see her, as much as he needed to know she was sleeping better, he couldn't make himself go check on her. He didn't want to see them touching. He didn't want to see them sleeping side by side.

He didn't want to see her in bed with anybody else at all.

Tony moved away from his charge and slowly circled the bed. "Work thing, my ass. It *is* a woman."

A woman he couldn't have. Derek swiped a hand across his face. If Shea had been available, he'd have made his move a long time ago. The problem was that she wasn't on the market, and he wasn't one to break up a happy couple. From the very first, ever since he'd met her and felt the tug of attraction, he hadn't been able to get past her partner. The guy was always around at the office and off-site meetings. The two were seemingly inseparable. He'd even answered the door at Shea's condo when Derek had gone to work on her home computer system. It was their familiarity with each other, though, that told how deep their relationship went. No coworkers he knew touched that way.

And the fact that Phillie-boy seemed to be a nice guy? Well, that just made it all the worse.

"Man, you never say anything!" Tony was standing right in front of him, reading every expression on his face. "You never talk. You're like the stoic king when it comes to this stuff."

You bet he was. His brothers could be worse than a church's knitting circle when it came to gossip, and he didn't want them talking about Shea. He didn't want them to know how he felt about her—especially if the feelings weren't returned. Just the idea of them feeling sorry for him had his skin tightening.

Only Tony didn't seem to get the message. "Who is it? Do I know her?"

"No." Fortunately, the only contact Derek had with her was through work. Although when he really considered it, that was unfortunate as hell. As much as he wanted to, he didn't really know her. All he knew was that she was high-class, beautiful, and intelligent.

And his dick got hard whenever she walked in the room.

"Woo-eee." Tony rubbed his hands together. His voice dropped, but the smile remained on his face. "Come on, D-

Man. This is good for you. You need something to shake up your nice, controlled little world. What's the lucky lady's name?"

"I told you, it's a business problem."

"A business problem that sashays when it walks. Hey, is it Ellen?"

"No, it's not Ellen!"

"But it is someone—"

"One of my clients may be having sleeping problems. That's it. Now let it go."

Tony grinned. "You first."

Derek let out a sound close to a growl. "I've got to get back to my rounds."

"You don't fool me, Machine." The grin turned into a full-fledged smile. "Going to see the mystery woman?"

"No," Derek snapped as he began to disperse. It was only through astral projection, the splitting of his spirit from his corporeal form, that he could visit all his charges. At the moment, he was happy to be able to disappear.

Because his brother was a little too close to the mark.

To the sound of Tony's laughter, Derek left the room and went off to find Tamika Hendricks. Shea's admin assistant was another sleeper under his care. Sometimes if he got really lucky, he could tap into her dreams to learn more about what was going on at Biodermatics—or with her brainy, beautiful boss. Long-legged, sleek, and athletic, Tamika usually slept like a log. Lately, though, she'd been showing signs of insomnia. At least, she'd been calling for him later and later.

After meeting with Shea this morning, the similarities had him concerned.

So far tonight, he hadn't heard Tamika calling for him, and it was getting late. Homing in on her bedroom, Derek let himself manifest again. He just wanted to check on her. The moment he looked around the room, though, he knew he wouldn't be bestowing any dreams. Tamika wasn't sleeping.

Her bed was empty.

* * *

The night was heavy when the creature materialized in the room, hovering beside his beloved. Atom by atom, his form gathered, yet he had no mass. No weight. No substance. The fluorescent light coming from the overhead fixtures streamed right through him, and he looked at his faint shadow on the floor. All he saw was a shifting mist. She'd given him power last night.

But he needed more.

Turning, he evaluated the room. This was a strange place to find her, so cold and impersonal. He was surrounded by stark machines, glassware, and computers—yet she was here, his lovely. His molecules swirled as he drifted closer to her, itching to get to what he needed.

She sat on a high stool, her body slumped over the counter in front of her. Her arms were crossed on the tabletop bench, nestling her cheek. Her hair spilled down her back, glistening in the artificial light. The brightness made him squint. He didn't like it when she fell asleep with the lights on.

He preferred moonlight. It was cooler, mysterious and intriguing.

Like her.

His pretty girl.

Reaching out, he stroked his hand over the soft strands of her hair. He growled deep in his throat when he couldn't feel them. In this form, he couldn't touch, couldn't experience physical sensations.

That was why he needed her.

For the life force she gave him. For her abilities.

A sound outside suddenly caught his attention, and he cocked his head. He had to be careful. The night was in full swing. Others could be around. But no. This room was quiet, except for the sound of her breathing. His nostrils flared as he sniffed the air to make sure. All he smelled was the lotion she put on at night.

It made his toes flutter.

Already he was aching. Prickly all over. He couldn't stay

away from her long, not in this state. The mist that formed his essence was already starting to dissipate and scatter.

"My She-a." He leaned down over her, his white mist ebbing and flowing. He could feel her power, her energy. He breathed in deeply. "Mmmm…"

He'd missed her so much. They'd been apart for so long.

He looked at her eyes, and excitement buzzed within him. They were still. No dreams filled her head. There was room for him. With a deep inhale, he hovered over her and slowly let himself drop into her.

"Ahh," he sighed as his power swelled.

He opened his eyes—her eyes—and blinked. She couldn't see as well as he could in the dark. Yet he'd seen something through her eyes last night, something she wouldn't have liked.

The memory of the window peeper flared in his head and, at once, he became angry. So angry, her body arched upright. He clenched her fingers around the edge of the tabletop. His She-a was his. His to watch. His to play with. His to—

He suddenly noticed how hard the bench was, how smooth and how cool.

Distracted, he ran her fingertips over it. Out of everything they experienced together during his visits, he liked the sense of touch best. He loved the textures, the tingles, the pressure…

And the pain.

He licked her lips. Oh, the things they could do together now that they were both grown up. He unlooped her legs from the stool, letting her muscles do the work.

"Come, my pretty one," he said as he moved them clumsily around the room. He wasn't used to her size or weight yet. She was so much bigger than the last time they'd been together. She felt different—more capable, more sensitive, more developed…

More delicious.

Power hummed through his veins.

What could they do tonight? What trouble could they

cause?

Items on the table suddenly caught his interest. Curious, he used her finger to nudge a beaker on the table. Liquid sloshed. He saw another device sitting on the bench. He bent closer to it, and her blonde hair slipped forward over her shoulders. It brushed against her face softly, tantalizingly. Reaching up, he fingered the soft strands and rubbed her face against them.

A scent drew his attention back to the strange equipment on the table. Her nostrils flared as he smelled something. He leaned closer, touching the rubber tubing and running her nose against it. He could smell better than she could, too, and he inhaled the tart tang of gas. Using her finger, he traced the knob at the base of the device.

"Ahhhh," he gasped, lurching backward with her when a flame jumped.

Fire!

He hissed at it.

His She-a hated fire. It scared her. Yet he couldn't stop watching as the flame flickered and danced. Yellows, oranges, and reds. He started to sway with the colors. So pretty, so alive, so hot... He was reaching her hand toward it when the noise outside caught his attention again.

He whirled around with her, hissing louder until the sound became a screech.

There was someone out there. Infuriated, he closed her fingers into fists. Why couldn't they leave them be? Why must they interfere?

The red from the flame filled his head.

Turning, he began moving her toward the door, gliding along as her steps became surer. He knew well the dangerous things that lurked in the dark. Mean, caustic things liked to hide in the shadows, but none of them were as dangerous or as mean as him.

Especially when his She-a was with him.

* * *

A crash filled the air, the sound loud and close.

It jarred Shea awake. Her eyes popped open, her muscles tensed, and her heart gave one big thud. Then it was off racing. Inhaling sharply, she looked around the room. Only she wasn't in a room this time, and it wasn't so dark she couldn't see.

Her nerves started to scream. Where was she?

The loud screech continued, making it hard to get her bearings. She was surrounded by an eerie green light... and numbers... and a padded leather wheel...

Oh, dear Lord, she was looking at the dashboard of her car.

And it was running!

Her spine straightened with a snap, and she clamped her hands down on the steering wheel. The sound. The rumble was loud and constant. She was dragging something! Her gaze jumped up to look out the front windshield. No, not dragging... pushing. She'd hit the Dumpster and was forcing it across the lot.

She jammed on the brakes, her foot almost sliding off the pedal. She dug her heel into the floorboard and worriedly looked at the rearview mirror. Had she hit anything else? The streetlight at the far end of the parking lot looked small and distant, but she didn't see anything lying in her tracks.

That didn't make her feel any better.

She looked at the path she must have followed. In order to get here, she must have walked out to her car, put her key in the ignition, backed out from her spot, and driven two hundred feet.

The tension she'd fought all day came back hard, and her vision started to narrow. She breathed through her mouth and forced herself to focus on one thing at a time. The car was stopped. That was good. The green lights on her dashboard showed the speed at zero. The Dumpster rolled another foot or so, before coming to a halt. She stared at it, the accusing silence almost louder than the noise. It looked no worse for the wear, although she couldn't tell how well her car had fared.

A loud thud made her jump.

Her head snapped to the right, toward the source, and she let out a surprised scream.

Somebody was standing right beside her car with their gloved fists lying on her hood! The figure was dressed all in black, with the hood of its sweatshirt pulled over its head. With the way the figure stood outside of her headlights, the shadows nearly swallowed it.

But she saw it, and it looked like the angel of death.

When its head slowly swiveled her way, Shea couldn't contain her raw fear. Her hand flew to the gearshift. There was no hesitation in her movements as she threw the car into reverse and hit the gas. Her tires screeched against the asphalt as she backed away from the person, stopping only when she was a safe distance away.

Breathing hard, she watched the figure. He stared right back at her, his face hidden in shadows.

Afraid to take her eyes off him, she patted for her purse, looking for her cell phone.

It wasn't there.

Tearing her gaze away from the figure, she looked to the passenger seat. It was empty. A cold sweat broke out on her forehead. Where was her purse? She looked frantically to the building that housed her laboratory. Was it in her lab? Was that where she'd fallen asleep? She had her keys. Had she locked the door on her way out?

Oh, God. Her stomach lurched. She couldn't believe it had gotten to her there. Her equipment! Her in-vitro tests! What damage was she going to find?

Her gaze snapped back to the figure in black.

It was gone.

"Oh, no." Shea looked around the parking lot. She hit the locks, making sure they were activated, and twisted in her seat to scan what she could of the Solstice Industrial Park. Where had he gone?

What had anybody been doing here this time of night?

"Think!"

DREAM WALKER

She wanted to check her lab to make sure everything was all right. Last thing she remembered, she'd been right in the middle of analyzing the re-epithelialization rates in her latest replication runs. The research she had going on in there was so important, but so was her safety. She hated the idea of leaving all that confidential information potentially exposed or ruined, but she wasn't getting out of her car for anything. The soft rumble of the engine that had started out feeling so threatening now seemed like her safety net.

But she never should have been here in the first place. She'd woken up behind the wheel!

"Oh my God!" Her gaze flashed back to the spot where she'd last seen the figure in black. Had she hit that man? Was that why he'd been angry, hitting the hood of her car?

She scrubbed her hands over her face. She couldn't make sense of anything. Too many thoughts were in her head—one more menacing than all the rest.

Shakily, she put the car into drive and headed for the exit. She had to get help. She couldn't make this situation right by herself. For a moment, she thought about finding Derek.

"No, Phillip." He'd know what to look for in the lab, and she wouldn't have to face that piercing, questioning look. Questioning why she'd left her purse behind, why she'd left her experiments half finished, why she'd left the building unlocked, how she'd found herself in her car...

Shea stepped harder on the gas. She knew the answer to those questions, only it was her worst fear come to life.

Dread bubbled up inside her chest. Finding herself in her basement the other night hadn't been a fluke. It hadn't been a one-time deal. She was sleepwalking again.

She was sleep-driving!

Her Somnambulist was back—and, apparently, back with a vengeance.

CHAPTER FOUR

"What happened?" Derek demanded as he strode into Shea's lab. In the dark predawn hour, the question came out too loud and too worried, but he couldn't take it back, even if he wanted to. He'd been concerned about her sleeping, but he hadn't expected something like this.

He found her sitting on a high stool next to her lab bench. Even with what had happened—or maybe because of it—she was absorbed in her work. She glanced at him distractedly, and then did a double take. "Derek? What are you doing here?"

She couldn't be serious. "Phillip called. He said you might have had a security breach."

Her face paled, and she glanced back to her work. "Oh, that."

"Yes, that," he practically growled.

She hooked her hair behind her ear. It was pulled back in a ponytail, but several soft strands had escaped. "I told him nothing was missing. I thought you'd just check to see if our computer firewalls had been breached or something."

Derek's eyes narrowed. She knew better than that.

"Just because nothing is missing doesn't mean somebody didn't get in here and poke around." He let his gaze rake over her. She looked okay, physically. That had been his primary concern as he'd driven, raced, across town. "Why didn't you

42

call me?"

Her gaze swiveled away to the lab book lying open beside the microscope. Purposefully, she began writing notes. "Phillip did call you, and I contacted Industrial Park Security. They just left."

That wasn't what he'd meant.

He curled his fingers around the back of another empty stool. The job was one thing. His concern for her was something entirely different. She'd been alone, and it had been so late at night. She didn't know what lurked out there in the darkness, but he did. "I need to know what happened. All of it."

She sighed. "What exactly did Phillip tell you?"

"He said you encountered a prowler in the parking lot. That was pretty much it."

"That *was* pretty much it." Her fingers tightened around her pencil. "I'll admit, though, he gave me quite the start."

"Why were you even here?"

"I came in to run a few more tests."

"They couldn't wait until this morning?"

"I couldn't sleep."

"Again?" He took a step toward her.

She met his gaze, for once, impatient. "I had another nightmare. Please don't push this, Derek."

Nightmares two nights in a row? That was starting to go beyond the normal. What issue had her so wound up? Had they had troubles here that he didn't know about? Someone looking for drugs? Or wanting to steal her ideas? Was that the source of the fear he'd seen at their meeting? "What was it about?"

She flushed. "Nothing."

"Try again."

Her cheeks turned even brighter. "I don't remember."

The electricity between them suddenly returned, the heat and the awareness. She remembered, all right, yet her reaction made no sense—until Derek remembered who gave her those dreams. His jaw tightened. If Zane had tried to give her an erotic dream that she hadn't wanted...

She turned off the microscope, extinguished its light, and recorded additional notes in her lab book. Derek took the hint. She might not want to talk about it, but he and Zane were going to have a close, personal chat.

Right now, she had him concerned. A prowler was nothing to take lightly, yet it almost seemed as if she didn't want him here—and that stung.

Well, want him or not, it was his job to make sure both she and her work were safe. That was why she paid him. "What time did you come in?" he asked.

"Around one o'clock."

Way too late to be here alone. "When did you first notice something was wrong? Did he try to get into the building?"

She blew out a breath. "I don't know. I tend not to notice things around me when I'm working. It wasn't until I was in my car that I saw him."

"So you were leaving? But Phillip said the building was left unlocked. That's why he called me."

Her fingers paused in the process of screwing the top back onto an open Petri dish. "Like I said, I can get pretty engrossed."

He watched as she stowed the Petri dish in its rightful place, lining it up with similar ones and making sure the label showed clearly. "Right," he said. "So that's why the Bunsen burner was left on, too."

Her gaze flashed to the burner. The color that had pinkened her cheeks drained out, and she nervously licked her lips. "I did that."

"Shea, you wouldn't—"

"I did."

She closed her lab book with a snap. She pulled the glass slide out from under the microscope's lens, stored it, too, and turned on the faucet over the sink.

Derek watched her closely as she washed her hands. The absent-minded professor she was not. Her movements were confident and precise, and, suddenly, he understood. This was her world, her domain. Here, she was in control.

But last night, all that had been threatened.

No wonder it had been so hard to pull her out of her work. She used it as an escape.

"You must have left in a hurry," he said gently.

She wiped her hands and tossed the paper towel in the trash. "I honestly don't remember."

He looked around the lab, his interest suddenly piqued. Usually when he came to Biodermatics, they met in the office building's conference room. This was the first time she'd invited him to her inner sanctum. It showed things about her, things she didn't even realize.

Everything was clean and tidy. The room was cluttered due to lack of space, but obviously organized. Yet there were personal things, like the mechanical pencil she used. It was hot pink. Soft rock poured from the radio atop a file cabinet, but it was the Mets calendar hanging on the far wall that really caught his attention. He'd wondered about her name...

"What?" she asked pointedly.

She'd caught him snooping.

He shrugged. "I've never seen you work before—not in your scientific capacity, that is. It's like watching Einstein in his natural environment."

She blinked. "Einstein was a theoretical physicist, and a man."

"Then Madame Curie."

Her lips parted in surprise. "She studied radiation."

"Take the compliment, Shea."

They stared at each other for a long, quiet moment. "Thank you," she whispered.

Derek's fingers actually ached. He wanted to pull her into his arms so badly, he could hardly stand it—but it wasn't the right time or the right place.

"So when you and Phillip came back, nothing was missing?" he said gruffly. He gestured about the room. "Was anything out of place?"

Her gaze locked on the Bunsen burner again. Almost

compulsively, she reached past him to check it was fully off.

"Except for that, no." Moving stiffly, she headed for the door. "I was in my car when I noticed the man outside. I'll show you where I saw him."

Derek glanced at the burner. It made him almost as uneasy as it made her. He couldn't imagine that a competitor would try to burn her out. Not only was it extreme, it ran directly against the work that everyone in her field was trying to do. Yet he couldn't see her accidentally leaving it on, either—unless she'd been frightened.

He touched the hot pink pencil.

Turning on his heel, he went to catch up with her. She was just opening the door to the front staging room when he turned into the hallway.

"Here, let me." He stepped up to help her take off her lab coat.

She hesitated as his hands went around to the lapels of the white jacket. The move put him close to her, so close her scent wafted around him and invaded his senses. Her ponytail swept over his hand, and his fingers stiffened on the cotton material. He wanted to be touching her skin.

He wanted to hold her.

"Are you sure you're okay?" he asked quietly.

For a moment, a split second, he sensed her leaning back toward him. But then that moment was gone.

"I'm fine," she said.

He wasn't convinced. He could feel the energy rumbling inside her: the nerves, the questions, the awareness... Goosebumps had popped up on the back of her neck.

Trying to keep his touch easy and platonic, he pulled the lab coat off her shoulders and down her arms. Even so, he couldn't stop his fingers from lingering as they brushed against her hands. "Next time you call me," he said, his voice rough.

She inhaled softly, but didn't respond.

He put her lab coat on a hanger, but noticed that her hands weren't steady as she tugged the rubber band out of her hair. She retrieved her lab book and held it in front of her, with both arms crossed over her chest. "I'm sorry, Derek."

"Sorry for what?"

"For not following any of your security protocols last night. I'm sorry for bringing you out here so late." She glanced to the window. The first rays of sunshine were peeking over the horizon. "I mean, so early."

That was it. He couldn't keep away from her anymore. Reaching out, he caught her by the shoulder. "I don't give a rip about the security protocols. The most important thing is that you're all right."

A muscle in her temple fluttered, and he moved his hand to the nape of her neck. Gently, he rubbed his thumb against her racing pulse. "Are you okay, Shea? Really?"

She swallowed hard and nodded.

He brushed the pad of his thumb along her jaw line, and she straightened her spine. She nodded again and then moved by him. He got the door for her, and it seemed only right to settle his hand against the small of her back. When she didn't pull away, he left it there. Together, they walked out to the parking lot.

"He was over there." She pointed to the Dumpster. "Dressed all in black."

They were heading that way when the door to the adjacent office building opened. Phillip Morrison stepped outside, looking tall, handsome, and concerned. He quickly walked over to join them. "Figure anything out?"

As much as he hated doing it, Derek pulled his touch away from Shea's back. "She's just walking me through what happened."

Shea stepped away to stand at Phillip's side, and her partner swung his arm around her shoulders. Derek's hand automatically curled into a fist. He wanted to rip that arm right out of its socket. Where had Mr. Comfort been last night when she'd needed him? She'd had a nightmare, and the guy had let her walk away from their bed? He'd let her drive across town to be alone? What kind of a relationship was that?

Phillip cleared his throat. "Uh, do you think it was just a passerby, Derek?" He nodded toward the trash bin. "Strange place for a late-night walk."

"Is Biodermatics still shredding its documents like I recommended?"

"We try, but some things might slip through. Why?"

Shea looked at the trash bin, and her eyes widened. "You think he was going through our trash."

Derek was pleased that they were on the same wavelength. He'd noticed the twin lids hanging over the back of the Dumpster the moment she'd pointed it out. "Garbage companies like to keep these bins closed. It keeps the smell in, and rain and animals out. I'd say your unexpected visitor was Dumpster diving. You might have caught him in the act."

Phillip didn't look convinced. "Skin care is a competitive business, but do you really think somebody would go that far?"

Derek let an eyebrow lift. "Think about it. What was your profit last quarter?"

The man grimaced. "Enough to hire Audrey Lowe for our commercials."

"And how much do you estimate Shea's medical applications will bring in, once they hit the market?"

His point landed.

Shea rubbed her forehead, and her partner patted her back soothingly. Derek fisted his hands against his hips, and he turned to look at the Dumpster instead. For the first time, he noticed a smudge of silver along its front. His forehead furrowed, and he glanced at her car. It was silver, too. "Did you hit the thing?"

"The guy startled me," she mumbled.

Phillip looked at her sharply. "Tell him the truth."

Derek frowned. "Shea?"

Finally, her head came up. "The truth is I almost hit him.

He probably has more against me than I have against him."

"Did you get a good look at him?"

She wrapped her arms around her lab book. "He had his hood pulled up. I never saw his face. I was too busy peeling away."

Derek's muscles tightened. He hated to think of her coming up against someone like that. "That was the best thing you could have done."

"Absolutely." Phillip ran a gentle touch over her hair. When he caught Derek's look, the caress stopped, and he dropped his arm to his side.

Just then, a car pulled into the parking lot, surprising them all. It was still early. The sunrise was just shooting swatches of purples and pinks across the sky.

"It's Tamika," Phillip said.

Shea frowned. "She's awfully early."

Derek looked at his watch. Yes, awfully early—especially considering what time she'd gotten to bed last night. He watched as his charge got out of her car. She had a heavy bag swung over one shoulder and a large cup of coffee in her other hand. When she saw them, her eyebrows jumped above the line of her dark sunglasses.

"What's going on?" she asked. Her voice sounded husky and unused.

"We had an intruder last night," Phillip said.

She stopped mid-step. Lifting her sunglasses to the top of her head, she gave them a worried look. Yet it was a tired look, too. As stunningly beautiful as she was, her eyelids looked heavy and her eyes lacked their normal luster. "Who was it? I mean... What did they want?"

"We don't know." Shea frowned. "Did you skip your run this morning?"

"Uh, yeah." Feeling the weight of her bag, Tamika shifted it on her shoulder. "I'm not training right now. Too busy."

Doing what? Derek wondered.

"Have you noticed anyone snooping around here lately?" he asked. "Have you taken any strange calls?"

"Strange calls? *Oh*, yeah." She gestured with her coffee, showing some of her normal spunk. "That pushy woman you want to hire is getting on my last nerve."

"What pushy woman?" Phillip asked.

"Lynette Fromm."

"I'm sure she's just excited at the prospect of getting back into her field," Shea said.

"I didn't realize you needed a degree in chemistry to work in a business office." Tamika pulled her sunglasses back down, and her scowl darkened.

"We'll make a decision on that soon," Phillip promised, "but this matter has to take priority over everything else."

Like it hadn't already? Derek bit back a cutting remark when he saw the look on Shea's face. She was staring at the Dumpster and clutching her lab book protectively.

"I really don't care if somebody steals my work as long as it gets out there to help people." She swallowed hard. "I just need to know that my data won't be corrupted or lost. We've got to make sure that doesn't happen. Please, Derek."

When she asked him like that, he was ready to surround the place with armored tanks. "I'll take it on personally."

She looked at him swiftly. "Oh, I didn't mean that. I'm sure one of your staff would be just fine."

"You need me."

"But you have your company to run."

"I always do your work myself. You know that."

Phillip's eyebrows rose, and Tamika watched the scene with interest. Phillip caught her by the arm and, together, they moved away.

Shea shifted uncomfortably. "I think this was just an isolated incident, Derek."

"And I'll be pleased as punch if you're right. I don't like it that somebody was nosing around here, for any reason. I'm going to look into this whether you pay me to or not."

Her blue gaze locked with his.

"You need me," he told her. "Like it or not, you've got me."

* * *

"Wow." Phillip watched Derek's dark SUV pull out of the parking lot. "I don't know if I just got singed or frostbitten."

Shea looked at her partner. "What are you talking about?"

"The looks he was giving me. What is going on between you two?"

"Between Derek and me? Nothing."

Tamika nearly choked on her coffee. "You call that 'nothing'? I want some 'nothing'!"

"Me too." Phillip grinned. "Does he have any more brothers?"

Heat crawled up into Shea's face. She'd thought she was the only one who'd noticed that Derek had been even more intense than usual. The waves of energy coming off him had been powerful.

And sexy as sin.

When he'd helped her take off her lab jacket, she'd almost melted all over him. All she'd been able to think about was her dream and the way he'd held her, kissed her, and touched her...

"Hello," Tamika said. "Earth to Shea."

She let out a quick breath.

"Is there anything you want to tell me?" her partner asked. "What happened at that meeting yesterday?"

"I'm not sure." She dragged a hand through her hair. She'd always been aware of Derek, but now... She'd worried that letting him see her at less than full strength would damage his impression of her. Instead, it was as if her vulnerability had brought out his protective side.

Phillip was still looking toward the road. "I don't envy that prowler, I'll tell you that."

"Can he really do anything?" Tamika asked.

"It wouldn't surprise me if he tracked down the guy's name, address, Social Security number, and shoe size. Believe me, he has the skills to back up that macho attitude." He winked at Shea. "Lucky girl."

Her cheeks grew hotter. "The industrial park's security

staff is looking into it, too."

Tamika looked at them, stunned. "How serious is this?"

Phillip's bemused expression hardened. "We're not taking any chances. Shea's lab might have been compromised."

Their assistant nodded slowly. "I'll go make more coffee."

Turning on her heel, she strode toward the office's door.

Phillip waited until she was inside before turning to Shea. "He wants you."

She took a step back, startled. "I—"

"Wants you *bad.* I thought he might chew my arm off when I put it around your shoulders."

"So why didn't you let me go?"

Her partner smiled slowly. "To see how far I could push him. Which wasn't much, by the way. He had me shaking in my shoes."

Derek could do that, Shea thought. With just a look, he could make her shiver, cause her nipples to tighten and her belly to squeeze. Flustered, she smoothed her hair.

"So that's the way it is, huh?" Phillip's grin widened. "Well, as far as I'm concerned, it's about time."

Her chin snapped up. "What?"

"What do you mean, *what?* You look at him like you look at Baby Ruth candy bars—like you want him, but you won't let yourself have him. And the way he looks at you? I'm surprised he hasn't taken you down to the floor in front of everyone."

"Phillip!"

"I'm not saying anything that isn't the truth. You two have been quietly wanting each other forever. I just don't understand why he's held back." Phillip tilted his head, eyeing her speculatively. "Something's changed."

Shea's grip tightened on her lab book. Her partner could back her into a corner when she least wanted it. "He's concerned about a possible breakdown in our security protocol."

"He's concerned about you."

"Semantics."

"I don't think so." Phillip crossed his arms over his chest, settling in like he always did when he got stubborn. "Why didn't you tell him the whole story?"

A warning tingle ran down her spine. "We told him everything he needs to know."

Nobody knew the whole truth—not even Phillip. Shea exhaled carefully. Oh, he knew about her sleepwalking, but she'd never told him her deepest, darkest secret—her belief that her nighttime actions were not her own. Every time she thought about what could have happened last night, it nearly made her sick. Her Somnambulist could have made her burn down the entire building.

It had happened once before.

Her throat thickened. As a child, she remembered waking up to find herself completing strange tasks, like making banana and teabag sandwiches or stacking all her clothes in the middle of her bed. The disorientation had always been the worst, especially if she woke up in strange rooms or closets. It was why she feared the dark so badly.

Yet nothing had been as horrible as waking up with night dew coating her skin, smoke filling her lungs, and the sound of metal popping in her ears. Her family had lost its home that night. Their trailer had been a total loss, but the price her dad had paid was even steeper.

Tears blurred her vision as she looked around the Solstice Industrial Park, seeing everything she'd worked so hard to achieve. She had so many plans for her business, so many goals for her research. Had her Somnambulist been trying to do it again? Was that why it was back?

She felt herself wobble.

Phillip caught her arm and moved her toward the monument sign that boasted Biodermatics' name. He made her sit down on the sign's base. "Ah, sweetheart. You've got to get some decent sleep."

Shea ground her teeth together. Did he think she didn't know that? "I will," she said determinedly. "I have an appointment next week with my doctor."

Every problem had an answer. Sometimes you just had to go after it with systematic, logical steps. She'd been a child the last time her Somnambulist had come calling. She was an adult now and a highly trained scientist. She just needed to keep a cool head and think objectively.

She would get rid of it.

"I still think you should tell Derek," Phillip said.

"That I'm sleepwalking? What would that accomplish?"

"If he knew, it might help him separate your actions from the prowler's. Your story didn't exactly add up. You didn't see the way he looked at you when you couldn't give him more details—not to mention the fact that hitting the Dumpster with your car isn't like you."

"Enough." She lifted her hand to stop the litany. "We're not telling him. He doesn't need to know."

"But he wants to know. It's clear on his face. Why don't you let him in, Shea? He's a good guy. You don't always have to be perfect."

"I'm not perfect. I'm not even close." She knew that better than anyone.

Unfortunately, her particular flaw just happened to be more dangerous than most people's.

She let out a ragged breath. All the literature warned that sleepwalking adults could be even more volatile than sleepwalking children. Her Somnambulist had already taken her driving. With their history, she hated to think about how bad it could get.

"Did you ever think your sleepwalking could be the result of something as simple as stress or sexual frustration?" Phillip tapped her on the knee. "Maybe it would calm you down to have Derek in your bed—or, at the very least, tire you out."

Shea's skin prickled, the chill going straight to the bone despite the summer morning heat. As much as the idea turned her on, she couldn't even let her mind go there. Everyone was vulnerable while they were asleep, even a strong, competent man like Derek.

Hadn't they seen that with his brother, Cael?

And her dad? Look what she'd done to him!

Her fingers raked against the cement, rubbing her nails raw. She'd come very close to hitting that trespasser last night. She couldn't bear to think of waking and finding Derek in her headlights.

Or worse.

"He can work the prowler issue," she whispered. "Everything else is off-limits to him."

Especially her. Until she found a way to fix her restless sleep habit—to regain control of her own body—she couldn't let him get near her. Nobody was safe, not while her Somnambulist was around.

Not while she was being used as a weapon.

CHAPTER FIVE

It was early Sunday morning when Derek arrived at IHOP for breakfast. As soon as he set foot inside the front door, the scent of pancakes and bacon wafted over him. He inhaled appreciatively, but he surveyed the restaurant with a critical eye. He and his brothers tried to plan their weekly get-togethers when the crowds were low, and the food was hot.

They needed the privacy to talk about Dream Weaver business.

With a quick sweep of the room, he noted only two tables of night shift workers grabbing a bite to eat before they went home to bed. Up front, a trucker was getting ready to hit the road. Other than that, business was slow. The after-church crowd wouldn't arrive for a while.

Apparently, neither would his family.

He glanced at his watch and realized he was early. That didn't surprise him. He was usually one of the first to arrive, but he'd kicked it in the butt a little more today. Irritated, he tugged at his shirt cuffs. He still hadn't been able to make contact with Zane. He wanted to talk with his delinquent brother one on one if he could.

Too bad he usually strolled in after the rest of them had placed their orders.

"Morning, Derek," Sally called as she came through the swinging door that led to the kitchen. The pretty blonde was one of their regular waitresses. Still, the fact that she remembered his name was something. With as many of them as there were, she usually resorted to "honey" or "darlin'."

"Want some coffee?"

"Bring a pot."

"Oooh," she said with a wink. "Long night?"

"Long week." She wouldn't believe it even if he could tell her.

"I pushed two tables together for you guys. Will that be enough?"

"If it's not, we can help ourselves."

"Thanks, hon." She smiled and walked past him with a steaming order of eggs and hash browns hoisted up near her shoulder. "I'll bring that coffee to you in a minute."

Derek nodded, impatience eating at him. He really didn't have time for this today. He was busy looking for evidence that one of Biodermatics' competitors might have gotten their hands on Shea's proprietary data. It was the weekend, but he'd talked with the garbage company and determined when they'd made their last pick-up. He'd also spoken with the Bio staff to learn what might have been in jeopardy during that time frame. Already this morning, he'd been on the computer checking again to make sure none of the company's data had been tampered with.

For probably the first time ever, he didn't want to be here, family duty or not.

Unfortunately, Shea wasn't his only concern.

Pulling out a chair, he sat and straightened his tie, readying himself for business. Things hadn't yet settled down in the nighttime world. The people of Solstice were still having problems sleeping, including one of his charges who was calling for him later and later every night. The fact that this particular charge was Tamika Hendricks had him on edge. Was it a coincidence Shea's assistant was also having sleep problems, or was he missing something entirely?

He and his brothers needed to keep each other updated on what was happening so they wouldn't be caught off guard.

Not again.

"Here you go." Sally set a coffee pot in front of him. "And look who I found."

On her heels were two of his younger brothers, neither of whom was Zane.

"Hey, Derek." Wes sat down across the table. "How's it going?"

AJ just nodded.

"Busy," Derek said. "Do you guys know if Zane is coming?"

"There's food, so it's probably a good bet." Wes took the menu Sally gave him with a smile. "Why? You need to talk to him?"

"Yeah."

His brother's eyebrows rose. "What did he do this time?"

"Nothing, maybe. I'm not sure." Derek took a drink of coffee and tried to remain objective. He didn't know if Zane was to blame for Shea's problem or not. He didn't even know what her problem was—and to be honest, that was driving him crazy. He didn't like being in the dark, not like this. He was the guy everyone always turned to for help. He was the one who always got answers. Unfortunately, she was only turning to him for work issues.

She had Phillip for everything else.

"Whew," Wes said. "Whatever Zane did, it must be bad."

Derek traced the lip of his coffee cup with his thumb. "I just need to talk to him, the sooner the better."

He glanced at AJ. He needed to talk to him, too. "Do you know Tamika Hendricks? Tall, beautiful black woman who runs in those 5K races you do?"

AJ's head snapped up. "Long legs?"

"That's the one."

His brother eased back in his chair. "I might know who you're talking about. She didn't run yesterday, though. I haven't seen her for a while."

That was what Derek had been worried about. When Tamika was training, she slept like a baby. But for her not to be running at all… Something was up.

"Everything okay with her?" AJ asked.

"Maybe. She's not getting a lot of sleep. Can you keep an eye out for her? See if she shows up on the running paths?"

AJ nodded. "Sure."

"Hey!" Wes scooted his chair back and stood. "Look who's here."

Derek hoped it was Zane making an unexpected early appearance, but it wasn't.

Tony had brought Cael.

"Hey," Derek said, pleasantly surprised. "You made it."

"I'm not an invalid, Wes," Cael said as their younger brother pulled out the chair at the head of the table for him. Still, he did sink into the seat a bit gingerly. "Thanks," he muttered.

"How are you doing?" Derek asked.

"Better." Cael looked more comfortable now that he'd taken a seat. Derek knew that he'd been pushing the physical therapy to the limits, but it would take a while before he was back to one hundred percent. At least his color was better. In the hospital, it hadn't been good. Not good at all.

"Big brother was out on the curb waiting for me." Tony took the seat on the opposite side of the table. "I think he has ants in his pants."

"Let's hope he's got a little more than that for Devon."

Cael stiffened as the dry comment came over his head. Zane had arrived, smart attitude intact. He cuffed their oldest brother on the shoulder affectionately before scooting behind Derek and taking the chair on his right.

Derek's attention was immediately split. He knew that Cael should be his main focus, but he'd been trying to get in touch with his other brother for days. He glanced at Cael. He didn't look like he was going anywhere. Zane, on the other hand, could be out of here in two seconds flat if a pretty girl swished her skirt the right way.

"Is there a problem with your cell phone?" he asked as Zane hooked his feet around the front legs of his chair and leaned forward for the pot of coffee in the center of the table. "I've been trying to get in touch with you."

"I lost the thing," Zane said with a shrug. "Somewhere on that pub crawl Wednesday night, I think."

Sally showed up with her order pad at the ready. She placed a hand on Cael's shoulder and squeezed. "It's good to see you, hon. The girls here all missed you."

"Aren't we good enough for you, Sal?" Tony said with a pout. Somehow, the expression didn't match well with the massive biceps stretching out the arms of his T-shirt.

"Oh, you're all dreamboats, and you know it."

"Dreamboats," Wes repeated with a smile on his face. He let out a laugh, and AJ quickly elbowed him.

"Are you guys ready to order?"

Derek rolled his shoulders. So much for his one-on-one time with Zane. Now he'd have to wait until after breakfast, when things broke up. He just didn't know if he could wait that long. He wanted to know if Shea was sleeping better. Two nights had passed since he'd seen her. Two long, endless nights. Reining in his exasperation, he folded his menu and tapped it against his thigh.

One by one, they went around the table, ending with Tony, who got teased when he placed a side order for "girly" peach crepes.

Derek just couldn't laugh with the rest of his brothers. His brain was churning over other things, like Shea hitting that Dumpster. It didn't make sense. Had she tried to run the guy down? That didn't sound like her at all, unless it had something to do with the fear he'd seen in her eyes at his office. Was someone threatening her?

The thought was like a hot poker in his gut. He needed some answers now.

"Can we get this meeting called to order?" he asked the moment Sally was out of earshot.

Zane looked his way. "Looks like Cael's not the only one with ants in his pants."

"Zip it, Zane." Derek had waited as long as he could.

"How are things going on your rounds?"

His brother's forehead furrowed, and he looked around to see if anyone was within listening distance. "Fine. What's up with you?"

"Are you sure there isn't anything unusual going on?"

"Unusual?" Understanding lit his brother's eyes, and he smiled. "You don't want to have this conversation with me here."

Derek scowled. The hell he didn't. If something was going on during Zane's rounds as a Dream Weaver, they all should know. "Are you having problems?"

"No." Zane's congenial mood started to harden. "But it sure sounds like you are."

Their stares locked, neither of them willing to back down.

"Just ease up on the nightmares, okay?" Derek said softly. "I'm talking about Shea Caldwell."

Zane set down his coffee with a clatter. Splotches of the hot liquid hit the table and formed little pools. "I know exactly who you're talking about, and, while they're certainly nightmares to me, she seems to get off on them."

That was it. Derek turned in his seat so they were nose to nose. "Just stop playing with her head. It might be fun for you to toy with some of your other charges, but you will not do this to her. You hear me?"

"Hey," Tony snapped from the other side of the table. "Keep it down. And who's *her*?"

Neither Derek nor Zane paid him any attention. Their stares were locked and unblinking.

"What are you accusing me of, Mr. By The Book?" Zane asked.

"She's feeling the effects," Derek growled. "You need to back off."

Zane knocked his fist against the table, making even the carousel of syrups jump. "I don't know what you're talking about. She's had one nightmare—and it didn't start out that way. I haven't been leading her."

"Then what the hell is going on?"

His brother laughed, the sound sharp and humorless. "If you don't know, I'm certainly not going to tell you!"

"Whoa." Cael's fingers bit into Derek's shoulder when he started to lunge forward. For as incapacitated as their older brother had been, his grip was strong and his voice was stern. "What's going on here?"

Everyone had stopped talking and was staring at them—including the trucker at the front table. Derek picked up his napkin from his lap and carefully wiped his hands.

"A client of mine has been having trouble sleeping," he said tightly. "She won't tell me exactly what the problem is, but she's tense and scared."

He looked pointedly to his right. "She's Zane's charge."

"So it's my fault?"

Derek let silence answer for him.

Zane's expression turned belligerent. "Hey, if it's anyone's fault, it's yours."

He sat forward and poked Derek in the chest. "She's dreaming, all right, but those so-called nightmares are about you, buddy boy. She's having erotic dreams about the two of you together. Hot, get-naked, heavy-petting, erotic dreams."

Derek caught the finger and was ready to cause some major pain when the words sank into his brain.

And froze it.

His little brother gave him another nudge. "I've never known you to be dense before. Do you need me to spell it out for you? She wants you, Derek. That's probably why she's getting all tense and weird around you."

Zane cocked his head. "I know it would freak me out."

Tony leaned forward, that grin back on his face. It didn't take him long to figure out the lowdown. "What's her name? Is this the woman you didn't want to talk about the other night?"

Zane yanked his finger out of Derek's limp grip and folded his arms triumphantly across his chest. "Shea Caldwell."

"Shea." Tony looked around for input. "Anyone got

anything?"

Whispers went back and forth. Still, Derek couldn't move. Shea was dreaming about him?

"Co-owner and head research scientist for Biodermatics, Inc.," Zane supplied, helping everyone out.

Everyone but Derek, that was. Suddenly, he couldn't put two coherent thoughts together in a row.

"Biodermatics," Wes repeated. "Hey, that's that lotion company with the commercial. You know the one—all kinds of good-looking women lie back, point their toes in the air, and smooth that stuff all over their legs. Hey, is she in it?"

Derek snapped out of his stupor. "No!"

"No way. She's top grade all the way," Zane agreed. "Classy, quiet, and smart as a whip. But you know what? If she'd wanted to be in that commercial, she would have rocked it."

Tony's eyebrows rose. "So she's a looker?"

"Blonde and flat-out gorgeous."

Cael leaned forward onto his elbows. He looked as pleased as the rest of them, but the expression was tempered with concern. "Derek, what's wrong with you? You usually read people like books."

Derek felt like he was swirling; his thoughts, his head, his body… Then that one, all-too-important fact slammed into his head, shutting everything down, and leaving him cold. "She's taken," he said flatly.

None of this mattered. Hell yeah, it turned him on to know she was dreaming about him, but thinking about that would just give him a hard cock and a headache. The dreams obviously weren't wanted. Look at how stilted everything had become between them. They were making her uncomfortable, because she was in love with someone else.

"No, she's not," Zane said, taken aback.

Derek looked at him so quickly, he nearly wrenched his neck. "Yes, she is. Her partner. Phillip."

Zane shook his head. "She sleeps alone. In some mighty sexy lingerie, I might add."

Derek had his hand fisted in his brother's T-shirt before he knew it. "Phillip Morrison. They've been together since college."

"Morrison?" AJ piped up. He shook his head. "No."

"Yes." Derek looked toward the end of the table.

"Morrison's one of mine. They're not together."

"But…"

"He's gay."

"What?" Derek's fist dropped from Zane's shirt.

"Mostly closeted, but gay." AJ shrugged and sat back in his chair.

For the second time in one minute, Derek couldn't think. There wasn't one clear thought in his head.

Cael's voice sounded close by. "What are you still doing here?"

Derek looked at him blankly.

"Do you want her or not?"

Everything clicked into place, and Derek's chair skidded back. "I've got to go."

Laughter, hoots, and words of encouragement erupted from the table, drawing the attention of the growing restaurant crowd. Sally skidded to a halt with their order lifted high on her shoulder as Derek strode past. He paid no attention to anyone as he slapped a ten-spot on the counter by the cash register. He was reaching into his pocket for his keys as he headed out the door.

Behind him, he didn't see his brothers smiling.

* * *

Tony tapped Cael on the shoulder as they watched Derek's car peel out of the parking lot. "I told you so."

"It's about time that guy got laid," Zane said dryly. "He's wound tighter than a spring."

Cael turned on their little brother. He might have been out of action for a while, but in no way, shape, or form was he weak. "Were you telling the truth? Did you do anything to influence those dreams?"

"Like I'd have her dream about him instead of me." Zane

ran a hand over his ruffled hair, obviously more affected by the confrontation than he wanted to admit. "Close it down. Here's our food."

Tony got up to help Sally, who was still looking curiously at the front door.

"Is something wrong?" she asked.

"Nah," he said. "Something's very right."

Together, they served breakfast, making sure the crepes were close at Tony's side. Sally finally moved away, picking up the money Derek had left behind. She tucked it into her apron, still looking out the front windows with interest.

She wasn't the only one who was curious. The moment she was gone, Wes sat forward. "You can't leave us hanging. Tell us more."

Zane took a quick bite from a bacon strip. "When that little gem of a movie first started playing in her head, it about knocked me out of my boxers. At first, I thought Derek had something to do with it. You know, like he was pulling some kind of long-distance trick you guys haven't told me about."

He rolled his eyes. "But then I remembered I was thinking about The Machine."

Tony licked syrup off his thumb. "Do you think there's something else going on with her, though? He seemed to think she's having sleep problems."

For once, Zane got serious. His brown eyes lost their twinkle, and the perpetual smile on his face faded. "Maybe. She's gotten very unpredictable. I'll find her sleeping in odd places, or she won't call for REM sleep until late in the night. Something's going on. I just don't know what it is."

He gestured with his fork. "I was going to ask you guys about it today. Tactfully, though."

"That's you, all right. Mr. Tactful." Tony glanced toward the door and rolled his shoulders uncomfortably. "I've never seen Derek like that before. Is she really worth all the drama?"

"Oh, yeah," Zane said without hesitation. "Totally drama-worthy."

Tony looked across the table steadily.

"Hell," he finally said. He nudged a plate across the table. "Have some crepes."

CHAPTER SIX

The morning sun was bright as Shea came down the staircase. Bright, happy, and buoyant, but she felt none of those things. To her, it might as well have been the pitch of night.

It had gotten to her again.

She clenched the banister tightly and braced herself as she took one step down and then another. She was rock steady, but every muscle in her body was tense. Half of her wanted to hurry, to just get it over with, but the other half held back, afraid of what she might find.

She'd woken up in her closet, clutching her fire extinguisher to her chest.

As if that weren't enough to send her into a blind panic, a path of her shoes led out the door. She was following them now.

One by one, they led out of her bedroom, down the hall, and down the stairs. The placement was methodical. Left, right, left, right… All in pairs. It was almost as if she were following the Invisible Woman's footsteps. But where did they lead? And why?

Holding the extinguisher under her arm, she sniffed the air and listened intently. When she reached the bottom landing, her toes dug into the plush carpeting. She took a quick, ragged breath and did a quick check of her living room. The coffee table in front of her sofa was cluttered with industry magazines and reference books. Her laptop was lying askew in front of the chair, open, but powered down. For no good reason whatsoever, the television remote was propped up on the windowsill.

In a word, everything was perfect. In its place and as she'd left it—except for the trail of shoes that led into the kitchen.

She moved deeper into the room, the pathway calling to her. "Please not the basement," she whispered. "Not the basement."

She turned into the kitchen and stopped.

Her brow furrowed. The trail just ended, right in front of the kitchen sink with her favorite pair of blue and white zebra-striped stilettos. She stared fixedly at the scene, trying to comprehend it. Her shoes were lined up perfectly next to each other, facing the sink. It was as if she'd stood staring out the window—and washing it down with the sprayer from the faucet.

"Oh, no." There was water everywhere.

Snapping out of it, she put the fire extinguisher down on the counter and grabbed the dishrag. She mopped up the puddles as best as she could.

Why had it done this? Was there a message here? It made no sense.

But when did it ever?

Her chest tightened. After the sleep-driving incident, she'd started taking something to help her sleep. She'd hoped the pills would ward off her unwanted night visitor, but they'd only given her a two-night reprieve. Two measly nights.

She'd known better than to let them make her complacent.

How many trips had it taken to bring all those shoes down? The snow boots on the stairs had to have come from storage downstairs. How long had it had control of her?

"God help me," she whispered, bracing her hands against the edge of the sink. She needed to move up that appointment with Dr. Wainright. It was what the scientist inside her told her to do. She had a sleep disorder, a bad one.

She just couldn't quiet the words in the back of her mind,

the curse that had been spat at her so long ago.

Demon child. Demon child!

Mrs. Lupescu had insisted she was possessed.

Shea shook her head. She didn't want to go there. She didn't want to remember. Yet the more she tried to push the memory away, the clearer it got.

Shea didn't know what awakened her, the noises or the hardness of her bed. Her eyes felt heavy as she tried to open them, but the noises wouldn't let her go back to sleep. Loud cracks and pops sounded in her ears, but it was the howling of her alarm clock that made her groan. It was too early to get up for school. She felt like she'd just fallen asleep.

Groaning, she stretched, pointing her bare toes. The sheets of her bed scratched and clung to her hair. She pushed them away, but her hand came away wet and dirty.

Her eyes popped open. Darkness pressed down on her, the air sticky and heavy. It caught in her throat as she bolted upright. Her heart pounded as she looked around, disoriented. She'd done it again. She'd walked in her sleep, and this time, she'd wandered outside.

Standing up, she frantically brushed the dirt off herself. She tried to get a fix on where she was. It felt like she was in a hole, but she could see bright lights up higher. Lights flashed in reds and blues, and suddenly she recognized the wailing of her alarm clock for what it was. A siren!

Something was wrong, very wrong.

Stumbling, she headed for the flickering light that seemed to be in the center of it all. The terrain was uneven, though, and her feet slipped on the dirt and grass. She finally realized why she was so much lower than everything else. She was in the ditch. Turning, she scrambled up the slope.

The moment she came topside, she knew where she was. Guiltily, she looked down. She was right in the middle of Mrs. Lupescu's prized herb garden. She scrambled to the side, but not before a puff of wind betrayed her, ringing the bells that hung over the woman's door.

Out in front of the trailer, she saw a flurry of movement. Shea cringed when she recognized the flare of her neighbor's full skirt. She tried to avoid the rosemary, but Mrs. Lupescu gasped when she caught her. The woman's face paled, and Shea's chin wobbled.

"I'm sorry." She tiptoed her way out of the garden. "I didn't mean to."

"My heart and soul," Mrs. Lupescu breathed. Her dark ringlets of hair swung as she looked toward the bright, flickering light and then back to Shea. Muttering, she reached into her pocket and clumsily pulled out a piece of bread. She held it out in warning. "Stay away from me."

Shea took a cautious step forward, not understanding. "Mrs. Lupescu? What's wrong?"

"You demon child. That Somnambulist got hold of you again. Stay back."

Shea froze, the awful words going right to her stomach. Her neighbor had told her stories of Somnambulists and evil spirits, but she'd never looked at her like this before. "What happened?" she asked, her voice tiny.

"Demon," the widow said. She waved the bread to ward off supernatural spirits. "Demon child!"

Shea took a step forward, and the woman backed up. Another step, and she turned with a twirl of her skirts and ran. Shea's legs felt like noodles as she walked toward the main road. It was bad. Whatever had happened, she knew it was bad.

Another soft breeze stirred the air and ruffled her nightgown. The bells jingled in the background, and the hair on the back of her neck rose. Turning stiffly, she looked toward the source of the commotion.

The crowd blocked most of her vision, but above their heads, she could see why everyone was so stunned. There was a fire!

Her head tilted back as she watched the flames shoot into the air. They were bright against the black sky, all oranges and reds and yellows. The way they danced took her breath away.

Demon child.

The accusation rang in her ears. Oh, no. Please don't let her have done this. Please.

Her leaden legs carried her forward as she weaved in and out of gawkers on the scene. She had an awful feeling in her gut, a terrible cold sensation. She squeezed between a policeman and a fire truck, and her mouth dropped open.

Her trailer. It was her home!

"Shea!"

Her head snapped to the side, but it took a second or two for her to recognize her dad's voice. He sounded frantic. She opened her mouth to respond, but the breeze changed direction and blew smoke into her face. The bitter air choked her throat and grabbed her lungs. Tears filled her eyes as she heard her name again.

"Shea? Are you still in there?"

Someone walked in front of her, and she pushed her way around them. When she finally spotted her dad, he was kicking at their trailer's door. A fireman tried to pull him away, but he kept screaming her name.

"Dad!" she choked out.

With the sirens and the fire, he didn't hear her.

"Dad, I'm here!" She started to run toward him, but she screamed when the door gave way. She watched as her dad rushed into the shuddering, flaming mass of metal. "No! No!"

"No," Shea repeated, pulling back from the nightmare. "No!"

A cold, hollow, helpless feeling came over her, cinching up the tension around her ribs until she could hardly breathe. It was a feeling she remembered all too well, a feeling she'd always hated. Reaching up, she rubbed her breastbone, trying to ease the ache beneath it.

Forcibly, she kicked the memory out of her head. She had to deal with *this* now.

Focusing, she picked up as many shoes as she could carry. Dwelling on the past wouldn't help anything. She needed to concentrate on the here and now, and she had a problem. It was as simple as that. Problems could be solved by taking planned, logical steps, so she'd move up her appointment with Dr. Wainright and schedule a visit to the Solstice Sleep Clinic.

One way or another, she would take care of this.

She'd barely climbed halfway up the staircase, though, when a knock came on her front door. Only *knock* didn't really cover it. *Boom* was closer to it. The sound was loud and demanding, much too insistent for so early on a weekend morning.

Shea looked down at herself. Her arms were full of shoes, but she hadn't taken the time to get dressed yet.

The pounding on the door started coming like a jackhammer. It lifted that red flag of warning inside her head. Oh, God. Had she done something worse than an impromptu footwear show?

She dropped her shoes in a pile over the railing and hurried to the front door. Her heart was in her throat as she looked through the eyepiece.

She nearly came right out of her nightie when she saw Derek bearing down on her.

He looked riled.

Her mouth went dry. Even through her distorted, fish-eyed view, she could see the fierceness in the line of his jaw. His eyes sparked of midnight, and his dark hair was rumpled. Most riveting, though, was the sense of impatience that radiated right through the door.

Her hand fluttered to her chest. What had happened? What had he found? Nerves clanging, she looked down at herself. Her chemise didn't leave much to the imagination.

"Shea! Open this door."

"Oh, God." Please don't let anything have happened to her research. Or her buildings. Or her friends...

She slid the chain lock off its mooring and opened the door against her chest. "Derek, what's wrong? Why are you here?"

His dark gaze fixed on her, and her heart did that funny stutter step inside her chest again. He had a hand propped against each side of the doorjamb, and his body was so tense, his muscles looked ready to explode. "Why did you let me think you and Phillip were together?"

Whatever she'd been expecting, that wasn't it. She blinked, trying to pull her scattered thoughts together. "We are together. We're partners."

"Business partners," he said, his voice like a knife.

The tone had her muscles clenching. She didn't understand what he was getting at, but his anger and impatience had the morning air crackling. Something had rocked him off his calm, and she could feel him all the way to her core. Her belly squeezed, and she pressed herself so tightly against her shielding, she nearly stubbed her toe. "Yes," she said, her voice going quiet. "What does that have to do with anything?"

"Not bed partners," he said, ignoring her question.

She nearly lost her grip on the doorknob. "Of course not. I never— Why would you—"

She didn't know how he moved so fast, but one moment he was outside her door. The next, he was inside her home.

She gasped and pulled the door open as wide as it would go. Squeezing herself between it and the wall, she tried to hide her skimpy state of dress. She'd never faced him in anything less than a power suit and three-inch heels. Without them, she felt vulnerable and exposed.

On edge, she stared at him. His hair was mussed. It looked as if he'd raked his hands through it a couple dozen times. His suit jacket was almost as rumpled. It sat crooked on his wide shoulders, straining under the tension in those thick muscles. Most telling, though, his tie was almost undone, and his collar was loosened.

She'd always wondered what would happen if he stepped outside his business persona. She had the thrilling feeling that she was about to find out.

"Why the big façade?" he demanded.

"What façade? I don't know what you're talking about."

"Were you trying to keep me at arm's length?"

"No." Maybe.

He took a step forward. "Because if that was your goal, you're going to have to stop looking at me like that."

Sexual excitement oozed through Shea's body. Pressed against the door as they were, she feared her nipples might drill their way right through.

Derek swore and raked a hand through his hair, mussing it

even more. Making her want to give it a try...

"I said stop—" He went dead still when he caught a glance at what she was wearing. Muscle by muscle, his face crumpled. "Oh, hell."

He moved like a blur again. She felt the door's weight lessening against her... the handle slipping out of her damp palm... his hand catching her lower back... and the nape of her neck...

And *oh God*.

Her heart began pounding hard as his mouth came down hot against hers. His lips pressed tight, devouring her, as his tongue swept deep. Shea couldn't move. Couldn't think. She was rooted in place as he took possession of her mouth in one hot, fell swoop.

But then a groan bubbled up from deep inside her throat.

All that fearful energy that had built up inside her quickly changed to arousal. It was sharp and intense. He was offering her an escape, and she grabbed him with both hands. "Derek," she whispered.

The hand at the small of her back tightened, bringing her up solidly against him and a very thick, very hard erection.

He grunted at the contact and turned them to brace his shoulders against the wall. The way he pulled her toward him had her rocking up on her tiptoes, off balance. He took her weight easily as he kissed her again. Harder, with more hunger.

"Why did you try to put the brakes on this?" he asked against her lips. "Why?"

"I didn't." She gasped when his hands ran down from her waist to her thighs. His touch against her bare flesh was startling. "You just always... put me off kilter... It's... *ahhh*... intimidating."

His head snapped back, and his hands froze against her.

"Not in a bad way," she rushed to say. "You just always watch me so closely."

His dark eyes narrowed.

"Like that," she whispered, shifting self-consciously.

The move only rubbed her stomach more intimately against him, and his hips swiveled right along with hers.

"Can't be helped," he said.

She bit her lip when his hands started moving again. They cupped her bottom, and his teeth caught her earlobe in a sharp pinch.

"You look at me the same way," he said, soothing the hurt with a sweep of his tongue. "The only difference is you try to hide it."

Her body heated as his touch swept upward again, this time right under her nightie. He traced the crease where her legs met the curve of her bottom, and she let out a soft cry. The *whoosh* of excitement made her realize just how serious things were getting.

And how out of control she was, too.

"Do you want me as much as I want you?"

"Yes." She caught his wrists when his thumbs hooked around her panties. "But should we maybe think about this?"

"That's the problem." He stole another quick kiss. "We both think too much."

When his hands began their determined sweep downward, her panties went with them. Their gazes connected as the little scrap of nothing disappeared, sliding over her knees and down to the floor.

"It's time," he said.

Shea heard the clock ticking on the wall as their gazes held. He was here, and it wasn't a dream. She was so tired of being scared and trying to hold everything together on her own. "Past time," she whispered.

He groaned in relief and tugged her chemise upward. The ice-blue piece of silk went sailing, and she suddenly found herself standing naked with her arms raised sexily over her head.

Derek's gaze swept down her body, and a tight, urgent ball of need gelled in her stomach. For a second, she thought she felt his hands tremble against her waist. But then he picked her up and began heading for the couch. She grabbed at his shoulders and wrapped her legs around his waist to keep her balance.

"No more holding me off," he said as he dropped kisses onto her shoulder. "No more of the strictly business routine. If you need help, you call me."

Shea started tugging at his clothes. She wanted him naked. Before she could get more than his tie off, though, he'd laid her down and backed away.

Her breath seized inside her chest when she looked up at him.

He was standing over her in the bright morning sunlight, looking like something she'd only seen in her nighttime dreams. His face was hard. His chest was expanding and contracting with each ragged breath. What caught her attention most, though, was the big erection tenting the front of his pants.

"Derek," she said shakily.

He began stripping out of his jacket and shirt. Her nipples tightened to the point where they hurt, and her belly sucked in. This was all so fast. So unexpected. So out of character for him. Or maybe she was just seeing the real side of him, the side that wasn't kept lashed down and tied up in rules. The side that was straining to get out.

She knew what that felt like.

He went for the zipper of his pants. "You've had me worried as hell."

He was naked before she could process the words, and then, she couldn't think at all. He was built, *GQ* underwear model built.

"I need you to talk to me," he whispered as he grasped her ankles in each hand.

Her heart began to pound. It was the hard, desperate, I-need-to-get-out-of-your-chest kind of thudding that made everything more vivid, more real.

This was just about as real as she could stand.

He spread her legs. Leaning down, he kissed her inner ankle.

"Oh, God," she said, her voice jumping.

His lips slid ever so slowly up her shin, and his tongue swirled around her kneecap. "I need you to trust me."

"I do trust you."

"Not enough." His mouth moved up her leg to her quaking inner thigh muscles. "I want to be closer."

She clutched at him. One hand found the top of his head, while the other bit into the straining muscles of his shoulder. He used it to nudge her legs wider to make room for himself between them. Then his hot breath touched the most private part of her. "Let me behind those walls."

The first touch of his tongue blew her mind into a million pieces. Her breath heaved in her chest as it swept upward, licking at her pussy lips, probing her opening, and then sliding over her sensitive clit.

"Ohhh," she groaned, so aroused she was shaking the entire couch.

Or maybe they were doing that together.

Derek was trying so hard to keep himself contained, his muscles were jumping.

He'd never felt anything as intoxicating as Shea's skin. He couldn't get enough of it. He continued his journey up her body, dipping his tongue into her belly button and giving it a swirl. She trembled against his face, making him just want to rear up and plunge into her.

But there was so much more to explore, so much more to revel in. He wet his tongue, and when he let it touch her belly again, it was for one long, destroying lick.

He wanted her so badly he was nearly going blind. She was perfect. So stunningly perfect. He let his weight come down on her more heavily, and his breath hissed out when she touched him.

He hovered over her breasts, trying to slow down. It just wasn't going to happen.

"You're so beautiful."

He finally gave in and did what he'd wanted to do forever. He licked. He stroked. He sucked. Her shoulders pressed hard into the cushion beneath her. Still, she stayed poised as his mouth closed over her nipple and gave a hard pull.

"Ahh!" she cried.

He turned to the other one and suckled even harder, but his own body couldn't take much more foreplay. He felt like a racehorse heading down the straightaway.

And she was right there with him.

"Oh, please," she groaned, her body heaving beneath his.

Derek ran his hands up her sides as his mouth slid up her middle. Then he was finally over her, atop her completely. He settled into the cradle of her hips. His abs pressed intimately against hers, and his chest found the cushion of her breasts. He caught her hands and locked his fingers with hers, palm to palm. Their knuckles dug into the cushion on either side of her head, as the head of his cock nudged at her opening.

He just had to know one thing.

"Do you dream about me?"

"Yes!"

He thrust into her, and the feel of her had him gasping for air. She was tight. Tight and white hot. Her silky grip almost pushed him right over the edge, but then he felt her moan against his lips.

"Shea," he said with a rasp.

The sturdy couch squeaked as he began to pump into her. Friction built between them, skittering along his skin. She was holding on to him with everything she had. Her fingers bit into the backs of his hands. Her legs wrapped around him high, catching him about the ribs. And her pussy. She gripped him hardest there.

"Oh, hell. Baby."

They'd wanted each other for too long. Neither of them could take a drawn-out seduction. It was a hot, fast, wet fuck that had them both panting and straining.

Shea's orgasm hit first. Her body arched, and she cried out as she tumbled into the abyss. Derek kept moving atop her, his cock dipping deeper and harder with every thrust.

"So good." He pressed his face into the crook of her neck.

He couldn't get enough of her. He wanted this to go on forever. "Shea, I——"

Forever ended with a bang. He let out a shout, tensed, and then was spurting into her.

And that moment did seem like forever.

When he finally sank back onto her soft body, Derek's mind was blank. His tension and agitation were gone. That never-ending ache of wanting had eased. Nothing was pushing at him or demanding something from him. He let himself relish the emptiness for a long time before he realized he didn't feel empty at all.

Gradually, he eased his hold on Shea's hands, but he didn't let go. He rubbed his palms against hers, enjoying the sensation. Slowly, he lifted his head. She looked as stunned as he felt.

Stunned and more than a little self-conscious.

The room went quiet. A bird might have chirped outside. A car might have started up in the parking lot. Neither of them heard any of it. Sunlight streamed through the window as they studied each other, both achingly aware of what they'd done. What they were technically still doing...

Derek felt the muscles at the base of his spine tighten. This hadn't been his plan. It hadn't even been close. They'd ventured onto totally new ground here. Barreled onto it, actually, without thought or caution.

"You make me lose control," he said, surprised.

"Me too," she whispered.

He never turned himself loose. It was just too difficult. Expectations always held him back. Responsibility. Yet the moment he'd touched her, he hadn't been able to rein in. Even now, he was feeling the urge to start all over again. One signal, one touch, one look from her was all it would take.

Yet she acted uneasy. Wary.

Squeezing her hands, he levered his chest off her so she could breathe more easily. "I didn't mean to jump you like that."

Her lips slowly parted. "Oh... That's... It's..."

"Like *that*. I came over here fully intending to bed you. I just should have said hello first."

"Oh," she said breathlessly.

The look on her face turned his muscles to putty. He couldn't help it. She was the most beautiful thing he'd ever seen, especially now with her body warm and welcoming under his. He was entranced by the way the sunlight glowed in her hair.

"Tell me you want this, too."

"I do," she said. "I've been attracted to you since we first met."

Warning signs flared in his head. "But?"

"But... I..." She bit her lip. "It's not a good time for me to get involved with someone."

Time? What did time have to do with anything?

"Why not?" he asked.

"There's just too much going on. The prowler, my research..."

Her gaze flicked across the room toward the staircase—and stuck. Her pupils dilated, and she quickly looked away, but not before he recognized the look. He'd seen that fear on her face before. He looked to see what might be causing it, but all he saw was a pile of shoes on the floor.

"What's wrong, Shea?" His body shifted instinctively, trying to cover her and protect her from harm. "Is someone threatening you? Why are you so scared?"

"Threatening me?" Her eyes widened. "No, it's nothing like that."

"Is it me?" he asked roughly, hating the idea. "I know I can get intense, but ..."

"Oh Derek, it's not you."

He could see the turmoil on her face, but then her worried gaze dropped to his lips.

"It's *not* you."

His heart took off again when she lifted her head and kissed him. The touch of her lips was gentle and erotic, and it melted him from the inside out. Entranced, he ran his touch up her arms and over her shoulders. She turned her head, adjusting the slant of her mouth across his, and his hands fisted into her hair.

"You don't scare me, Derek. You just surprised me."

But something did scare her. This close, he could see the slight widening of her eyes and feel the tension running underneath her skin. Her hands brushed against his back, and he made a decision fast.

"Spend the day with me."

He knew it was impulsive and that he hadn't thought everything through, but he didn't care. Hadn't he just learned that good things could happen when he didn't overanalyze them? That going with his instincts sometimes felt better than anything else in the world?

She glanced again toward the pile of shoes, but he caught her chin and made her look at him.

"You need to stop overthinking this, Madame Curie."

They both did.

"Ask me to stay." His muscles tensed as he waited for her response. He'd just put himself out further on that limb, and her answer was a bit too slow in coming. The worry in her eyes cut deep. Slowly, he started to pull away.

Her fingers dug into his back. "Stay."

He couldn't remember ever getting so hard so fast. "Where's the bed?"

CHAPTER SEVEN

He'd let her fall asleep.

It was the first clear thought that ran through Shea's mind when she opened her eyes. That and the fact that Derek was still with her. His heat pressed against her back, and his arm draped heavily across her waist. They were lying side by side on her bed, with her body tucked up close against his.

Yet even as she responded in pleasure, she tensed.

Darkness was falling. They'd spent the day making love, and now the sun was setting. Night was creeping in. She stared at the oil painting that hung on the wall until her nerves began to crawl. Even the littlest thing could set her Somnambulist off—and today had been anything but normal—yet she'd let herself be lulled into sleep.

What had she been thinking?

"There you are." The hand against her stomach flexed, and she was pulled more tightly against the big male form behind her.

His muscled thigh slipped between her legs, and Shea arched when he kissed the side of her neck. The intimate embrace had her groaning. Obviously, she hadn't been thinking. Her brain had been shorted out, disconnected, and thrown right into the bathwater.

How could she have let her guard down like that? The freedom had been fantastic, arousing and intoxicating as fine wine, but how could she have forgotten what had been happening to her? What had happened just this morning?

Had she... Oh, no. Had she done anything in her sleep? With Derek here?

"How long have I been out?" she asked in a rush.

"Not long."

That rumbling voice was too disconcerting, too sexy. She had to look into his eyes. Tucking the sheet up high under her arms, she rolled over to face him. When she did, her breath caught in her chest. His short hair was mussed, and dark shadows lined his jaw. The bad boy look didn't fit his character, but it was so incredibly hot she had to press her thighs together.

Unable to help herself, she let her gaze drop. She took in the well-drawn lines of his body, his muscled chest and rippling abs, but the sheet sitting low on his hips wasn't what made her look up again. It was the relaxed look on his face. She'd never seen him so calm, so relaxed, so at ease in the moment. It made her belly warm.

Relaxed had to be good, right? If she'd gotten up and danced zombie pirouettes around the bedroom, he wouldn't be relaxed.

Or so obviously ready to make love to her again.

"You were out like a light." His gaze slid over her face, alert as always. One of his eyebrows twitched when he saw the tension she was trying to hide. He pulled her closer to him. "Maybe that last time in the shower was a bit too much."

Shea's racing thoughts skidded to a stop.

The shower.

She remembered that. In fact, it was the last thing she remembered before she'd woken up face to face with her Tasha St. James original. Nerves singing, she glanced over Derek's shoulder toward the bathroom. Even as wound up as she was, her body melted as memories of that wet encounter flashed through her mind. She remembered how cool the tile had felt under her fingertips as he'd bent her forward... how warm the water had been as it had stung her back and bottom...

Her teeth caught at her lower lip.

Mostly, though, she remembered how big he'd felt as he'd thrust into her from behind... How widely his hips had arced and how deeply he'd gone... She'd come so violently, her knees had buckled.

But after that?

"Yeah," he said softly.

She placed her hand against his chest, her fingers tingling for him. Yet as she pulled her gaze away from the bathroom, it accidentally skimmed over her walk-in closet. Darkness filled up the back corners of the tiny room, and the doors stood wide open. Her shoes were still arranged as she'd found them this morning, one stepping out after the other.

"Shea?"

The chance she'd taken! She wasn't the only one vulnerable when she slept. He was even more at risk. For goodness' sake, she'd almost run over that stranger with her car.

His hand slid down to cup her hip. "What's wrong?"

One look at his ruffled hair and sexy eyes, and she stopped herself. Why ruin what had been the most erotic and sexually fulfilling day of her life? She had the perfect man in her bed: strong, smart, and sexy as all get out. Why spoil this?

"Nothing's wrong."

"Are you sure?"

She trailed her fingers over his hard chest. "It's just waking up to find you here, in my bed. We seem to have skipped right over the dating part."

His dark eyes flared. "We'll date all you want."

He kissed her again, rubbing his mouth against hers slowly, taking the intimacy deeper by degrees. By the time his tongue swept across hers, her fingers were digging into his back.

"I can't get over how good you feel." He kissed his way under her chin, and his hand stroked up her side to cup her breast. "Your skin is incredible. You know your business, Curie."

Curie. Shea's nipple peaked hard when his thumb brushed over it. He said the name like an endearment. The inflection was so close to *chéri*, she looked up to see if he realized what he'd done.

He did.

"Phillip and I have worked very hard," she whispered.

"But you two never…"

She shook her head, blushing a little when she remembered how worked up that had made him. Still, Phillip wasn't ready for the world to know. Only she and Tamika knew the truth, and it made her uncomfortable that Derek had somehow found out. Yet that was what he did. He found out the truth, no matter how uncomfortable or inconvenient. An uneasy jitter ran down her spine. "We're just friends. Best friends ever since college."

"Don't worry. I won't out him. That's his business." His thumb settled over her nipple and lingered. "I just don't think you realize the part you've been playing in keeping his secret. We could have been together long before now if I'd known."

Shea leveled a look on him. "You're no open book. Our meeting the other day was the first time I realized you might even be interested. Other than work, I don't know that much about you."

"I'm interested. What else do you want to know?"

"Are you serious?"

He plumped the pillow under his head. "I want to know about you, too."

This all just felt so strange, lying here naked with him, their skin brushing and their breaths mingling. The darkness in the room deepened, surrounding them and drawing the intimacy even closer. "Derek, you must have done a background check on me. That's… Well, that's what you do."

"I know the basics, the things that are kept track on paper, but that doesn't tell me about you as a woman."

Shea's lips parted. For some reason, that was the sexiest

thing he'd said to her all day. Unfortunately, it was also the most unsettling. All he must see was the image she'd worked so hard to create, that of the polished professional. "You like throwing me off balance, don't you?"

He smiled softly. "I'm beginning to find it one of my favorite things."

She shifted, and her legs tangled with his. The more she thought about it, the more disconcerted she got.

"Your turn," he said.

"For what?"

"To tell me anything and everything there is to know about Shea Caldwell." He snuggled against the pillow, looking as sexy and lazy as a tiger settling down for a nap. "Why biochemistry?"

The question surprised her, but it eased her as well. "It always clicked for me. Chemistry makes sense. Sometimes it's the only thing that does."

"Can't argue with you there." The look in his eyes told her he wasn't thinking about the kind of chemistry that required a periodic chart.

"There's so much good I can do with it," she said. "So many people I can help. I want to do more. I want to—" She stopped and licked her lips. "What about you? Why corporate intelligence?"

"Because privacy is important to me, I believe in rules, and I'm very protective of what's mine."

She tried to think as his hand stroked over her skin. "But your brother is a newspaper editor. They like to get information out."

"We're all different."

"There's more than just the two of you?"

He smiled. "I have more brothers than you can count, but no sisters—at least that I'm aware of."

She smiled with him. "Your poor mother."

"Don't feel sorry for her. She's a force to be reckoned with."

"What's her name?"

"Nyx."

Shea's fingers paused on his collarbone.

"What?" he asked.

She looked at him bemusedly. "I took a course in Greek mythology when I was an undergrad. Do you know the story of the Oneiroi, Derek?"

She felt the energy gather in him. It practically swirled around the bed. "I'm familiar with it," he said carefully.

The power coming off him was heady. Shea inhaled, absorbing it as her mind went back. "They were dark-winged daemons sent up by gods from a cavern in Erebus, the underworld. When they appeared to humans, it was in their sleep. The Oneiroi could take whatever shape they wished, but true dreams emerged from a gate made of horn while false dreams came from a gate made of ivory."

He cleared his throat. "Something like that."

"They were said to rule over sexual dreams most of all."

The room seemed to shrink, and Shea felt him everywhere they touched. If anyone ruled her sexual dreams, it was him. She cleared her throat. "Anyway, the mother of the Oneiroi was said to be Night, or Nyx."

He edged closer. "What do you think of all that?"

"The coincidence is fascinating. Derek Dream," she said, caught up in the whole idea of it. The mysticality. The sensuality. Slowly, she shook her head. He probably thought she was silly. "I loved that class, particularly that myth."

"Myth." His gaze dropped, yet his hand rubbed gentle circles at the small of her back. "Any reason for that?"

This time, she was the one who got careful. "I've just always been interested in stories that tried to explain things... the ones that predated the science that told the real truth. Folklore, I guess. Mrs. Lupescu used to tell me all kinds of fairy tales and legends."

"Mrs. Lupescu?"

A puff of air escaped Shea's lips. She usually did everything she could not to talk about that time of her life. He really had a way of slipping past her defenses.

Or just storming her castle walls directly...

Discomfited, she pulled the sheet higher on her chest. "She was our neighbor in the mobile home park."

"Here in Solstice?"

The blank, unassuming expression on his face took her aback. "You had to find that in your background check."

That had certainly hit the papers.

"Tell me about this neighbor."

That probably wasn't a good idea, especially now. Still, he'd be like a bulldog with a bone if she didn't give him something. She knew how he was about digging out information. "Mrs. Lupescu was this larger-than-life woman," she said, choosing her words with care. "She'd tell me all kinds of fantastical stories when my dad was on the road, but she could get a little over the top about it, too."

"Your dad traveled a lot?"

"He was a truck driver. Well, actually, he's driving again. For Biodermatics." Her gaze dropped. "He... uh... took a break for a while."

"Are you two close?"

"Very." Her eyes stung. "I think that's enough show and tell for today."

Derek's eyes narrowed, that familiar spark of curiosity flaring. Yet then he did something she'd never seen him do; he tamped it down. "Maybe enough telling, but definitely not enough showing."

Moving in, he kissed her again. The hand at her back slid down her spine, the fingers caressing each vertebra with care. It sent her system into an uproar. After a day of making love, her body was beginning to know when he was serious.

"So soft," he whispered against her lips.

Shea groaned as he touched her sensitive flesh, stroking and building a hunger she hadn't even known existed.

His fingers stroked over her waist and then slid down between her legs. One dipped into her, its entrance shallow and smooth. The moment he discovered how wet she was, he came back for more. His fingers pushed in further, burrowing deep to caress the walls of her vagina.

Shea arched in his embrace. He touched her like nobody else ever had, like he knew she was his.

"I can't believe this is happening between us," she whispered.

"It's happening." He kissed her. "Touch me."

She felt his heart pounding against his ribcage. Looking into his eyes, she saw his need. He was as responsive to her as she was to him.

And, oh God, was she responding to him.

Her hips pushed down to meet each plunge of those thick, determined fingers. She let her knuckles drag down his chest, over his belly, and across his six-pack abs. The heat of his cock was so unexpected, she paused.

A thrill went through her when he flinched.

"Don't stop," he groaned.

Shea fought for air as she rubbed her fingers along the top of his heavy cock from its base to its blunt tip.

"Fuck," Derek panted, his fingers slamming into her almost roughly.

Shea let out a cry as her hips jumped in pleasure, and she wrapped her hand around him, taking hold of him for real.

"Stroke it," he said.

Eagerly, she pumped her hand up and down. He felt hot in her hand. Hot, hard, and silky. He was big, and her pussy squeezed at the thought of taking him again.

She gasped when he suddenly pulled his fingers out of her. The loss left her aching, but not for long. He caught the back of her thigh and pulled her leg over his hip.

"Now."

Her hand trembled as she directed his erection to where she needed it the most. The moment the bulbous head dipped into her notch, though, he took over. Rolling his hips, he pushed into her.

Her breath caught in her lungs.

"Okay?" he asked, his hand catching her by the lower back.

She lifted her leg higher over his waist. "I love the way you feel."

She felt his muscles clench, and then he was filling her again. His thick cock burrowed slowly up into her, stretching long-unused muscles, until he was seated all the way inside her. Her leg wrapped snugly around his hip, and she held him close. His whiskers scraped against her cheek as he took a long, slow breath.

"I'm glad we didn't stop to date first. I don't think I could have waited."

"Me either."

Their mouths met as he began to thrust into her slowly, sensually. She found his rhythm and met him stroke for stroke. Their bodies sealed tightly, her breasts plumping against his chest. Their body temperature heated the dark air around them, and the night became sultry. Still, they kept it slow until their skin slickened... Until their bodies were straining... Until neither of them could stand it.

"Ah!" Shea cried when Derek thrust a little harder, a little faster.

She looked into his dark eyes and saw pleasure.

"Yes," she agreed.

His thrusts became more urgent, quicker and rougher. She took him greedily, and the rhythm translated up the bed until the headboard was knocking against the wall.

"Oh, God. Derek!"

"Curie."

Shea arched as her orgasm hit her hard. The waves just kept coming over her as the headboard knocked and banged. Derek propped himself up on his elbows and dropped his head as he fucked her right through it. When his release came, it was hot and sticky. His shout of completion was even sexier.

His weight finally came down on her and pinned her in place. Their skin clung as they both struggled to catch their breath. Slowly, he pulled back. His hand was unsteady as he brushed her hair off her face.

Shea felt shaky, too. His weight felt good against her. Right. The darkness around them was complete. Night had fallen. It was the first time in years she'd felt comfortable in it, safe. Yet she could feel sleep sneaking up on her again, coiled and ready to pounce.

Anxiety hummed over her skin.

She looked into Derek's fathomless eyes. She didn't want to hurt his feelings. She didn't want to jeopardize the tenuous relationship they'd just started.

But all of that took a back seat when it came to protecting him.

"It's getting late," she said gently.

His brow furrowed. "So?"

"So tomorrow is a work day. I'm sure you want to get an early start."

"I'd rather sleep in with you."

Shea shivered when she saw the closet gaping like a huge, dark mouth. "You said just for the day..."

"Are you asking me to leave?"

She smiled sadly. "I've loved being with you today, Derek. I really have, but... I think it's time you should go."

* * *

The mist started collecting in the corner of the room. Particles gathered, shifting as the form took shape. Yet even assembled, the being was amorphous. Free-flowing. The Somnambulist entered his She-a's room carefully, putting out feelers as he went. Sniffing the air...

The scent of Weaver filled his brain, scrambling his thoughts. It was the most-feared scent for his kind, a killing scent.

Yet the room was empty, save for his beloved.

His pretty, pretty girl.

She lay on the bed, her blonde hair flowing around her shoulders. Her toes peeked out from under the rumpled covers, and excitement licked through him. She was too tempting for him to leave, even with the threat of danger lurking.

He edged toward her, aching to be with her again. He wanted her power, craved her ability for physical touch. His particles fluttered in anticipation as he crept forward, but he stayed on guard. The Dream Weaver had left, that much was clear. Yet his She-a wasn't dreaming.

The creature's eyes narrowed.

What was a Weaver doing here if not bestowing dreams?

Possessiveness heated him from the inside out. His She-a was his. His to be with, his to enjoy. Reaching out, he stroked his fingers over her shoulder. He watched as they disappeared into her body, and he wished he could feel the resiliency of her skin.

He wished he felt something else, too.

A growl bubbled up inside his thin chest.

Something was wrong. Again.

He wiggled his fingers, pulled them out, and delved into her again. Her arm was like a bag of sand attached to her torso. Heavy. Dead. For nights, it had been like this. Ever since they'd taken that drive in her car, she'd been fighting him.

A hiss left his thin lips. Was the Weaver responsible for this?

The creature bent down over her, so near that her breath pushed right through him. He peered at her eyelids more closely, but they were smooth and still. Dreams weren't what held her down.

What had the Oneiros done to her?

"Arggggh!" the creature screeched. With a lurch, he powered himself up over her. He hovered for a moment, before letting himself slowly drop. He filled her up from head to toe, letting his essence congregate.

His anger was immediate.

She felt heavy and cloudy. Cobwebs filled her head. Frustration had his particles shaking. Why was he having to work so hard to get her to respond to his commands? Why was she keeping her delicious, wonderful power from him?

After all that he'd done for her, how dare she treat him

this way?

He tried to sit her up, but he couldn't. Snarling, he tried to move her head. Open her eyes. Lift a finger. Wiggle her toes.

Panting, he stared at the backs of her eyelids. He needed to focus. It was how he'd taken charge of her last night—last night when he'd needed to show her that the face in the window was back. Yes, yes, there it had been, hateful eyes glaring. He'd shown it to her, and he'd left a path of breadcrumbs to remind her. They'd taken their time setting out all her pretty, colorful shoes.

He licked his lips, remembering how it had felt to be corporeal for that long. How sumptuous it had been. He wanted that control back.

Closing his eyes, he held on to his anger. He let it feed him, hone his concentration. The moment he did, he realized her body felt different. Something had changed. Tonight, it wasn't only heavy and cloudy, it was hot and... tickly. Sensitive.

"Hmm." What was this?

Trapped as he was, he could sense every inch of her. Beneath the weighted fog, he detected something. Something pulsing with energy. The red bumps on her chest... They were all pointy and tingly. And that special spot between her legs felt awake.

His Somnambulist heart began to pound. This was new.

He went very, very still, concentrating on that tender spot. Was that slickness? Between her thighs? He tried to rub her legs together, but she remained frozen in place.

"Aarrrgggh," he cried in frustration.

There was a secret here, a power that he craved.

He had to find a way to tap in to it.

His determination built. He shook his head inside She-a's, trying to clear out the cobwebs that had tangled up her brain. "Let me in!"

He needed to blast through those sticky webs and find a way to connect with her. He focused all his concentration downward, but flinched in surprise when those red nips throbbed and that awake spot squeezed.

He paused.

He tried it again, and those achy spots on her body sang. So did he. This was better than pain... almost. He sent the impulses down over and over again until—

Her toes wiggled along with his.

He gurgled deep in his throat. He loved her toes.

Soon he had her feet.

Excitement made him work harder. If he could wiggle her toes, could he wiggle her fingers? He sent his concentration through her and the red bumps on her chest tightened almost painfully.

He whinnied gleefully.

Oh, this was working better than anything else had. He flicked her fingers back and forth, feeling the circulation build. He circled her wrists and bent her arms at the elbows.

Finally, he managed to lift her head.

Those red tips were pointing so high into the air, they looked as if they were trying to poke right through her clothes. Curious, he used her hand to reach over to touch. The blue material was slick, soft, and slippery.

"Oooh," he crooned. He liked that.

He hissed when her fingertips bumped up against that pointy tip. He liked that better, and so did she. He jabbed at the soft point again, and electricity coursed straight down to that magic spot between her legs.

The sensation made them both shudder.

Oh, the power. He licked her lips. It was luscious and potent. He had to have it. He needed more.

He latched on to the red bump. Using her fingers, he squeezed and plucked at the naughty nub, feeling the power lash through them both. Wanting more, he let her pinch and twist it.

With a cry of pleasure, her body lifted right off the bed.

The Somnambulist stopped, stunned.

She'd done that, not him.

Using her hands, he pushed them under the slippery

material and excitedly caught both the full mounds. She squeezed them, pinched them, and rolled them. The red bumps beaded up until they were tiny and hard. The power was so scintillating, he could hardly stand it.

An idea flashed inside his head, a brilliant idea. If it felt good touching her there…

He had both her hands diving down when warning signs suddenly clanged in his head. He jerked her head up. Nostrils flaring, he took a quick whiff.

"Dream Weaver!"

Not now!

The creature's particles instinctively jumped, trying to scatter. The room was taking on a different charge, and a shimmering had appeared on the opposite side of the bed.

Fear warred with pleasure. Wants clashed with instincts. Knowing he couldn't stay, the Somnambulist lurched out of his hostess' willing body. The quick disconnect was painful, ripping.

Looking at the bed with regret, he started to disperse. He hated to leave now, just as they were on the verge of… something. "I'll be back for you, my pretty lady," he promised.

Oh yes, he'd be back for her soon.

Real, real soon.

CHAPTER EIGHT

She'd made him leave, just asked him to go. Any way you put it, Derek was pissed.

He was also worried as hell.

The day had been perfect—or so he'd thought. He'd gotten closer to Shea than he'd ever believed possible, and she'd wanted to be with him, too. He didn't question that. Nobody was that good of an actress. Her body had warmed when he touched her. Her eyes had softened. She trusted him with the physical, that much was clear.

It just didn't go beyond that.

He punched his pillow and tried to get more comfortable. Something had put her on edge. Something had made her want him out of the house, but he didn't think it was anything he'd done. She'd seemed troubled as she'd closed the door behind him. Troubled and sad. The look in her eyes had just about killed him. Why would she want to be alone at night? If something was scaring her, wouldn't she have asked him to stay?

None of it made sense.

Rolling onto his back, he tried to relax. He'd gone along with her request for one reason only. He could go right back.

And he would, if only he could get to sleep.

He rested his wrist against his forehead as he stared up at the ceiling. Insomnia wasn't usually a problem for Dream

Weavers. They slept differently from humans. Tonight, though, he was just a little too worked up to get into that state of relaxation he needed, the one that put his physical body into stasis and let his spirit fly.

Letting out a deep, cleansing breath, he forced his muscles to relax. Trying to stop his brain never worked. Instead, he squeezed his fists, then let the tension flow out of his fingertips. He did the same with his toes. He worked his way through his body until, finally, he concentrated on simply inhaling and exhaling. Inhaling and exhaling.

Suddenly he was there, detached from the human world. His spirit split from his sleeping earthly form, and he astral-projected into the dream realm.

Calls from his charges immediately hit his ears.

"Shit." He'd forgotten about them.

For a long, conflicted moment, duty pulled at him. He'd never ignored his responsibilities before. The thought had never even occurred to him. For once, though, he didn't conform. Pushing his guilt away, he headed straight for Shea's condo. He'd get to the others. He'd just be worthless to them until he figured out what was going on with her. The moment he sensed her brain wave pattern, the rest of the din faded into the background. He materialized in her bedroom, concentrating solely on her.

The mistake could have meant his end, because he wasn't the only one there.

Zane spun toward him, hands lifted. His brown eyes were fierce, and his jaw was like granite. Automatically, Derek stepped back and braced himself.

"Damn it, Derek."

Whirling back around, Zane faced the bed. Shea slumbered on, beautiful and unaware. Yet every muscle in Zane's body was tense as he scanned the room.

Derek quickly went on the alert and turned the other way, guarding his brother's back. Concentrating, he tried to pick up on whatever Zane was feeling. He caught it immediately. The vibrating hum was strange. Close. It started in his hands and traveled to his chest. It echoed there, faint but sinister.

And it wasn't fading.

"Do you feel that?" Zane said.

"I feel it." Derek's hands came up, ready for an onslaught. "Find it."

* * *

The Somnambulist hadn't gone far.

He couldn't, not after what he'd just found.

Feeling greedy and territorial, he hovered outside the windows of his She-a's home. Awful Weavers. They might think they owned her, but they didn't. He'd found a way past the foggy haze they'd put inside her head. But what were they doing back here? And why two of them?

Taking care not to get caught, he let his form stretch to the point where it could barely be seen. Barely be detected...

He peeked inside, but one of the big Weavers turned sharply, and his hands came up. The creature cringed, elongating and stretching until he nearly came apart. Deadly hands, those were. Hands of sizzle and burn.

"You sense something?" the first Weaver asked.

A growl rumbled up inside the creature, making his particles quiver in outrage. That was the one who'd chased him out of his beloved's room... out of her very body... Just a few more minutes with her, and he would have found something momentous. He knew it.

The scary Dream Weaver didn't answer. His attention focused on the window, and, for a split second, the Somnambulist's particles froze in place. It took everything he had not to shriek. The Weaver's eyes burnt and gleamed. He moved closer to the window, and the Somnambulist trembled in fear.

He knew he should disperse. One Dream Weaver was dangerous. Two were deadly. And they were obviously attached to his pretty, pretty lady.

But so was he.

Moving carefully, the creature shifted to the next window. His gaze raked over his lovely's blonde hair and rounded shoulders. The red-tipped bumps on her chest were covered, but he knew the power they held. He needed it.

Another host wouldn't suit him. He was old, ancient for his kind. With age came a need for more energy. Easy targets like the young couldn't give him the juice he needed. His She-a was an adult now, too, and he'd just found a power source in her so vast, he could survive without her for nights.

Or even better, stay with her longer and longer. Why, with that kind of power, he might even be able to be with her all night.

And she needed that.

Anger flared inside him when he remembered the face in the window, that figure in black. His beloved hadn't known anyone was peeking inside her home night after night, but he had. Without him, she never would have been able to chase the nasty bugger away.

No, no. The Weavers couldn't protect her like he could. They couldn't have her.

Brazenly, the Somnambulist watched his enemy. They wanted to play hide-and-seek? He was the best. For years, he'd slipped out of their reach. Unfortunately, others hadn't been so lucky. He'd heard what they did to his kind.

Sizzle, sizzle. Regular or extra crispy?

It was a risk he was willing to take. Knowing he'd pushed his luck far enough for tonight, though, he let himself vaporize and disappear.

But he'd be back.

The Dream Weaver with the tough eyes couldn't be here all the time. He had other sleepers to attend to.

Fortunately, Somnambulists only needed one.

* * *

"I don't feel it anymore," Zane said.

"It's gone."

Zane let his body relax from the defensive posture he'd taken. Still, he was on guard. "What was it?"

Derek wished he knew. The vibration had been odd, familiar yet not. With it so faint, he couldn't be sure about anything other than that a night creature had been nearby.

That was bad enough.

He peered out the window for any signs. Dark clouds were stamped against the moon. The air was heavy with humidity, but nothing moved. The leaves hung limp on tree branches, and the grass beaded up with moisture.

A bad feeling niggled at him. As he turned back to the bed, his gaze immediately went to Shea. She was sleeping soundly. He could feel the delta waves from where he stood. She was in stage three, ready to be led into REM sleep.

It wasn't a good sign. Too many night creatures liked to strike early in the night before he and his brothers made their first appearance.

"I felt it as soon as I manifested," Zane said. "But then you appeared, and I lost the trace. What the hell are you doing here, Derek? She's my charge."

"I know."

"But you still think I'm messing with her dreams?" His brother's jaw hardened. Moving fast, he came across the room and got in Derek's face. "I know you're The Machine, and I'm The Screw-Up. That's the way everybody likes it, clean and simple, but I take care of her, Derek. No matter what label you throw on me, I'm good at what I do. Damn good."

"I know that." Derek rolled his shoulders. He was the one who wasn't doing his job tonight, yet he identified with his brother's anger. He was sick of being labeled, and he wasn't an unfeeling robot. A machine wouldn't invade his brother's territory and avoid his own. When he looked at Shea, though, he knew there wasn't anything else he could do. "This isn't about you. It's about me."

"You think you're better than I am?"

"No. I think I couldn't stay away—not even when she asked."

Zane blinked and took a step back. "Did things not go well between you two?"

Derek glared at him. What had happened between him

and Shea was private, yet just as he was about to inform Zane of that, he realized his brother was acting almost disappointed. Disappointed and kind of sympathetic.

Hell, was he that pathetic?

"Hey, I'm not implying anything." Zane lifted his hands. "I expected you to be here—just in that bed with her, not floating in the dream realm with me."

Derek looked at the empty space at Shea's side. "Yeah. Me too."

What else could he say? It was where he still wanted to be.

"So... what happened?"

Derek shifted uncomfortably. "She kicked me out."

"She did not." Zane tried to hold back, but that just wasn't the kind of guy he was. "Are you serious? What did you do? You can't tell me the sex wasn't good."

He gestured about the room. Pillows, bedding, and shoes were strewn everywhere. Lotions had been scattered across the dressing table, and two damp towels were draped over the side of the tub in the master bath.

Derek stiffened, but proof was proof. "We were... compatible. She just didn't want to sleep with me. Now I think I understand why."

They both looked to the bed. "When she said sleep, she meant sleep."

"She knows something's after her." Moving instinctively back to her side, Zane set up guard. If anything was out there stalking her in the night, he was the one bound to protect her.

But damn, Derek wanted to be in his place.

He rubbed the back of his neck. He should have pressed her harder. She'd told him that she hadn't been sleeping well. She just hadn't let him know how bad it was. With night creatures lurking, it *had* to be bad. He swore underneath his breath. His instincts had been right the first time, yet he'd let himself get distracted with that trespasser. Although that was a bad scene, too...

What the hell was going on?

He stared hard at the floor. He needed to think with the

head on his shoulders, not the one that seemed to pop to attention whenever she walked in the room.

"Check the dresser," he said as he went into the bathroom. A nightlight glowed steadily. "Is this always on?"

"Yeah, she's afraid of the dark."

Derek shook his head. The darkness was where he was most comfortable. It was his home, his retreat.

His spine stiffened. The most-telling sign of all sat on the counter beside the sink. "Sleeping pills."

"Prescription?"

"Over-the-counter." Feeling tense and ready to pop, Derek leaned his arm against the doorjamb and stared hard at the bed. Asleep, Shea looked sweet and vulnerable. Her lips were parted as if awaiting a kiss. She'd put that ice-blue nightie back on since he'd left, but the sheet had drifted low across her breasts. She'd been fighting this scourge on her own and fighting hard. If only he'd known... If only Zane had known...

But they hadn't.

Now, they had to play catch-up.

"She's a scientist," Derek said flatly. "She doesn't know she's a target. In her mind, she thinks she has a parasomnia, a sleep disorder."

"Yeah, but which one?"

The vibration seemed to reappear in Derek's hands, and he had to flex his fingers to shake it. The hum had been low and powerful, like a big bass amplifier. Frustration filled him when he still couldn't place it. "How does she normally sleep? What's a typical night like?"

Zane shrugged. "She's a lot like you, if you really want to know. When it comes to sleep, she has very strict routines. She goes to bed at the same time every night, and she takes dreams easily. In the past few weeks, though, something's changed. I don't sense her until late."

Derek paused. He wasn't sensing Tamika until the wee hours of the night either.

"It could be due to her work," Zane said. "I've found her

sleeping over her papers or with a book falling out of her hand."

"She works too hard," Derek said with a frown. "How have her dreams been? Any more nightmares?"

"Other than the wet ones?"

He hadn't known he could growl.

Zane's lips twitched. "Sorry."

His brother ruffled his mop of hair. "She has really unique dreams," he confided. "She dreams in equations, man. Chemical formulas and reactions. I'll find her walking all over a molecule, trying to find where to attach a carbon element."

Derek hadn't needed details. Good or bad... normal or disturbing... that was all he'd wanted, yet the details were irresistible.

"She's brilliant," Zane said quietly. "I can't make heads or tails of what she's thinking, but it's impressive. You know?"

"I'm just surprised you know what a molecule looks like."

"I'm not a complete idiot."

"No, you just play one sometimes." Derek let out a long breath. Bantering with Zane made him feel better, like things were on a steadier keel than they really were.

"What else?" he asked, his voice rough. She hadn't told him nearly enough as they'd rested on that same pillow only a short while ago. He wanted to know more about her. He needed to know more if he was going to help her.

"She's terrified of fire."

Derek looked up sharply, his stomach taking a dip in the opposite direction.

"Most of her nightmares center on it," his brother said.

The Bunsen burner. He remembered the way she'd stopped to double-check that it was off. She'd seemed almost obsessive about it.

"She loves Baby Ruth candy bars," Zane offered. "If you want to find a way back into her bed, that might be a good way to sweeten her up."

"But she's a Mets fan," Derek said absently, rubbing his chest.

"A Mets fan who craves a chocolate bar named after the biggest Yankee ever. That's why it's a secret."

She had a lot of those. Too many.

Derek closed his eyes. So did he.

He could help her with this, but how could he explain that to her? How could he tell a top-notch biochemist that he wasn't quite human? That he was a Dream Weaver who traveled through another realm at night to bestow dreams? She might like the fantasy, but she'd never accept the reality. At best, she'd think he was mocking her.

At worst, she'd think he was insane.

Zane's arms dropped to his sides. "Go ahead."

Derek looked up. "What?"

"Take a swing at me. You've got every right."

"What are you talking about?"

Guilt rippled across his brother's boyish face, but then he stood a little straighter. "I screwed up. I obviously let something get by me."

"Ah, hell. So did I." Derek pushed himself away from the wall. "I missed it, too."

And for that, they both should be kicked.

Moving automatically to the bed, Derek reached for Shea's forehead. The best way to help her was to get her back into a normal sleep cycle, starting with REM sleep. As his fingers brushed over her brow, though, he remembered his place. Muscles protesting, he made himself take a step back. "Take care of her. Please."

Zane looked at him sharply. "Are you sure?"

"She's yours."

"My charge, maybe."

Yeah, life sucked sometimes.

Still, Zane held back. "I don't think so. You should take over with her."

The offer was unexpected, and it made Derek's pulse jump.

Still, he looked at his little brother. Really looked. "I trust you, Zane. I might not like your methods sometimes. The way you play around in people's heads drives me nuts, but it also makes me realize how good you are at this."

"But you want her."

"Yeah, I do."

"So take her."

Just like that. Take her.

Zane lived by impulse, but it was harder for Derek. He wanted to grab the opportunity with both hands, but there was more to consider. Would it put him too close? And how would it affect his relationship with his brother? For all his nonchalant attitude, Zane had been Shea's Dream Weaver for a long time. If he really believed Derek didn't think he was good enough for her...

Zane cleared his throat, obviously uncomfortable at the silence. "I've got to warn you, though, it's going to cost you."

Derek braced himself. That cocky, self-important look was back in his brother's eyes. It drew over him almost like armor. "Cost me how?"

"You'll have to give me someone for her."

"You want to trade?"

"One hottie for another." Zane's gaze slid over Shea's form. It was soft and protective, yet he smiled wickedly. "A woman like this? Hell, you might have to give me two."

"You reprobate," Derek said.

Yet he had an uncanny suspicion that he was being let off the hook.

His brother did have a point. They'd been struggling to balance out the workload. He really couldn't take on Shea, knowing she had sleep issues, without giving somebody up. He might not have the time to treat them all equally—and he knew that she was going to get his best.

"Somebody sexy," Zane said. "Somebody smokin'."

An idea hit Derek, and it was perfect. "Tamika Hendricks."

"Really?" Zane said, perking up. "I mean... Sure. Is there anything I should know about her?"

Derek rounded the bed, deadly serious about this. It

would kill two birds with one stone. "She works with Shea, and she's been calling for me late, too. She'll take dreams when I give them to her, but finding her asleep has been a problem. When I saw her the other day, she looked troubled."

His brother's humor left fast. "Do you think there's a connection?"

"I don't know. Maybe." Either way, Derek didn't like it. "You know what this thing feels like now. You can be on the lookout for it. I'd do it, but—"

"But you'd rather be here." Zane planted his hands on his hips, yet one eyebrow cocked. "Is Tamika good-looking?"

Derek felt the familiar desire to knock his brother upside the head. It made him feel so much better about things. "She's unbelievably hot. Long, lean runner's legs. High, perky breasts. And she can have some pretty kinky dreams."

"You had me at legs."

"It's a deal, then. Tamika's yours, and Shea's mine."

Together, they looked at the beautiful blonde on the bed.

Unexpectedly, Zane cuffed him upside the shoulder. "Machine Man, I think you might have finally met your match."

CHAPTER NINE

Shea didn't want to throw Derek out of her bed ever again.

She'd hated the look on his face as he'd stood on her front stoop under the moonlight. He hadn't complained or argued. He'd simply kissed the daylights out of her before saying goodnight. Yet she'd seen the look in his eyes. He'd been disappointed and worried. She knew that glint, and she was tired of being responsible for it.

She was tired of so many things: being scared, being out of control, and being vulnerable. No more. She was determined to get her life back, and she'd just taken the first step.

She lifted the brown plastic bottle up to the sunlight and gave it a jiggle. The sleeping pills inside rattled. She hoped this prescription medication worked better than the over-the-counter stuff. As far as she could tell, she hadn't sleepwalked last night, but she had a strange, uneasy feeling she just couldn't shake. Her Somnambulist might not have wandered with her last night, but it had visited.

The hair at the back of her neck rose. She hated to think how it was going to react to this.

The pills rattled louder as she shoved them into her purse and got out of her car. She needed to stop thinking like that. She had a sleep disorder—a sleep *arousal* disorder, to be precise. As her doctor had explained it, she was coming too close to wakefulness as she progressed through the sleep stages. There was a scientific, clinical explanation for what had been happening to her. She was not a victim of some long-ago childhood monster.

Although, deep down, she still might feel like it.

Lifting her chin, she opened the front door of Biodermatics and stepped inside. As serious as her problems were, they were personal. She'd worked too hard to get where she was, and she wasn't about to let her professional life suffer for it. Worse, she didn't want to set a bad example for her employees—the newest one of which was sitting at a desk not twenty feet away.

Tamika's head popped up when she heard the *whoosh* of the door's piston, and she quickly shoved something in her desk drawer. Their newest employee, however, was engrossed in something. Shea headed over to the desk that had been set up across from Tamika's main reception area. "Good morning, Lynette. Welcome to Biodermatics."

The woman looked up from the list of ingredients she was reading on the label on the back of their wrinkle cream. "Oh, Dr. Caldwell."

She quickly stood and tugged at the hem of her sweater, trying to get the material to smooth over her hips. "My stepmother used to love that stuff."

Shea smiled. "Feel free to take some samples."

Lynette's eyes widened, and she pushed the bottle away. "Oh, no. I mean… I couldn't."

"Of course, you can. You work here now."

"And I'm so happy to be here. Thank you for giving me this opportunity."

"We're glad to have you. We've needed more help around here for a while."

Lynette nodded solemnly. "I'm willing to contribute wherever I can. With my chemistry background, I'm sure you'll find me useful. I could even help out in the lab if you'd like."

Shea blinked in surprise. "Let's start with the front office work first."

"Oh, of course. I didn't mean anything."

"You're enthusiastic. I appreciate that. Has anyone shown you around yet?"

"Phillip did." The phone on Lynette's desk started to ring. "He showed me the facilities and introduced me to everyone who was here. Do you always come in this late?"

Shea was taken aback. "I had an appointment. Usually, I'm one of the first ones here."

Lynette's forehead furrowed. "But I was just acquainting myself with the scheduling system, and I didn't see anything on there for you."

"Ahem," Tamika said loudly, clearing her throat like a gravel truck. "She doesn't have to clear her schedule with us. She's the company president. And if you're not too busy, that's Phillip's line."

"Oh! That's me." Lynette tilted her head sheepishly. "I'm not used to answering phones for other people."

"Yet," Tamika said.

Shea glanced her assistant's way. Tamika rolled her eyes and lifted up two messages. Shea's heart jumped. Were either of them from Derek?

"What am I over here, chopped liver?" her admin assistant said. She played keep-away with the messages when Shea reached for them. "You walked by without even saying hello."

"Hello, Tamika. Good morning." One look at her friend and Shea could see that she'd gotten up on the wrong side of the bed. She could sympathize. Discreetly, she tilted her head towards their new hire. "How's she doing?"

"Ms. I've-got-a-background-in-chemistry?"

Inwardly, Shea sighed. Oh, this was not what she needed. "What's wrong?"

With a flourish, Tamika rolled back her chair and crossed her arms over her chest. "She's annoying, that's what wrong. She's just such an eager beaver—and I do not mean that in the good, kinky way."

Lynette wasn't showy, that was true. She wore flat heels,

flatter hair, and no makeup. But that was neither here nor there. They needed someone who was loyal and dependable. Tamika was both, *and* she could stop a Mack truck dead in its tracks.

Wearing a turtleneck.

It was those legs, Shea thought.

"Give her a chance. She's excited about having a new job."

Tamika leaned closer. "I don't like her."

The angry hiss startled Shea. Usually her assistant was outgoing and effervescent, yet that sunny personality had faded recently. More and more she was becoming snippy and guarded, definitely short-tempered. "Are you okay?" Shea asked.

"I'm fine."

Fine wasn't usually displayed with a scowl and lowered eyebrows.

"Tired," Tamika admitted, shuffling papers on her desk.

"I'm counting on you to help train her," Shea said.

Her assistant pressed her lips together. Nodding, she handed over the messages.

Shea looked through them and was disappointed when she didn't see Derek's name. She flicked the corners of the slips until the writing blurred.

He'd been frustrated when he'd left, but was he angry with her?

She bit her lip. As wonderful as yesterday had been, it had all been so sudden. And with her sleep problems, she wasn't ready to let him spend the night. It was going to be days before she was fully convinced that the new sleeping pills were the answer to her problems... That the dosage would hold against her nerves... That the formula gave statistically proven, reproducible results...

"There you are." Phillip stepped into the open doorway of his office. He looked crisp and professional in his blue shirt and red tie. "We need to iron out the production schedule. Remember?"

110

Shea's shoulders slumped. What had ever happened to tackling one problem at a time? "Give me a minute. I'll be right there."

As she headed to her office, the production schedule was the last thing on her mind. With each step, she thought of Derek. Every brush of her skirt against her thighs brought back memories of his hands on her. Her lips were swollen under her lipstick, and her nipples were sensitive against the cups of her bra. None of that compared, though, to the intimate tenderness between her legs.

Her body felt as if it had just been jump-started, but she hadn't expected this. She didn't know how to handle it. Although one thing was for certain. You didn't *handle* Derek Oneiros.

Unless he asked you to.

"Flow cytometry, confocal microscopy, polymerase chain reaction," she chanted.

Time to get her mind on other things.

Knowing that Phillip would soon be in to get her, she set down her briefcase and stashed her purse. She grabbed her notebook, but she couldn't find her favorite pen. She patted down her desk, searching for it, but finally gave up and pulled another out of the drawer. Pushing her decidedly unprofessional thoughts out of her mind, she headed to the hallway. Her footsteps slowed when she glanced down.

"Darn it." She'd picked up her lab book, not her business notebook.

She backtracked to her desk, where she found her business notes sitting atop the latest issue of the *Journal of Dermatological Science*. It made her frown. That was the research-related pile. She was very organized, especially when it came to separating the two aspects of her job. Still, she had been harried recently.

But not enough to leave her chair pulled out and sitting at a cockeyed angle.

She took a slow, uneasy step backward. Tucking chairs away was an ingrained habit of a sleepwalker. She did it unconsciously, but she also did it habitually. Especially recently. An unwanted feeling turned her stomach, and her gaze was pulled to the window. The Dumpster sat in clear view.

This was not how she'd left things. Somebody had been at her desk.

Instinctively, she nabbed her lab book and hurried to her partner's office.

"Phillip, has anyone—"

Lynette suddenly appeared in the doorway. "Do you need me to take notes?"

Shea's nerves nearly snapped. Drawing into herself, she stiffly moved to the back corner of the room. Phillip moved between her and their overeager staff member. "We're really not that kind of an office. Not enough staff, not enough airs."

Lynette looked chastened. Over her shoulder, Shea could see Tamika smiling smugly.

"Tell you what." Phillip reached into his pocket and pulled out his keys. "If you could load my car with those samples in the conference room, I'd appreciate it."

Lynette lips twisted. "The moisturizer or the eye cream?"

"Both of them, and organize them, please."

She sighed. "Yes, sir."

She left, and Phillip quickly closed the door after her. "What's wrong?" he asked as he whipped around.

He knew her better than anybody.

"Has anyone been in my office today?" Shea asked.

"I don't know. It's been a busy morning. Why?"

She put her notebooks down on his desk. They might not look like much, but inside they tracked all the blood, sweat, and tears that had gone into making Biodermatics the profitable company that it was. Worriedly, she traced the edge of her lab book's leather cover. "Did you check our main offices the night I saw that trespasser on the property?"

"Yes, and this building was locked up tight."

"And our security system hasn't shown any unusual entries?"

Her partner's brow furrowed. "Don't you think Derek would have been all over that?"

"Derek," she repeated softly. "Right."

Phillip stepped closer. "Let me try again. What's wrong?"

Shea let out a shaky breath. She had an eerie feeling that her Somnambulist had come calling last night, but could it have actually brought her over here, gotten inside the building, done whatever, and returned her home to her bed without her knowing? She raked a hand through her hair. "Somebody was in my things."

Her partner's handsome face tightened. "Are you certain?"

"It was subtle, but things had been moved. Little things might be missing. You know how you just know?"

Phillip grabbed his phone. "Derek was right. Someone is after our company secrets."

Shea caught the phone. "Wait."

"He has to know. It's what we pay him for."

"Just stop." His grip loosened, and she put the phone back in its cradle. "We need to look at the check-ins to see who came in over the weekend."

Derek had set up a security system that required all employees to swipe their ID cards to enter during off-hours.

"Good idea." Phillip opened up the computer program and began to type in rapid hunt-and-pecks.

"See if I logged in," Shea said.

His shoulders hitched. "Did somebody steal your card?"

"Not in the way you think."

It took a moment, but when he swiveled toward her, understanding was in his eyes. "Honey, you couldn't have sleepwalked all the way over here. There's no way."

Shea's throat thickened. She'd done a lot of things without knowing, things she'd never even told Phillip about. "It's not outside the realm of possibility. I've already driven my car… Just look, okay?"

Phillip's concentration returned to their security log. Neither of them realized they were holding their breath until he let out a long sigh. "The only person to check into the main office this weekend was me, and I didn't touch your things."

Shea was surprised. The only other option was that somebody had snooped around her office this morning.

Hesitantly, they both looked toward the door.

"No," she said. There had to be a perfectly good, benign explanation. She trusted their employees. "Maybe it was just Bonnie."

Phillip shook his head. "She's always very careful not to disturb things when she cleans my office. What was missing?"

"Just a pen and perhaps an envelope I scribbled some formulae on. I didn't see it." Shea reached up to pinch the bridge of her nose. "Maybe I'm making a mountain out of a molehill. Somebody probably just knocked the things off my desk and put them back in the wrong place."

"The same somebody who dressed like a ninja to go through our trash the other night?" Phillip reached again for the phone. "I'm calling Derek."

"No, don't." Shea flushed when her partner looked at her sharply. "I'll go see him. I... I need to talk to him anyway."

Phillip's eyebrows rose. He could say so much with a look.

"He came over this weekend," she confessed.

"And?"

She shrugged uncomfortably.

"If you don't give me more information than that, I'm going to hide all your pipettes."

As far as threats went, it was a pretty good one. Shea found her friend's protectiveness touching.

"It was... Derek was... perfect." Shea took a bracing breath.

"Did you two hook up?"

Heat poured into her face as she nodded. "But I had to send him home. I had no other choice."

"You sent him home?" Phillip looked at her as if she were insane. "What were you thinking?"

"I was thinking that I'm a sleepwalker who rams her car at people."

Her partner let out a strangled sound. "Just tell him you've got a sleep disorder."

She looked away. "Think about it. Derek is a fixer. He solves problems and protects things. If I told him about this, he'd be unable to help himself, but he's not a doctor or a therapist. I can't have him around, not when I'm sleeping. It's too dangerous for both of us."

"Come on, Shea. I know you like him. Don't break the guy's heart—or your own."

She blinked, stunned. Was Derek's heart really in the game?

Just the idea had her own heart pounding faster.

"Go see him. Tell him the truth."

The idea was almost tempting, until she noticed how protectively her hand sat on her notebooks. Suddenly, all Shea could think about was the figure in black and the angry way the person had stood over her car. If that trespasser had put his hands on her research... She shook her head, feeling sick. "He needs to know about this more. He's got to find whoever is doing this and stop them now."

* * *

"Damn," Derek said under his breath. He stared at the computer screen, hating what he was reading, but unable to stop. This was not what he'd wanted to find.

Paging down, he continued reading the newspaper article he'd found in the *Sentinel* archives. He'd been at this all morning. While it didn't make him proud, he'd learned a lot about Shea. He'd read about her schooling and the accolades she'd received as a young researcher at the university. The business section had boasted the successes of her startup company, but this story went further back—back to the time she was that little girl in the trailer park.

What he was reading made his chest tighten to the point where it was hard to breathe.

He stared at the black-and-white photograph that showed the melted, buckled wad of metal that had once been her home. Bracing himself, he continued with the story.

Unknown ignition source. One injury. Total loss. Firefighters had originally been unable to locate the young girl who lived in the trailer, but she'd eventually been discovered outside the scene.

He ran his hand across his face. No wonder her nightmares were about fire.

Guiltily, he looked at the file he'd created. He didn't like the tactics he'd had to take, but after his discussion with Zane, he'd had to know more. Shea had given him tacit approval. She'd told him she'd expected him to do a thorough background check on her.

She'd just seemed happy that he hadn't.

His pen bounced when he tossed it on the desk. There was no way around it. He was a snake in the grass. He could justify it every which way to Sunday, but she'd gotten into his head and under his skin. He wanted to know everything there was to know about her. He wanted to know her favorite colors, the breakthroughs she was making in her laboratory, the sexual positions that got her off...

And why she was taking those damned sleeping pills.

His fingers flexed. If only he could place that strange vibration he'd felt in her bedroom. It had just been a tingling, a rattling on the edge of his senses. There were too many night creatures that could be haunting her. Taunting her.

Possessiveness roared up inside him. They wouldn't be having their way with her much longer, not once he caught them.

But that was the problem, catching them.

He gave the mouse a shove, and it rolled across the mouse pad. Like a good, dependable Dream Weaver, he'd completed his rounds last night, including taking Zane to Tamika. She'd only been in the first stage of the sleep cycle, though, just barely starting to slumber. It made him uncertain. Had he missed something? Was there more he could be doing?

A tap at the door had him looking up. "Come in," he called, automatically closing the manila file folder.

The door opened, but instead of Ellen's dark head, he saw

the shine of natural blonde. He was on his feet before he remembered the information he still had pulled up on his computer. Feeling caught in the act, he abruptly closed the screen. "Shea, come in."

She closed the door behind her. "I'm sorry to pop in, but I need to talk to you."

"You don't need an appointment." He watched her cross the room and picked up several things at once. She was polished and reserved again in her tidy blue suit. Too bad all he could think about was stripping it off her. Yet there was an edginess to her, an aggression she couldn't hide. "Is this business or pleasure?"

"Business." Her steps paused. "Not that... I just really need to talk to you in your professional capacity right now. I might have more information about that prowler."

Derek snapped to attention fast. "What happened?" he asked.

She put her briefcase on the floor by a chair. "Somebody has been snooping around my office."

"Your office?" He had enough security features in place that that shouldn't happen.

"It wasn't as I left it." She wrapped her arms around her waist, and outrage practically radiated from her. "I think somebody went through my things."

"No alarms were set off recently." He turned toward his computer. "Let me check the card swipes."

"Phillip already did that. He didn't notice anything out of the ordinary."

"Was someone careless with their ID?"

"Either that, or they had permission to be there."

His eyes narrowed. She suspected one of her own.

"What about your lab?" he asked, his voice going hard.

"It seemed undisturbed."

"What about your employees? Have you noticed any unusual behavior lately? Have attendance habits changed? Is anyone having fiscal problems that might make them susceptible to other's interests?"

She paled. "I didn't really believe you when you said somebody was trying to gain access to my research. I thought it was... something else. But first that prowler and now this..."

She was upset, and it made it hard for him to focus. "Do you remember anything else from that night?"

"No." For some reason, that seemed to infuriate her even more. "I should have paid more attention, but I... *He hit my car.*"

"He did what?"

"The person in black slammed his fist right into the hood. I forgot about... I mean, I forgot to tell you that."

She most definitely had.

That changed everything. Someone trying to dig up information would have made himself scarce, not acted out like that. Derek didn't like this, didn't like it at all. The aggression directed toward her wasn't a normal sign of corporate espionage. It was much too personal.

She rubbed a hand across her forehead. "I want this to stop, Derek. I want this person caught."

"Breathe, Curie. Getting this worked up isn't going to help anything."

"Maybe not, but this is something I can fight."

He saw the determination she hid so well underneath the businesslike exterior. This wasn't just about an intruder. She was talking about her sleep issues. She didn't like feeling helpless or vulnerable and, after reading about what she'd survived, he understood why. A girl from the wrong side of the tracks didn't make it big without having a bit of scrappiness inside her.

"We'll fight it together," he promised. "All of it."

She didn't look so sure.

Unable to keep things strictly business any longer, he moved closer and cupped her cheek. "You're so wired, you're about ready to spark."

"I can't help it. I'm angry."

"I can see that." He brushed his lips softly against hers.

"Want to work off that head of steam?"

Her eyes rounded. "Here?"

The corners of his lips twitched. "We don't have to keep things professional anymore."

It had been a long night alone without her, and he'd wanted her for so long. Now that he'd finally touched her, it was impossible to stay away.

Shea nibbled at her lower lip. Her gaze went to the sofa, but then it pulled away guiltily. They were two of a kind, he realized. Two people wrapped up in straitjackets of responsibility. They were always expected to be conscientious, to do the right thing, to stay on the straight and narrow.

Well, he was tired of playing by the rules. He wanted to experience the thrills and risks that others seem to take without hesitation.

And he wanted to do it with her.

"Nobody has to know but us."

"What about Ellen?"

That problem was easy to fix. He walked over and locked the door. "She won't bother us."

"But Derek…"

He walked toward her slowly. Her blue suit had some sort of wraparound jacket, one that tied at the side. He was more interested in the deep vee between her breasts. He pressed an open-mouthed kiss against the center of her breastbone and felt her shiver.

"Be irresponsible with me," he said as he nuzzled against her. "Let me make you feel better."

Anyone else and neither of them would be able to let go. Yet all that energy was pulsing inside her. He could feel it. When her fingers threaded through his hair, he knew he had her.

He kissed her full and deep, letting his tongue slide against hers. When he finally pulled back, her blue eyes were smoky.

"Take it off." Her hands shook as she reached for his tie. "Take it all off."

"You first." The tie on her suit jacket gave way with one pull. She stripped it off her shoulders, and like a heat-seeking missile, his gaze locked on her breasts. They bounced in the confines of her lacy bra, nearly spilling out of it. He unbuttoned his shirt and unzipped his pants, but he went still when her skirt loosened and slid to her feet.

Everything on her matched. From her suit to her thong to her sexy high-heeled shoes, everything was a vivid royal blue.

But *those shoes*. With the suit, they'd been an intriguing spark. With the bra and thong combo, though, they looked downright racy. Blue and white and striped like a zebra, they were sexy as hell.

He caught her by the waist, set her on his desk, and stepped up close.

"You should star in your own commercials. You're sexier than any of those professional models you've got on there."

She gave him a shy smile, but she became bolder when she pushed off his shirt. Her soft hands ran down his chest, and Derek's stomach cinched in.

He nuzzled his face into the crook of her neck. He'd never felt anything softer or sleeker than her skin. She was all woman, and he couldn't get enough of her. He cupped her breasts in his hands and felt her arch against him.

"Is this what you've been wearing underneath all those suits of yours?"

Her big blue eyes were heated with arousal. "You asked that in my dream, too."

Her dream… That did more for him than she could know. "What else would a red-blooded man ask?"

As much as he liked her in the lingerie and stiletto heels, he wanted her naked. He undid her bra and palmed her breasts, lifting them higher. The pink tips jutted out and he rubbed his thumbs over them. She groaned, and he let his hand slide down over her ribcage and across her trembling belly. They both watched as his fingertips slid under the blue lace of her thong.

"Derek," she gasped, her voice going tight.

Using his knees, he spread her legs wider. He slid a finger into her and pressed his lips against her ear. "Want to know my fantasy? It involved bending you over this desk."

She squirmed and moaned so loudly that, for a minute, he did worry about his secretary checking on them. Then one of her arms came up and circled around his neck. Anything and everything outside his office disappeared.

"Deeper," she begged, rolling her hips higher.

He let his fingers plunge, and she let out a sharp cry. His patience stretched thin, and he caught the skimpy thong with both hands. "Lift."

Her chest rose and fell as he peeled the stretchy silk off her. Pushing down his pants and his briefs, he stepped back between her spread legs. Her eyes were wild with lust and need. He positioned himself and then pushed into her with one long stroke.

"Derek," she moaned.

She wrapped her arms around his neck, and her legs encircled his hips. Their mouths sealed tight as their bodies pressed flush. Derek had never felt anything so hot, so wet. She was tight, gripping him like a velvet fist. Inch by inch, she ate him up until he was seated right in the cradle of her lap. Her heat licked at him, and he deliberately ground himself into her.

"I missed you last night," he said, his voice rough.

Her cheeks turned pink. "I'm sorry I made you go."

"I'm glad you came to me now."

He kissed her. He understood better now. She'd sent him away because she'd thought she was protecting him. He wasn't angry, but he was going to do everything he could to make her change her mind.

He wanted to be in her bed.

He pulled her hips forward until she was balanced right on the very edge of the desk. Her thigh muscles bunched, but then she relaxed back onto her elbows, trusting him. He felt her sexy shoes against the small of his back. The dangerous heels poked against his ass every time he thrust.

It was the most erotic thing he'd ever felt. Over and over again, he thrust into her. Bumping, grinding, squeezing, and releasing...

He murmured hot words to her. Harder and faster, he worked inside her. Her breasts bounced as their bodies came together, and her thighs quivered from exertion. He could feel the storm gathering within her, building and screaming.

"Derek!" she suddenly cried out.

Her back arched, and her hair swung back in a long waterfall. He buried his cock deep as her pussy spasmed around him. He felt spurts of his own pre-cum escape, and his head spun.

When she sagged against the desk, the mating instinct just reached up and grabbed him by the throat. His hips began pumping hard, in sharp, deep thrusts that he couldn't control. He slammed into her repeatedly, obsessively.

She moaned and clutched at his arms. Her legs squeezed, and one of those sexy shoes poked him in the butt. That was all it took to set him off. He jammed home one last time, seating himself deeply, and lost all sense of time and space.

All he knew was her, his Shea.

When the world finally returned, he found that the desk was the only thing keeping them upright. His hands were braced on the desktop beside her shoulders, and his elbows were locked. She lie limp atop his day planner, with one thigh still locked around him and the other leg dangling off the desk. That sexy shoe still clung to her pointed toes.

"Wow," she murmured. She settled her hand on his chest over his heart. "If I'd known being irresponsible felt so good, I would have tried it before."

"Me too." Their bodies were still locked together, but Derek couldn't bear to leave her. Not just yet. He knew he'd just thrown the rulebook out the window—but only with her. "We'll get the bad guys, Curie, I promise."

"All of them?" she asked softly.

"Every last one."

CHAPTER TEN

The creature was livid, incensed. A growl left his lips as he lie unmoving inside his beloved.

Why wouldn't she be with him anymore? The fog in her head was thicker, the weight of her body heavier. It had been nights and nights since she'd responded to his commands. He'd thought he'd found the answer to making her pliable, *functional*, but he couldn't keep working so hard. It used too much of his already dwindling power. He could feel his need growing… the tension and the friction. It was getting harder and harder to keep himself together. He needed her power, or he was going to pull apart and become nothing. He'd lived too long to fade away like that.

"Weavers," he hissed. "Weavers numbering two."

This was their fault. They'd put a double whammy on her. It was the only answer. The cobwebs in her head were made of tension wire, and her muscles were like lead. The Dream Weaver with the mean eyes had been hanging around, glomming on to her. It was getting harder and harder for the Somnambulist to find a way in, to find time to be with his one and only.

But the mean Weaver wasn't here now…

"*My* She-a. *Mine.*" Closing his eyes, the creature concentrated on her body—her wonderful, luscious power source of a body.

His determination built. They had to be together again. It had to be her. Last night he'd gotten so desperate, he'd tried walking with the little boy next door. He'd needed the juice, yet the little squirt had only given him a squirt. And when they'd pulled that kitten's tail, the boy had woken up. One delicious slash of claws across his wrist, and the crybaby had started sobbing.

The pain had only carried the Somnambulist so far.

He focused on his precious girl's achy spots. Those sensitive red tips on her chest—that was where the answer lay. That and the beguiling spot between her legs...

He summoned what power he had and sent it downward, concentrating on making her feel. The red nubs tightened, squeezing hard.

Yes, yes! That was what he needed.

He kept going, his power waning, until he finally gained control of an arm. He bent it, and her hand fell limply against the slick gown she wore. Using her fingertips, he rubbed one of the tickly buds through the material. Back and forth he flicked it, circling round harder and faster, pinching...

A moan left her throat, and relief swamped him. It was working. Bit by bit, he was gaining control. He moved her other hand to her chest and played with both the naughty nubs until they felt like they were on fire. Burning, aching, pulsing...

"Fire," he crooned. Visions of orange and yellow danced in his head.

He wanted to heat her up even more. The power she was giving him was invigorating, but it wasn't enough. He pushed her hands down, loving the water-like feel of what she was wearing. Yet when he got to the spot he so dearly wanted to investigate, the gown was in his way.

It made him snarl.

Pushing the material between her legs, he felt for her anyway. One blunt brush of fingertips left him gasping. Oooh, he needed to get at that!

Rolling and contorting, he yanked the clothes off her. At

last, she was bare, and all that wonderful skin was free to touch. Eagerly, he cupped her hands over the bumps on her chest and squeezed.

That magic spot down below squeezed, too, feeling all hot and tingly.

He threw one of her hands toward it.

"*Ayiiii!*" he yelped. What he found! She was soft and squishy down there. Plump, hot, and wet. Her hips danced as he poked and prodded with her fingers. She bowed up like a bridge, though, when he accidentally pushed a finger into a recess he hadn't expected.

But it felt so good!

He stuffed in another finger and drank up all the sensations he could. Heat, dampness, slickness, pressure, pleasure... He could feel what she was feeling inside and out.

Yet, even better, she was moving without him. Her hips were rocking, and her legs were spreading. She was doing things he hadn't told her to do. He'd never heard of such a thing. Tilting her head up, he watched.

The picture was so exciting, he could barely stand it.

He yanked her other hand away from the pointy red tip and sent it down between her legs, too. She groaned, and the sound went right through him. She bent one knee, digging her heel into the mattress, and she touched and stroked all kinds of magical spots. He gasped when she found a knot that sent spasms all through her.

"Oh," he moaned. The sound came out in her voice. The energy rolling through them was unlike any he'd ever felt. It made him want to weep.

Then, suddenly, she went dead still.

"She-a?" The Somnambulist felt her muscles clench without his order. Panic exploded inside his chest. He couldn't get trapped. He couldn't— "She-*ahhhh!*"

The most glorious thing happened. The power. It just exploded around him, its amperage and voltage almost more than he could bear. His head spun, and it took everything he had to keep from being kicked out of her. He held on to her tightly, lovingly, and gobbled it up until it was no more.

At last, her body collapsed on the bed and the power bled.

Right into him.

"Ahhhh," She-a sighed.

The creature's particles buzzed. She felt wonderful. Rejuvenated. The cobwebs were gone, and the heaviness had evaporated. He felt wonderful, too.

Unstoppable.

Opening his hostess's eyes, he stared at the ceiling. Her vision had never been clearer. And her body— He shook like a blender. She was ready to go.

So was he.

With a surge, he sat upright, taking her with him. As powerful as he felt, he almost didn't need her body—but he wasn't leaving it behind. No way, no how. He whipped her legs off the bed, planted her feet on the floor, and stood. She didn't sway or falter.

She wasn't fighting him anymore.

He crowed in victory. "Oh, what fun we'll have tonight."

He directed her out into the hallway, curious as to what they could find. He stopped quickly, though, when he heard something.

He cocked her head. Another sound drifted up from the first floor, and his happiness drained away fast. Anger bubbled up to take its place. *Why, why, why?* Why must others interfere when he and his lovely were together? The Weavers and the face in the window were always watching and intruding.

He started growling low in his hostess's throat.

He'd had enough of this. She was his.

He stomped back into the room and looked around. The talking device on the little table by her bed caught his attention. He snatched it up and stared at the numbers. His beloved knew the right ones. Using her finger, he punched them in. A voice answered.

"Help me," the creature said. He liked the sound of his She-a's voice, so smooth and pretty.

He headed again toward the door.

He wondered how it sounded when she screamed.

* * *

The breeze was the first thing Shea noticed. It was soft, cool, and slightly damp. It blew against her face and ruffled her hair. She felt the soft strands tickle her bare shoulders, and her skin contracted against the cool exposure.

The sensation was pleasant. Arousing.

Yet disconcerting.

Derek had left. Hadn't he?

Slowly, she became more aware of her surroundings. It was brighter than usual in her bedroom, even with her nightlight. And something prickly poked against her feet, something damp and gritty.

Uneasiness suddenly pricked at the back of her neck. She knew that feeling. She'd woken up feeling it once before.

She was outdoors.

That horrible awareness swept over her, the awareness that she was coming back into herself. Feeling vulnerable, she wrapped her arms around her middle. It was then that she realized she wasn't wearing any clothes. Her air caught in her throat, and she curled into herself.

Feeling unbearably vulnerable, she waited that interminable time for her senses to awaken and fully return to her. When they did, her body braced.

She was near the parking lot of her condo association, just at the edge of illumination of one of the streetlights. Frantically, she looked from side to side as she tried to orient herself. Suddenly, a car nearby roared to life. Her heart nearly burst out of her chest, and she jumped back into the shadows.

A whimper escaped her as it peeled out of the parking lot. Using her hands, she tried to hide her nakedness. She'd never felt so exposed in her life. She had to get inside.

She started backing quickly toward her home. She hadn't taken two steps, though, when her heel hit something big and solid.

"Ah!" she cried out as she lost her balance. Stumbling to her side, she nearly went down. Frightened, she spun around. She wasn't prepared for what she found. There, on her front lawn, was a body.

Air seized in her throat, and her brain scrambled to process what she was seeing. A man. Facedown. Unmoving.

Uncertain what to do, she edged around him. What had happened? Was he alive? Dead? *Had she had anything to do with this?* The band of tension around her ribs couldn't keep the panic at bay. When she saw the man's face, though, it snapped entirely. It sprang open and let her horror spill out into the darkness.

"Oh, no. *No, no.*" She surged toward him and dropped to her knees. "Phillip!"

She reached for him, so scared she could barely think. He felt warm. She ran her touch over him, searching for injuries. A cry left her lips when she found a knot on the back of his head. There was no blood, but the swelling felt big as a tennis ball.

"Phillip?" she said shakily.

She shuddered when she saw a thick chunk of landscape edging at his side. "Oh, God."

Leaning over him, she checked if he was breathing. Tears pricked her eyes when his soft air caressed her face. She felt for his pulse. It was strong and steady under her fingertips.

Yet he wasn't moving, and he wasn't waking up.

"Help me," Shea yelled.

Nobody answered.

"*Help me!*" she screamed.

And screamed and screamed and screamed.

Lights came on at the Rasmussen condo next door. The curtains shifted, and the door opened. Her neighbor, Kathy, peered outside. "Oh my word! Shea? What's wrong?"

"He's hurt. Call an ambulance!"

Spinning around, her neighbor opened her closet door and pulled out a long jacket. "Steven," she called. "Dial 911!"

* * *

Shea rubbed her temple and tried to concentrate as the policeman asked her questions. It was impossible. The hospital corridor was blinding in its whiteness. The place was so cold and stoic. It was almost as if it was purposely reflecting all her emotions back onto her. With every second that passed, her doubts and worries grew.

"So what time did you find Mr. Morrison?" the man asked.

"Around midnight." That much, she knew for sure.

"What was he doing there so late?"

Good question. "He's my friend."

"I see," the cop said. "Was he coming or going?"

"Coming." And she had no idea why.

"Have there been any other incidents in your neighborhood? Any break-ins or muggings?"

"No, nothing." Besides, it hadn't looked like a robbery to her. That EMT—Justin, she thought his name was—had found Phillip's wallet with his money and credit cards intact. It wasn't a good sign.

She hadn't found any good signs at all.

The cop scratched his ear with his pen. "Does Mr. Morrison have any enemies? Has anyone been harassing him or causing problems?"

Shea raked a trembling hand through her hair. She couldn't take this. She wanted to be in the emergency room with her partner. She wanted to apologize. She wanted to know if she was responsible!

"Dr. Caldwell? His enemies?"

She took a tight breath. "Not that I know of. Phillip gets along with nearly everybody."

"What about your business, this Biodermatics?"

"What about it?"

"Do you think the attack could have anything to do with that? Does anyone take issue with your products? Maybe that commercial with all the... *ahem*... naked legs?"

She started to shake her head until she thought of someone who might have an issue with them, someone who'd tried to put his fist through the hood of her car. "We did have a trespasser recently."

"Did you report it?"

"Yes."

Her whirling brain homed in on the possibility. Could someone else have done this? It was a stretch, a long one, but it gave her... hope? God, how could she think like that? Phillip was lying unconscious in the emergency room. He'd been *attacked*.

And *she* was the one who'd been standing over his body.

She started to shake. She needed to tell the policeman everything. She had to tell him she might be responsible. She just couldn't get the words out of her mouth. She could barely fit them into her brain.

"I'm sorry, ma'am. I know this is tough. I have just a few more questions, if that's all right."

Shea stared at his badge so hard, it seemed to pulse. She'd been wandering around naked outside while Phillip had been hurt on the ground. What had that thing been doing with her tonight?

A sick, uneasy feeling corroded the lining of her stomach. She'd known it wouldn't like the more powerful sleeping pills she'd gotten from her doctor. Was this her punishment?

"Did you see anyone?" the cop asked. "Did you hear anything?"

She shook her head miserably. "When I found Phillip, I panicked. I wasn't paying attention to anything else."

That was the absolute truth. She massaged the knot that had formed underneath her breastbone.

"I'll need to speak with Mr. Morrison as soon as he's able."

She nodded tightly.

She needed to speak to him, too. She had to know what had happened. She had to know if she was to blame.

Footsteps suddenly sounded down the hallway. A short sob escaped her when she saw Derek. She pressed her fingers against her lips. He must have flown to get here so fast.

"Hey," he said, coming right up to her. He folded his arms around her and pulled her up tight. "Are you all right?"

She sagged against him. "Better," she whispered into his chest.

His embrace tightened, and she closed her eyes. She was past the point of not wanting to look weak in front of him. She just needed to soak up his strength for a moment and recharge her own. Her fingers clenched into his back, and she realized he was out of his normal uniform. The suit and tie were gone. In its place were jeans and a black T-shirt. For some reason, she found that even more comforting and intimate.

"What's going on?" he asked the policeman.

"I'm just asking Ms. Caldwell some questions, Mr...."

"Oneiros. Derek Oneiros. I think she's had enough. Can you finish some other time?"

The cop scratched his ear with his pen as he looked at his notes. "I'd like to get answers while everything's fresh in her mind, but yeah. I'll contact you if I think of anything else."

"Thank you," Shea said. She pulled away from Derek and scrubbed her hands over her face. She couldn't take any more of the policeman's inquisition, although it had been tame compared to the one going on inside her head.

"Let's go sit down in the waiting room," Derek said.

She'd been on her feet ever since they'd rolled Phillip past those swinging doors at the end of the hall. How long ago had that been? Minutes? Hours?

"This way," he said, urging her along.

The room was empty when they entered, a medical ghost town. Shea settled uneasily onto one of the couches and noticed vaguely that hospital waiting rooms had improved over the years. The furniture was more comfortable. A television hung on the wall, and the magazines looked almost current. It hadn't been like this all those years ago when she'd waited to see her dad.

Another sob left her lips, and she dropped her head into her hands. It was inevitable that she'd think of that night, but it still hit her like a fist in the gut.

"Hey, easy now." Derek sat down beside her, almost as tense as she was. Watching her closely, he rubbed her back. "How bad off is Phillip?"

"He has a concussion for sure. They'll have to run more tests to determine if it's worse than that."

Somebody had hit her best friend. Hit him in the head from behind. Had he even seen his attacker?

She thrust her fingers into her hair. It couldn't have been her. She'd never do that, not even if she was under the influence of... *something*. She'd fight against doing anything so horrible. She knew she would.

Didn't she?

Derek kept rubbing her back. "He's young and strong. He'll be all right. You know he will."

No, she didn't. She didn't know anything at all.

She lurched to her feet and began to wander about the room. Staring up at the ceiling, she searched for control. She needed to figure out what to do next. She needed to think. She had a problem. What were the logical steps?

"I'm sorry," Derek said. "I should have been there."

She swung towards him. "Don't say that."

"I could have done something. I might have been able to stop it."

"No. It's best that you weren't there."

"The hell it is."

"It could have been you!"

The words bounced around the empty room.

"Shea, what happened?" Derek finally asked. "What was Phillip doing there?"

"I don't know," she whispered. "I swear."

She swallowed hard. Derek's hair was rumpled, but his eyes were sharp and intense. She'd gotten him out of bed, but he was here for her. He wanted to help her; she knew that. She just couldn't—

Why not?

Her breath hitched. Why couldn't she lean on him? Why

couldn't she tell him the truth? Was Phillip right? Was she too proud? Too ashamed?

The next logical step was sitting right in front of her. She didn't have to go this alone. She just had to do what Derek had always wanted: *trust him*.

She gathered her courage. "I have a new job for you."

"Anything. What do you need?"

"I want you to investigate someone."

His dark eyes narrowed. Slowly, he rose and moved toward her. "You think you know who did this."

"I need you to investigate *me*."

He stopped. "You?"

Trust him.

"I need to know what I do at night," she said huskily. She could feel the words gathering steam. "I need surveillance or something, but not in person. Film me. I know that's not your area of expertise. You're not a private investigator, but—"

"Shea. Slow down."

"The sleep clinic is booked solid. I can't get in, and—"

"Shea!" He caught her by the waist and gave her a little shake. "What are you trying to tell me?"

She took a short, shaky breath. "I have... I mean... I *am* a somnambulist. I walk in my sleep, Derek."

He sagged as if someone had just kicked him in the back of his knees.

Shea swallowed hard. "And I think I might have hurt Phillip."

CHAPTER ELEVEN

Derek was wound up tight when he pulled into the parking lot at Shea's complex. A Somnambulist. A fucking Somnambulist had gotten hold of her, entered her body, and taken her over. He was so pissed he was shaking. He knew what those things could do. He'd seen the havoc they caused. And to think of that leech toying with her—

He threw the transmission into park and ripped the key out of the ignition. When his hand slipped off the door handle, he realized he had to calm down and regain control. If he was going to track this thing down, he needed to think. It had circumvented him more than once. He needed to up his game, and he couldn't do that if he was seeing red.

Moving more precisely, he opened the door and faced Shea's condo. Slowly, he exhaled. He felt more contained— like a pressurized can ready to blow at the slightest prick— but that was the best he could do.

"Derek."

He was surprised when he saw Zane with Cael, but then he figured the more eyes and senses, the better.

So help him, when he got his hands on this thing—

"Man, I'm sorry about this." Cael raked a hand through his dark hair. "A Somnie… *Fuck*."

Yeah. Derek's fingers slowly curled into his palms. "Thanks for coming."

"Where's Shea?" Zane asked. "Is she okay?"

"She's at my place." He'd hated having to leave her, but at least he'd gotten her away from the hospital. "Now that Phillip has woken up and the doctors say he'll be okay, she's trying to rest. She just has too many questions."

"And she can't stop searching for answers?"

Derek looked at Cael in surprise. "You've met her?"

"Let's just say I know the type."

Okay, yeah. Derek admitted he couldn't get his mind to turn off either. Right now, though, he was relying on that as his greatest strength.

Zane came up beside him. He looked more concerned than Derek expected. "Is she alone?"

"Tony's with her. She's scared to even close her eyes now, but she took one look at him and figured he could reel her in if the worst happened."

"It won't." Cael's voice was calming. "Mack will watch over her from the dream realm like a pit bull."

That was the only reason Derek could let himself be here. He trusted that his brothers wouldn't let anything happen to her.

"So what are we looking for?" Zane asked as he scoped out the grounds.

Derek gestured across the lawn. He'd been strategizing during the drive over here. "She found Phillip over there by the streetlight. I'm wondering if we can pick up any remnants of the Somnambulist. Sometimes when they're weak, they'll leave a trail behind, particles of their essence."

"This one doesn't sound weak." Cael was already fanning outward so they could cover more ground. "Still, there was an altercation. Maybe we'll get lucky and some of it detached."

"Stretch out with your senses," Derek told Zane quietly. Full-grown Somnambulists were rare. *He* hadn't even caught on to what they were dealing with.

That low hum.

Without a word, they all started trying to pick up details. The condo association kept its grounds well-tended. The grass was trimmed, and the flower gardens were weeded. Everything seemed calm and peaceful. Knowing what had happened here last night, though, the bright morning sunshine felt out of place.

"I see you got rid of the noose."

Derek frowned at Zane.

His brother held up his hands. "I'm just saying… It's been a while since I've seen you in anything but a suit and tie. I didn't think you owned jeans anymore."

"Zane," Cael said tiredly.

"What? He's loosening up. It's a good thing."

Loose? Zane thought he was loose? Now that was enough to almost make Derek laugh. "Can we get on with this?"

"Yeah. Sorry, man. I'm just upset this thing got by me, all right?" Zane rubbed his shoulder. "I should have picked up on it."

"It's not your fault."

It was that sneaky nocturnal hitchhiker.

Derek headed for the streetlight where Shea had told him she'd first come back to consciousness. He hated to think of her waking up, not knowing where she was. How many times had that happened to her? It must be unnerving to go to bed at night and wake up somewhere else.

And that snake of a creature had taken her out of her home *naked*.

"Easy," Cael muttered.

Right. Easy. Control. *The Machine.*

It just wasn't working for him anymore.

As much as Derek tried, there was no way he could ignore the anger he felt or the sense of failure. The best he could do was compartmentalize it and use the energy to concentrate on what needed to be done.

Zane curled his fingers around the lamppost, but he shook his head when he felt nothing. "Did you ever find out what Morrison was doing here?"

"The creature called him," Derek said.

"The Somnie? Are you freaking serious?"

"Freaking."

That was a good way to describe Shea's reaction, too. When Phillip had told her that, she'd nearly lost it.

"Did he see her sleepwalking?" Cael asked.

"No, he was hit from behind." The question was, by whom? Shea was racked with guilt, but if it had been her, it hadn't been her fault. She'd been under the influence of the Somnambulist. "I'm getting nothing here. Let's go inside."

Together, they headed up the front walk. A few early morning risers watched them curiously as they came outside to pick up their morning editions of the *Sentinel*. In this neighborhood, ambulances during the middle of the night drew attention.

Derek reached into his pocket as he came to the door.

"A *key*," Zane said, missing nothing. "When did you get that?"

Derek's teeth ground together. He was not in the mood for this today. "Don't make me hit you."

"Are you sure it wouldn't make you feel better?"

He glanced at his brother. It probably would, and Zane knew it. He had a cocky grin on his face and a dare-you look in his eyes. The tension in Derek's shoulders drained. With a sigh, he knocked his brother upside the head. "You're a pain in the ass."

"That's what they tell me."

Still, it worked for him.

The distraction worked, too. When Derek slid the key into the lock, he felt more settled and centered. The door swung open, and he stepped inside with purpose.

Zane followed, but he stopped not two feet inside the condo. "It's here. I feel it."

Cael bumped him aside and entered, too. "That's not the Somnambulist. That's leftover power."

The place was practically throbbing with it.

Derek's fingers buzzed as he wandered into the living room.

"How did I miss this thing?" Zane wondered aloud.

"They're slippery," Cael said. "They catch sleepers before they call for us, right when they're most susceptible. Somnambulists slip in, take over, and draw the power they need."

Cael held his hands out, palms down, and searched for any remnants of the creature. There was the possibility that trace elements might lead them back to it. Still, it was a tough trick to pull off, especially after so much time had passed. Out of all the Oneiroi, though, he was one of the most powerful.

Derek followed suit. "This thing has to be old, especially if it has the power to take over an adult. If we haven't caught him by now, he's learned a lot of tricks to avoid us."

"It was there, wasn't it?" Zane said. "That night you took over with her?"

"Yeah," Derek said. "That humming vibration is their signature. It lowers as they mature, but I've never heard a bass like that. I should have figured it out."

Zane shook his head. "Let it go, man. Let it go."

He couldn't. Frustrated, Derek linked his fingers behind his neck. They'd made a connection, but Shea still wasn't letting him sleep over. He couldn't have been gone from her bed for an hour when the thing had overtaken her. It had moved in when his back had been turned. He'd been tending to other charges when she'd needed him.

Cael took one look at his face. "I'll go out to the car and get the cameras."

Derek wandered further into the living room.

"You don't want to think of it in there with her, do you?" Zane said quietly.

No, he didn't.

"I don't get it," Zane said. "I thought Somnies were playful, mischievous. Why would it smack Phillip around like that? He's Shea's friend."

"Somnies are playful when they're young." Derek stood over the sofa where he and Shea had first made love, and his fists clenched. "When they take over, though, they do it fully. There's no human consciousness there at all. The

Somnambulist just taps into their host's abilities and knowledge. That's why when they're young, they'll do simple things like walk through the house, color, or stack up blocks. If we don't eradicate them early, though, they grow into more complicated activities."

His stomach gave a miserable turn. "And they get more unstable."

Zane drummed his fingers against the kitchen counter. "Right. You look around here. I'll go upstairs."

Derek nodded.

As soon as his brother left the room, he drew himself up. Shea was trusting him to help her. She'd opened herself to him. She'd shared her most private secret, and he had no intention of letting her down. She just had no idea she'd put her faith in the one person—the one *family*—who could help her the most. He'd never been so grateful for his abilities and heritage.

Or so cursed for the knowledge he held.

This would be so much easier if he could just tell her what he was and that the myth was fact. He was a Dream Weaver, and her sleep disorder was a parasite. He could get rid of it. He could destroy it with one touch of his hand or scare it away forever. If she'd just sleep with him, she'd be safe. A Somnambulist would never come into a Dream Weaver's bed.

He just couldn't tell her any of that. He wouldn't even know where to begin.

"Shit." He rested his elbow atop the fireplace mantel and rubbed his forehead.

It was then that he noticed the photographs she kept there—one, in particular. It showed two smiling fans wearing matching Mets caps at a game at Shea Stadium. The man, though, had more of a half-smile. The left side of his face was disfigured, pulling his lip out at an odd angle. The arm he'd wrapped around Shea's shoulders showed scarring, too.

Burn scars.

Derek picked up the photograph. The man was older than

Shea, but his blonde hair left no doubt as to who he was. Neither did the love in his matching blue eyes.

"Ah, Curie," he said softly.

Her dad was the one who'd been hurt in that fire—the fire that had burned their trailer to the ground.

Carefully, Derek put the photo back in its place of honor. No wonder she slept with a nightlight on. No wonder the fireplace under the mantel was clean as a whistle. No wonder her nightmares always had flames.

"You all right?" Cael asked from the doorway.

Derek looked over his shoulder. His brother was juggling three cameras in his arms, and he went over to help. "Thanks for these," he said. "They'll make her feel better even though we don't need them."

"Thank Devon," Cael replied. "She begged and borrowed to get us three with motion sensors. For God's sake, don't drop the one you have. It's hers."

Derek nodded. Cael's girlfriend was fitting into their family just fine. Being a beautiful redhead, she had most of the Oneiroi panting after her, willing to be at her beck and call. Touch one of her cameras, though, and she could get cranky.

Derek fiddled with the camera's strap. "Listen, man. I think I came down too hard on you when you were going through that stuff with Devon. I didn't know. I didn't understand."

"It's all right."

"No, it's not. You didn't want to leave her. You *couldn't*. At the time, I didn't understand why you didn't just do your job and treat all your charges equally." He leveled his gaze on his big brother. "I get it now."

Cael's chest expanded as he took a slow, heavy breath. "Sounds serious."

"It is."

"Are those cameras for the bedroom?" Zane asked from the staircase. "Kinky!"

Cael rolled his eyes.

"You're the one who brought him," Derek said.

"Don't remind me."

"*I'll* handle setting up the camera in her bedroom," Derek said. "Let's set up one down here. She had to come down those stairs to leave last night."

As it turned out, it was a good thing both his brothers had come to help. Cael was a good photographer in his own right. He knew what camera angles would catch the most of the rooms. Zane, unfortunately, knew Shea's night habits better than anyone. Being barred from her nighttime bed, Derek could only defer to his little brother on that one.

That was going to change and soon.

"How's that?" Zane asked as he moved a pillow on the sofa out of the line of sight.

"Good. Right there." Cael's head came up from the viewfinder, and he pressed a button on the camera.

A phone suddenly rang, startling all three of them. Reflexively, they each checked their pockets, but the ringing was coming from the other side of the room. They began hunting, and Derek found what had to be Shea's phone near the foot of the stairs. "Hello?" he said, answering.

There was a long pause. "I'm sorry. I must have the wrong number."

"Hold on. Are you trying to reach Shea Caldwell?"

"Yes. Who is this?"

He checked the caller ID. It was the Biodermatics office. "This is Derek Oneiros."

"Oh, Mr. Oneiros. This is Lynette Fromm. Your security staff is over here right now."

The new assistant. Derek waved off his brothers.

"I'm trying to find Dr. Caldwell," Lynette said. "She said she doesn't make a habit of it, but she's late. Again. Nobody knows where she is."

Oh, hell. Where was his head? "I'm sorry nobody thought to call."

"What's going on?" she asked, irritation clear in her voice. "Your people have activated ID-only access to most of the offices, and they've limited my computer account. I can't do anything."

He pinched the bridge of his nose. "There was an incident last night involving Ms. Caldwell and Mr. Morrison. Neither will be at work today."

There was another long pause. "Are they okay?"

"Everything will be fine. Can you and Tamika handle things?"

Lynette let out a huff. "Well, that's the thing. Tamika isn't here either."

Derek caught Zane's attention. "Tamika hasn't made it to work yet?"

"No. What's going on?" Lynette asked. "And why are you answering Dr. Caldwell's phone?"

"Lynette, I know you haven't been there long, but do what you can. I'll make sure someone from my staff stays with you until Shea can get in touch."

"Okay… I'll do my best."

"Thank you," Derek said as he hung up.

"Tamika didn't call for REM sleep until late last night," Zane said.

"After the attack?"

"Yeah." Zane turned on his heel. "I'll go find out where she is and what she's been doing."

He never made it out the door. Just as he was about to grab the doorknob, it turned. He jumped back when the door opened, and a big form appeared over him. "Tony! You scared the crap— Oh! Hi, Shea."

Derek pivoted on a dime. There, in the doorway, stood Shea and another of his brothers. Compared to Tony, she looked petite and vulnerable. The look was deceiving. She was one of the strongest people he knew. Her eyes were as bright as anyone's in the room, and her jaw was set with determination.

He went to her quickly. "What are you doing here? You were supposed to try to get some rest."

"I couldn't sleep."

142

Her eyelids fluttered when he brushed a soft kiss against her cheek. Still, when he hooked an arm around her waist, she didn't lean on him. She didn't pull away, either.

When she saw so many strangers watching her, she smoothed the T-shirt and jeans she'd thrown on before going to the hospital last night. She took power from the clothes she normally wore, but she could have worn a potato sack and had his brothers at her feet.

"I'm sorry, but have we met?" she said politely.

"I'm Zane." The youngest Oneiros eagerly stuck out his hand. He looked enraptured, totally caught.

Shea shook his hand, but then held on. Tilting her head, she looked at him more closely. "Do I know you? You seem familiar."

Derek was just as surprised as Zane was by the question. She shouldn't have any recognition of her Dream Weaver at all... unless Zane had played one of his dream games. His brother shook his head when Derek shot him a nasty look.

"I've been around the neighborhood," Zane said, covering quickly.

Shea nodded, not quite convinced. She seemed to still be trying to place him when she caught sight of the other man in the room. "You must be Cael. Thank you for coming. This can't be easy for you."

Sleep problems had taken bad turns for both of them.

"You ask for the help of one Oneiros brother, you get us all."

"The Oneiroi," she said quietly, shocking them right down to their toes. Almost hesitantly, she looked around her home. "Did you find anything?"

"Not yet." Derek's fingers tightened against her waist, and he pulled her close. She looked so tired, yet so determined and brave. "Nothing looks out of place to me. Maybe we just need to wait for Phillip to—"

"Did you open those curtains?"

"What?" He followed her gaze across the living room to the dining room. He and his brothers had been searching so hard for supernatural evidence, he hadn't noticed anything so mundane.

"I close those at night. Did I go out the back?"

En masse, his brothers moved. Zane yanked on the sliding glass door, and it rolled on its fail. "It's unlocked."

"Check out the area," Derek said. "See if we can find out where she went."

They stepped into the backyard. Cael wandered out further in the communal space. Six condo units made up the building, and they all shared one large backyard. Each owner had tried to personalize their space, but other than a white picket fence at the far-end unit, anyone could wander around the area freely.

"Here," Derek said. There were footprints in the flowerbed under her kitchen.

Shea's brow furrowed. The impressions were clearly visible in the dirt, yet their placement was strange. They faced the building, as if the person who'd made them had been looking inside. But that wasn't the only thing that made her uncomfortable.

"Those aren't mine," she said.

"Are you sure?" Tony asked.

She measured her foot against the prints. "I'm sure."

"Whoever made them was wearing shoes," Derek said. "When you woke up, did you have anything on your feet?"

Pink splotches colored her cheeks. She'd told him she was naked. "I was barefoot."

"How old could those prints be?" Cael asked.

Zane scratched his temple. "Less than a day. We got that short burst of rain yesterday afternoon. Remember?"

Shea cleared her throat. "I walked in my sleep the other night, too. The next morning, I found my shoes lined up in front of the kitchen sink." She rubbed her arms. "They were pointed in this direction, as if looking out the window."

Derek exchanged a stunned look with his fellow Dream Weavers.

"Do you think it was trying to tell her somebody was out

there?" Zane whispered.

"*It?*" Shea asked, catching the slip.

"You and Phillip weren't the only people here last night," Derek said, changing the topic. "These footprints are proof. You had a Peeping Tom."

"Or a Peeping Tammy," Tony countered. "Those are small feet for a man."

Shea's eyes rounded. "The car! Oh my gosh, how could I have forgotten?"

She whirled toward them. "I heard a car in the parking lot last night. It might even have been what woke me. It was trying to get out of there fast."

"Could you identify it?" Derek asked. "Did you see the make or model? Did you get a look at the driver?"

Her face fell. "No. I just... I wasn't coherent then."

Derek didn't like the way things were coming together. First the trespasser at her place of business, and now this? "Baby, I don't want to scare you, but I think your problem is worse than an overaggressive business competitor. I think you've got a stalker."

"A stalker?"

"You've caught someone going through your garbage, rummaging around your desk, and now watching through your windows. Maybe worse."

Her eyes went wide. "Do you think the person who made those footprints attacked Phillip?"

The words came out hopeful, and she winced—but her feelings were understandable. She didn't want to be the one responsible for hurting her friend. She rubbed her brow. "But why? What did he ever do?"

"It might still have something to do with your company." Derek's brain was cranking through the facts. "Or it might just be that he's too close to you? Maybe he surprised them when he came over."

"I don't understand. Who would do something like this?"

"I don't know, but I'm not taking any more chances." This had gone on long enough. He braced his feet and lifted his chin. "I'm moving in."

She took an instinctive step back. "No."

"Yes." He caught her hand before she could step away again. "Either that or you move in with me. You're not going to be alone."

"I can't go to your place," she said tightly. "I don't know the layout."

Meaning she was sure she'd sleepwalk again.

Her honesty and her fear hit him in the middle of his chest. He knew what it had taken for her to confide in him.

"Then it's decided. I'll bring my things over today."

She looked up at him, her face drawn. He'd known she wouldn't like the idea, but she was a smart woman. She knew she was in danger. "Fine, but you're sleeping in the guest bedroom."

Zane coughed. He gasped for air even louder when Tony elbowed him in the gut.

Shea wasn't finished. "You'll be in another bedroom with the door locked and the dresser pulled in front of it."

Cael turned away and became inordinately interested in the garden hose.

"Oh, come on, Curie," Derek said.

"No. That's the way it has to be. I will not wake up to find *you* lying unconscious at my feet, and I refuse to find you standing in the headlights of my car when I'm sleep-driving."

His brothers' heads turned with a snap.

Shea kept her gaze on his as she fisted her hands into his T-shirt. "I just *can't.*"

CHAPTER TWELVE

Derek found Shea in her bedroom. Quietly, he set the camera Cael had loaned them onto her dresser. With the way the morning sunlight gleamed off her blonde hair, she looked angelic, yet the energy buzzing around her was anything but peaceful. He folded his arms across his chest and tried to ignore the tingling in his fingertips. Normally, a conscious mind was outside his abilities, but her brain wave patterns were so chaotic, his other half could sense it.

And it pained him.

Leaning against the doorframe, he simply watched her. He wished he knew what to say to her, what to do... Hell, he knew exactly what he had to do. He had to catch that damn Somnambulist before it got to her again and obliterate it.

But how could he make her feel better without telling her that?

"You're looking at me again." Slowly, she turned. Her arms were wrapped around her waist as if she was trying to hold herself together. When her tired blue gaze met his, Derek felt the kick right in his gut.

"Can't be helped," he said gruffly.

And it couldn't. She was easy on his eyes. She was easy on his soul.

"You shouldn't still be up," he said.

She shrugged. "Can't be helped."

147

She let out a long sigh. She was beyond tired. She was exhausted, mentally and physically. So was he. A night without sleep could do that to a normal person, and he was anything but normal.

Over the hours, the night had increasingly pulled at him. The darkness had called. His charges had called. Ignoring the relentless tug had him drained. Yet as much as the sunlight hurt his eyes and the rising temperature sapped his strength, he didn't care. He wasn't going to sleep until she did.

"Are your brothers gone?"

"Tony just left."

Cael and Zane had gone to check on Tamika a while ago—not that Shea needed to know that.

She nodded. "They're good guys. Handsome. If I didn't know better, I'd believe you *were* descended from Greek gods."

Derek's pulse jumped. If only she did believe that, yet he let the subject pass. She was in no condition to deal with any more shocks.

"I'm having trouble thinking straight," she admitted quietly.

"How can I help?"

Agitated, she drummed her fingers against her elbow. "I need you to be honest with me. Is there really a chance I didn't hurt Phillip? Even the smallest chance? Because if we're grasping at straws, I need to refocus and prepare. I can't do that now, because this feeling of hope is getting in the way—and I hate that it's hope."

She looked at him steadily, bracing herself. "I need to know if it has any merit, because if it doesn't..."

"Believe it." She hadn't done this. Of that, he was one hundred percent certain. The Peeping Tom or the Somnambulist was responsible. He didn't care which, but it hadn't been her.

He pushed away from the doorframe. The tingles of energy he'd felt randomly coming off her suddenly focused in his direction, and the jolt was magnetic. It drew him to her, and he stopped only when they were face to face.

"Somebody put those footprints there," he said. He ached to touch her, but knew she needed to deal with this first. "You didn't hit Phillip."

Her eyes flashed, but her chin came up. "That other person might have been coming to his rescue."

"Or you might have played that role. You said your hands were empty when you came awake."

"But Phillip said I called him. Derek, I lured him over here."

"No, you called him for help." Besides, she hadn't called anyone. The Somnambulist had pulled that little stunt.

Worry slowly dimmed that spark in her eyes. "But did I really need it? It's... I'm becoming more aggressive when I sleepwalk. I already told you that."

Her sleep-driving story still made Derek lightheaded. He couldn't believe how far the creature had gone with her. To put her behind the wheel of a car... He couldn't think about it. "Your stalker is becoming more aggressive, too. There were three people here last night."

Shea rubbed at her breastbone. "I can't believe I'm hoping you're right. I'm hoping I have a stalker. I'm hoping he or she attacked Phillip. It's wrong on so many levels."

Derek needed her to accept the fact, unpalatable as it might be. The Somnambulist was one thing, but this unknown third party threw everything out of whack. He needed her to help him figure everything out, and the sooner she stopped blaming herself, the better.

She rubbed at her breastbone harder with the heel of her palm. "I feel like I should have known. The face in the window... Maybe I did know."

"The face in the window?"

She jumped. Sighing, he reached out and cupped the nape of her neck. He drew her toward him and brushed his thumb against her cheek. "Sorry, it's just rare for Somnambulists to—"

She flinched again, surprising him.

"Sleepwalkers," he quickly clarified. "It's rare for sleepwalkers to remember anything they see or do."

Yet even as he tried to calm her, Derek's own mind was spinning. It was more than rare. He'd never heard of anything like that happening before. A Somnambulist never transferred its consciousness to its host.

An uneasy feeling settled in his chest. Was that thing so entwined with her? Were they meshing so completely? His fingers tightened reflexively in her hair.

Would hurting it hurt her?

And killing it?

He squeezed his eyes shut.

"Derek?"

He kissed her. He just pulled her against him and sealed his mouth over hers. Put him up against a Night Terror any day. Make him face an army of Lunatics. He could take a threat against himself. Just don't threaten her. He couldn't handle it.

His touch seemed to finally break her. With a soft cry, she wrapped her arms around his neck. Her body melted against his, and he pulled her even closer. He wanted to protect her from this. He wanted to shield her from everything bad and scary.

He pulled back to look into her eyes. The Somnambulist had obviously tapped into her consciousness. If she'd been in jeopardy... "I just wish you'd let me stay."

Any remaining color drained from her face.

"Don't say that." She clutched at his shoulders. "Don't say that."

Almost desperately, she pulled him down. Her kiss was deeper and rawer as she tugged his T-shirt from his jeans.

She needed this. They both needed this.

Derek fisted his hands in the soft fabric of her T-shirt. Breaking their kiss, they tugged off clothing and dropped it onto the floor. As if they'd been lovers for years, they came back into each other's embrace. His fingers found the clasp of her bra, while hers found the zipper of his jeans.

He groaned when she pressed her palm against his growing erection.

"I hate what's happening to me," she whispered against his chest. "I can't take not knowing what I'm doing and feeling so out of control."

He folded his hand atop of hers. "Baby, you can be in control of this."

Dipping his head, he stole another kiss. He'd needed to be with her like this ever since she'd first called from the hospital. The fear and anguish in her voice had been too much.

He'd do whatever she wanted, be whatever she needed.

He stripped off her bra and tossed it to the floor. Together, they worked out of the rest of their clothes.

When she stepped back up to him again, though, things slowed down. Their gazes connected, and the temperature in the room began to heat. Derek felt every degree. The tips of her breasts brushed against his chest, and her belly stroked against his swelling cock. It was all he could do not to pick her up and bury himself deep.

But she wanted to be in charge, and he'd given her the reins.

She gave him a nudge. The back of his knees hit the mattress, and he sat down hard. He let out a ragged breath when she stepped up between his legs.

"Derek," she sighed.

She placed one knee on the mattress beside his hip, and he slid his hand intimately between her legs. With a low groan, she let her head drop back. Her hair dangled behind her, and she looked so sexy he almost forgot to breathe. He rubbed her more possessively, and her breasts jutted up into the air.

"Come here, baby."

She climbed onto his lap, straddling him, and he cupped her bottom with both hands. The sheets rasped beneath her knees as he pulled her forward. The sound was erotic as hell, but it also made an unwanted realization pop into his head.

The bed was unmade. The last time she'd been here, the

Somnie had been inside her.

His fingers bit into her bottom. He was a Dream Weaver. She was his charge and his lover. He was supposed to stop things like that from happening to her. He kissed her harder, sweeping his tongue across her damp lips. She parted them and snuggled closer.

It was the most sensuous feeling in the world. His heart thundered as her hands glided down his back. Her breasts flattened against his chest, and her belly pressed tightly against his erection. His proprietary instincts surged, and he fisted a hand in her hair.

He hated the thought of anyone or anything else touching her. Permeating her.

Watching her.

"Ah, hell." He broke off the kiss and tried to shield her as best as he could with his hands.

"The camera," he said, breathing harshly. He glanced over her shoulder to the dresser. "It's motion activated. I was supposed to turn it off until tonight."

Her hair tickled his fingers as she slowly looked over her shoulder. Staring right at the camera lens, she took a deep breath. When she turned back to him, her eyes were heavy-lidded. "It's always best to run a test sample."

Oh. Fuck.

Shea felt Derek's cock jump against her belly—but she wasn't trying to be bold or outrageous. She needed this. She needed to be in control of something. In the light. In the heat. In the sunshine and in front of the camera, there were no secrets.

No doubts.

And she wanted him. She needed him to make her feel like she was whole, not splintering in two. At night, she turned into an unthinking zombie. In the crisp sunshine, she was Shea.

She knew he wanted her, too.

Aware of the prying eyes, she kissed him again. She loved how he felt, so big and tough. So solid. Sensuously, she rubbed herself against his muscled chest. She felt his hands settle on her backside again—not shielding her from the camera, but cupping her and caressing her.

She groaned and swiveled her hips against him. She shivered as his erection rubbed against her most sensitive flesh. "There was a time I thought I liked you for your brain."

He grunted. "Right now, I couldn't spell my own name."

Lifting herself up higher onto her haunches, she directed her breast toward his mouth. A delectable tension streaked through her body when he latched on and began to suckle. She watched as his mouth worked on her. She saw the indentations in his cheeks, felt the hot lashes of his tongue, and heard the wet slurps. She closed her eyes as she felt her pussy clench.

Then she was wet.

She moaned when the head of his cock brushed against her, and she started to lower herself onto him. He restrained the movement, keeping her lifted and poised for his mouth. When he moved his hot, wet attention to her other nipple, she squirmed in his grip.

"I thought I was in control."

"Curie," he said, raking his teeth against her swollen tip, "in case you haven't noticed, you've got me wrapped around your little finger."

Shea couldn't take the teasing any longer. Cupping his face, she kissed him. His hands were hot on her bottom, and his erection was tucked up intimately against her.

She wanted to feel it inside her. She wanted to feel him pumping deep.

She pushed at his shoulders. "Lie down."

Slowly, he lay back, watching her with those glittering, dark eyes. Feeling urgency grip her, she came up over him and braced her hands against the mattress by his head. He positioned the tip of his cock against her opening. Closing her eyes, she slowly pressed herself down onto that wonderful thickness.

His fingers bit into her hips as the pressure intensified.

Her nipples pinched, and she dug her fingers into the mattress. He felt big this way. Huge. The fit was tight and raw until a jolt of sensation went through her.

Her eyes popped open when she felt the pad of his finger settle over her clit. Her gaze locked with his when he rubbed her sexily. His eyes were heavy, seductive, and just a little wild.

"*Ohhh*," she moaned.

Frozen, she could only stare into his eyes as he stroked the back of her thigh with his other hand. He looked so dark and sexy. So *hers*.

Taking a deep breath, she tried to relax. He didn't help when that intimately placed finger stroked deeper between her legs to the spot where they were connected... to where she was stretching to accommodate him. Her inner muscles fluttered, making him groan.

And making her so wet, it didn't matter anymore.

Shea didn't think. She just began pressing herself downward onto his stiff, hot cock until she'd taken him fully. The fullness... It was... It felt... *Oh, God.*

She began to thrust. Her thighs clenched and released as she lifted and lowered herself onto him. Her heart began to pound uncontrollably, and her mind spun. She raked her fingers across his chest, and her nails scraped over his man nipples.

She cried out sharply when his hips bucked. He rammed into her, and her back arched. Their bodies strained, caught in the position, too racked with pleasure to give it up.

But his hands cupped her breasts.

And his legs churned.

And the need to move slammed into her.

Bracing her hands against his shoulders, she began to pump harder and faster. His hands settled over her breasts, and sweat built up between their bodies. Shea felt a droplet trail along her back where the camera was focused. The viewfinder was documenting exactly what they were doing.

Voyeuristic pleasure had her sitting up straight and

grinding down on him. His fingers dug into her thighs at that, and she let out a surprised cry. She came so hard her back bowed, and her face lifted to the sun.

Derek let out a shout. Then his hips were straining upward, lifting her right off the mattress. He thrust into her in ragged, rapid thrusts before he exploded. Pressing up into her, he held her immobile as he came for what felt like forever.

Dropping onto the bed as one, they fought for air. Coherency took its time coming.

Shea cuddled against Derek's chest, loving the lightness. She loved the safety she found there. He wrapped his arms around her, keeping her close.

"Better?" he asked softly.

So much.

She'd been alone for so long. She could be strong and self-sufficient, but it felt nice to share the weight with someone just once.

"Thank you," she whispered. "For coming to the hospital. For dealing with... everything."

"You should have told me about the sleepwalking before."

Maybe... or maybe she'd kept him from harm.

He pressed a kiss to the top of her head. "How long has this been happening?"

She hesitated. "Since I was little."

He pulled back sharply. "You've been walking in your sleep your whole life?"

"No, it stopped after... It stopped for a while." Absently, she ran her hand across his chest. It was hard to talk about this. Growing up, she'd had to deal with the laughs and the teasing—or worse, the frightened looks. Yet she felt so close to him, like she could tell him anything.

Almost anything.

"It just started again, actually... the night before I came to you for the background check on Lynette."

He stared up at the ceiling. "That explains the fear."

"What?"

"Nothing." He swept his hand down to her bottom, holding her put so their bodies wouldn't disconnect.

Even satiated, she liked the feeling of him inside her.

It made her feel secure and protected.

With her guard dropping, though, she felt the heaviness of fatigue falling over her like a blanket. Instinctively, she tried to push it off. It was just so difficult, wrapped in his arms the way she was.

"You know," he said quietly, "the Oneiroi don't like it when things mess with their charges."

Shea went still. Derek Oneiros didn't seem like the type to tell bedtime stories. "Their charges?" she prompted, wanting more.

"Those people placed in their care, the ones to which they deliver dreams. We fight to protect them."

She looked at him in bemusement. "I didn't think the Oneiroi took sides, neither good nor evil."

"We don't."

She smiled. *We.* She knew he was coddling her, indulging her, but she liked it. It was sweet and so very soothing. Her eyelids felt heavy, and it was getting hard to concentrate. Still, she watched him, entranced by the story he was spinning.

"We're very protective about our right to bestow dreams. Good or bad, we don't like it when something gets in our way."

"Like a Somnam—" She cut herself off quickly. God, she was getting tired. "Like sleepwalking?"

"Precisely."

She felt something flare inside her chest. He looked so serious, and she'd always wanted to believe in fairy tales. Good overcoming evil. The impossible coming true. "So what do you do about it?"

"We stop it."

The warmth in her chest spread. "And you're my Oneiros?"

"I am."

She liked the sound of that. Her heart pounded as she

cupped his cheek. "You'll protect me?"

"You know I will."

The promise touched her, with one exception.

"From the other room, though. Right?"

She was nearly under, but she forced her eyelids back open.

He sighed loudly. "From the other room."

"With the door locked." One last thought occurred to her, and she lifted her head sharply off his chest. "Don't let me fall asleep naked."

"Don't worry, Curie." He cupped the back of her head and drew her down. "I've got you covered."

CHAPTER THIRTEEN

When Shea awoke, it was strangely dark. Not quite night, but not quite day. The eerie grayness threw her, and she was disoriented as to time and place. A long, low grumble made her turn on her side.

She was in her bedroom. Alone—she glanced down quickly—and dressed. She smoothed her hand over Derek's black T-shirt. It was soft and comfortable. Comforting. Outside, she heard another low rumble.

Thunder.

There was no mistaking it now. She looked out the window. The sky was heavy and foreboding. This wasn't going to be another quick shower. A summer storm was about to hit.

She turned on her bedside lamp. The cloud layer was so thick, it blocked out the sun. The resulting darkness was nearly as unnerving as the dead of the night, yet she was surprised when she saw her alarm clock. It was still early afternoon.

She'd slept deeply, but had she slept soundly?

Sitting up, she looked around the room. Everything seemed in order.

Pushing off the sheet, she got up. Derek's T-shirt brushed low against her thighs as she headed toward the hallway. She found him asleep in her guest bedroom with the door wide open.

Peeved, she pushed her hair over her shoulder. Yet as she watched him, it was impossible to stay upset with him. He lay sprawled on his back, taking up most of the queen-sized bed. The bed linens were slung low across his hips. Very low.

She inhaled slowly, and the thunder outside seemed to growl. His body was muscled and tanned. His hair was rumpled, and his eyelashes looked long and soft against his cheeks. Her breasts ached when she saw the stubble darkening his features. Those prickly whiskers made him look rakish and reckless. Knowing he was the exact opposite made this private little viewing even more intimate.

Wind suddenly gathered and blew strong against the walls of the condo. She watched as Derek's chest rose and fell. He was sleeping deeply, oblivious to the impending wildness outside. He'd been as tired as she was, maybe more. He hadn't had adrenaline pumping through his veins the way she had, but he'd stayed with her throughout the night. He'd held her hand, calmed her nerves, and fended off his own fatigue.

Lightning flashed. Giving in to an impulse, she crossed the room. He didn't stir as she came to the side of the bed. Carefully, she crawled onto the open space beside him. He didn't budge an inch.

She hesitated as she watched him. He didn't turn toward her, he didn't adjust to the movement of the mattress, and he didn't grumble. Thunder cracked, making her jump. Still, Derek did nothing.

This wasn't just the sleep of the overly tired. She'd been right; he was vulnerable when he slept.

He slept like the dead.

As big, smart, and strong as he was, he couldn't defend himself against that which he didn't see coming. He was susceptible to dangers like her or anything else that wandered in the night.

She edged toward him. When he still didn't respond, she laid her head on his shoulder. Her arm found a comfortable spot around his waist, and she twined her leg around his. For a long time, she lay there thinking.

It was time she made some decisions.

When Derek suddenly stretched, it surprised her. His whole body shifted as if he'd just come back into himself. She watched in fascination. She knew how that felt, but she'd never seen anyone else do it before. As worried as she was, a pleasant warmth filled her when his dark eyes opened.

"Mmm." His arm came around her. "Now this is the way to wake up."

"Good morning," she whispered.

"More like good afternoon." Pulling her close, he kissed her. It was a long, slow, drawn-out welcome that stopped only when another blast of wind rattled the windows. Turning, he lay so they faced one another. "Did you sleep well?"

"I think so."

"Good dreams."

Her eyes narrowed. It didn't sound like a question, and she had had good dreams—insights about her research, actually. His bedtime story about the Oneiroi popped into her head, but she pushed it away. As tempting as it was to play make-believe, she had to face the truth.

"You didn't lock the door."

He glanced toward the hallway. "It's easier to hear if it's open."

"You didn't hear me at all when I walked in just now."

"I knew you were here." Once again, calm assurance was in his voice.

She just couldn't fight it, and she didn't want to. Wearily, she laid her hand against his chest. The rhythmic thud of his heart was steadying. "I've been thinking," she said.

"About what?"

"The things I need to do. The actions that will fix this situation." She looked into his eyes. "I need to tell the police the whole truth."

His hand tightened against her back. "Shea."

"I have a medical condition," she said, staying firm. "I'm

160

under a doctor's care. There have been court cases where sleepwalkers have been declared not guilty, because they weren't in control of their faculties at the time the crime was committed."

"But we don't even know if you did commit the crime."

"Which makes it even more important to get everything on the record." She ran her hand over to the biceps of his arm. The strength she found there encouraged her. "If somebody has been stalking me, I want to do something about it."

He watched her for a long moment. "All right. Whatever you need."

Whatever she needed… She was finding herself needing him more and more each day. That was why her next decision was so important.

"I've also made a decision about my sleepwalking."

One of his eyebrows lifted. "You have, have you?"

"I wasn't thinking clearly last night when I asked you to monitor me. It's not fair to you, and it's dangerous. I need to seek professional help." Her fingers curled against his smooth skin. "Since they can't get me into the sleep clinic here, I'm going to have Dr. Wainright refer me to somebody. I don't care if I have to fly halfway across the country. I want to see a specialist."

Derek propped himself up onto an elbow. "Stay with me. Just give it a little more time."

"I need to do this."

"Sleeping pills aren't the answer. You've already determined that."

"There might be something else wrong. I could have an electrical short of sorts in my brain, an out-of-time circadian rhythm, or even ment…" She took a deep breath. "Mental—"

His face hardened. "There is nothing wrong with you."

She cupped his cheek, feeling the tension in the room grow as surely as the storm outside. Feeling miserable, she looked at him. "Please don't fight me on this."

A muscle worked in his temple, and she could see the strain in his jaw.

"Fine," he said at last. "I'll come with you."

She didn't know why his offer surprised her, but it did.

"But your company," she said, trying to concentrate on the rational over the leap in her heart. "You've been spending so much time away from there already."

"I have good people. They'll cover for me."

So did she. That made this decision so much easier. She could trust them to carry on.

Or could she?

Bio! With a jolt, she sat upright. She couldn't believe she'd left her company stranded high and dry. "I forgot to call in. Everybody at Biodermatics is probably wondering where Phillip and I are. We should have shut down for the day."

Derek drew her back down. "I had my people step in. We didn't interfere with production, but we locked down your office, Phillip's office, and your lab."

Shea exhaled roughly and looked to the ceiling. "Thank you. I... I wasn't thinking."

"You were thinking plenty. You just had other things on your mind."

She had. She had too much to think about: Phillip, a potential stalker, and her sleepwalking. How could she have fallen asleep?

Derek's hand was gentle as he tucked her hair behind her ear. "Curie, we need to talk. Who do you think is behind all of this?"

Her stomach dropped. She didn't want to have this conversation. "I don't know."

"When we talked at my office, you were worried that this might be an inside job."

"That was when I thought someone was trying to access company info, not kill my partner!"

He wound a strand of her hair around his finger. As calm as he looked, the electricity crackling in the room nearly overpowered that outside. "I want you to think back to that prowler in the parking lot. I know you were disoriented, but could it have been a woman?"

The footprints. "You think it was the same person outside my window?"

"Just close your eyes and try to remember."

She didn't have to close her eyes. That part of the night was very clear in her memory banks. She remembered the dark shape and its anger. "The person was wearing a loose-fitting sweat suit with the hood pulled up. It could have been anybody."

"I'm just exploring all the angles," he said. "Someone— probably a woman—has been watching you. They gained access to your office, and Phillip was attacked. I'm trying to find the common link."

"But that narrows it down to Tamika or Lynette."

"If you have other thoughts, I'm open to them."

Shea swallowed hard.

"It would be difficult for anybody else to gain access to your office without drawing attention. Have either of them been acting suspicious?"

"Both of them." Shea rolled onto her back. She couldn't bear to think it was someone that close to her. "Tamika's whole personality has changed recently. She's always tired and cranky."

"Like she could be running around at night looking into other people's windows?"

Shea closed her eyes. "Can we not do this? She's a good friend of mine."

"Good friend or not, she wasn't at work this morning."

Shea looked at him sharply. "Where was she?"

"We don't know, but coming right after the attack, it looks suspicious. Lynette was there alone."

"Oh, no."

"You don't trust her."

Shea wrapped her fingers in the bed sheet. "I… Let's just say I don't know her well enough yet. She seems to want to get into everything."

"All this started when she showed up."

"But that could be coincidence. You did the background check on her."

He shifted. "Yeah, and, on the surface, she checks out. She has no criminal history, her credit is solid, and her former employers liked her. I'm not done, though. I'm still trying to get more information on her sabbatical during her stepmother's illness."

"I don't think she likes me," Shea admitted.

"Why do you say that?"

"She interviewed really well, but now that she's in the office every day, I can see that she's passive-aggressive. I thought it might be just a defense mechanism—you know, nerves on the new job—but now I'm not so sure."

"Does she do it to Phillip?"

"Not that I've noticed—but she sets Tamika off, and in a big way. Tamika's still upset that we hired her."

"Maybe you need to think about getting rid of both of them."

Shea sagged against the pillow. "How did things go so wrong so fast?"

"Just watch them, okay?"

Lightning hit, and thunder cracked.

"Watch everyone."

She shivered as rain suddenly lashed against the window. It was hard and driving. Relentless.

It was nothing compared to the look on Derek's face as he slid his T-shirt up over her hips.

"And not everything is going wrong," he said huskily. With a smooth move, he rolled on top of her and slid in deep. "Some things are finally very, very right."

* * *

The storm was in full swing when Shea finally made it into the office late that afternoon. She parked in her reserved spot and glanced up at the sky. A cold front was colliding with the heat and humidity that had sat on the city for days. The result was tumultuous.

Much like her mood.

Seeing a brief letup in the downpour hitting her windshield, she reached for her umbrella and briefcase. She made a mad dash to the door, but her skirt and shoes were damp by the time she made it inside.

"Shea!"

Looking up, she found the front office crowded. Almost simultaneously, a bolt of lightning lit the room. The faces of her employees were imprinted on her mind as well as if it had been photographic film.

Watch everyone.

Derek's words rang in her ears along with the crack of thunder that suddenly split the air.

"How's Phillip?" Tamika asked, rising from her seat behind her desk. "Was he really attacked?"

"We heard a news blip on the radio," Lynette said. "Do they have any idea who did this?"

The barrage of questions was expected. The feelings of doubt and suspicion they raised were not.

"No, and we can't figure out why." Shea concentrated on her umbrella. Giving herself time, she shook the rain off it and hung it from the coat rack. "I just came from the hospital."

"Is he going to be all right?" Bruce, her operations manager, asked.

"He has a concussion." Wind rattled the windows as Shea crossed the room. She brushed more droplets off her suit and ran a hand across her hair. "The doctors are planning to keep him overnight for observation, but they think they might be able to release him tomorrow."

"Does he need anything? What can we do?" The concern on Tamika's face seemed real.

"Just keep him in your thoughts."

"This is just so hard to believe," Bruce said.

"He didn't deserve this, not Phillip," Lynette agreed. "At least he's in a good hospital. They treated my stepmother well. It's just so terrible he ended up there."

"I know," Shea said. It was terrible that her best friend had been hurt, and terrible that she was looking at those closest to him with distrust. How could she let herself think like this? They all looked genuinely worried. Guileless.

Yet that made the hair on her arms rise even more.

"Should we be worried?" Bruce asked. He waved his clipboard at the parking lot. "First there was that prowler, and now Phillip's been attacked. Is there something going on that we should know about?"

"Mr. Oneiros had his security team crawling all over the place today," Lynette said.

Tamika's eyes rounded. "*You* were the target! That's why Derek's people were here."

Shea felt a pull between her shoulder blades. "The Oneiros agency added some security measures as a precaution. The police are officially handling the investigation."

Unfortunately, as Derek had warned her, their scrutiny was now on her. Her fingers curled more tightly around the handle of her briefcase. "I recommend you all be careful. Until then, let's concentrate on doing business. Phillip would hate it if we missed a sale because of him."

Bruce cleared his throat. "Well, I don't know if this is the right time to tell you, but we might have missed more than just a sale."

Shea looked at her operations manager. She really couldn't take much more bad news.

"With all the chaos here today, we ran behind. We didn't get that shipment of eye cream out to Cleveland. It's going to be late."

"How late?"

"A couple of days."

Thunder rumbled, and the vibrations ran up Shea's feet. Biodermatics' lotions were their bread and butter. The income they generated paid her employees' salaries and allowed her the luxury to do the research she wanted to do. Were things worse than she and Derek suspected? Was somebody trying to sabotage her entire company?

Watch everyone.

A chill ran down her spine. The thought of this particular research being in jeopardy rattled her almost as much as the sleepwalking. It was so important to her. It could help so many people in need.

Bruce scratched the stubble on his jaw. "If you've got a few minutes, we really need to talk about this new production schedule."

Production schedule?

He shook his head. "Things are only going to get worse if we switch to this."

"Let me see that." Shea took the clipboard and scanned the spreadsheet. With one glance, she knew that Phillip hadn't put this together. Neither had she. Her fingers stiffened on the clipboard. "Lynette, can I have a word with you?"

Stiffly, Shea headed down the hallway and badged into her office. She heard Lynette follow at a much slower pace.

"Yes, Dr. Caldwell?" the woman asked when she finally stepped into the private space.

"What is this?" Shea asked, holding up the spreadsheet.

Lynette's face faltered. "I was alone this morning. Mr. Oneiros said I should do the best I could, and I knew that was something you'd been procrastinating about."

After eavesdropping outside Phillip's office?

Shea felt her cheeks flush. "This is outside your authority. More importantly, it's wrong. If we tried running this fast, we'd risk machinery breakdowns and union problems."

"We would?"

Yes, they would! Not to mention that the overtime pay could put them out of business. Shea dropped her briefcase into her chair with a clatter. "Have you cancelled Phillip's appointments?"

"Uh... no."

"Please do so."

Lynette folded her hands together. "I was just trying to

help."

"I understand that." Shea held the schedule out to the woman. She could have helped more by just doing her job. "But tell Bruce we'll be going back to the old schedule until Phillip can get back on his feet. Thank you."

Lynette left with a frown on her face, and Shea raked her hands through her hair. How could she leave her company with nobody at the helm? Maybe it was best that the earliest Dr. Wainright could get her into another sleep clinic was the end of next week.

And maybe it wasn't.

Feeling trapped, Shea walked over to the window and gripped the sill tightly. Rain beat against the windowpane. The sky was darker than ever. Night was battling day—and darkness was winning.

"Shea?" The soft voice came from the doorway. "Are you okay?"

She closed her eyes and flat-out lied. "I'm fine."

Tamika's steps were muffled by the carpeting as she crossed the room. "Don't let Lynette bother you. I can handle her."

Shea rested her forehead against the pane of glass. "I'm just really on edge right now."

"That's understandable." Reaching out, Tamika rubbed her shoulder. "I know how close you and Phillip are."

"You're close to him, too."

"You found him, didn't you?"

The words were like an icy trickle of that dark rain going down Shea's spine. "How do you know that?"

"I just assumed... The news reporter said it happened at your complex."

"Where were you this morning?" Shea blurted. At the narrowing of her assistant's eyes, she folded her arms around her waist. "Derek said you were out. I could have used you here."

Tamika hesitated, the toe of one shoe twisting against the floor. "If you must know, I went to the bank to get a loan. I took vacation time."

Shea frowned. "Are you having problems?"

"No." Tamika fluffed her hair. "I just decided I needed something."

She walked over to the window to gaze out at the storm. Shea turned with her, intending to dig deeper, but her questions froze in her throat. She'd just gotten a good look at her assistant's shoes.

"I feel so bad for Phillip," Tamika said quietly.

Shea couldn't respond. All she could see were the black and white zebra-striped stilettos on Tamika's feet. They were nearly identical to her shoes, the ones that she'd found pointing toward her kitchen window the morning after she'd sleepwalked.

Had her Somnambulist been trying to tell her something?

Tamika rocked her foot back, pointing the toe of that crazy shoe into the air. "You just never think that something like this will happen to someone you know."

"No," Shea said weakly. "You never really do."

"It's scary."

Thunder rolled.

"Yes, it is."

CHAPTER FOURTEEN

The Somnambulist waited forever for his beloved to fall asleep that night. He floated back and forth next to her window, watching as she flopped and turned, rolling from one side of the bed to the other. Something had her perturbed.

Was it the storm? The lightning and thunder? He liked storms. He got a buzz from the swirling, the howling, and the sizzling energy. He loved the smell of burnt air, and the whoosh of pressure that rolled through him with every gust. It made his particles hum.

But not as much as she did.

He waited anxiously, raindrops falling through him, as his She-a settled into sleep. Still, he didn't enter the room. He felt twitchy. Weaver stench was in the air. There was one nearby—or had been—but the creature hadn't seen him.

He sniffed harder, yet the musky scent of her lotion tickled his senses. He swayed in delight. It was the yummy stuff that made her skin so soft. It made him ache. He wanted to be inside her. He wanted to feel.

Anger made his fragments thrum. Where was he, that peeking Weaver? It was the one with the mean eyes, he knew it. "Third wheel. Glom-onner."

Instinct told the creature he should leave. Greed made him stay.

He didn't need to be here tonight. He felt strong and fast. She'd done that for him. Last night they'd been strong together, faster than the wind. He could still feel the stairs pounding under her feet, hear the startled exclamation of their visitor, and smell the scent of fear.

It had excited him. He wanted more.

Annoyed, the Somnambulist let his toe slide through the wall and into the bedroom. He waited for that tingle that would tell him if a Weaver was about to pounce.

The prickle wasn't enough to stop him.

Tempted beyond caution, he slipped into the room. He waited, tensed, as his molecules reassembled. All was quiet. He floated closer. Paused. A little closer. Finally, he was suspended by his She-a's bed.

"Pretty girl. Smart girl."

She'd known what to do when he'd finally shown her the face in the window.

He bounced up over her, extended himself to her length, and slowly lowered himself into her. "Mmmm," he purred as he stretched.

Her body extended right along with him.

"Hm?" He pointed her toes. She was lighter tonight. The cobwebs had cleared from her head. He'd made her better! The Dream Weavers' hold on her had been broken.

Blew them away, he had! Like a match to a fuse. TNT to dust.

Excitement made him flutter, and he saw her nightie quiver. Lifting her hand, he caressed the pretty gown. It was soft and slick.

He knew someplace else that was soft and slick. Oh, the secret she'd shown him!

Pinching the material between her thumb and forefinger, he lifted her head and peeked underneath. There those red berries were. Hissing with eagerness, he slipped her hand underneath her nightie and gave one of the red bumps a pinch.

Her breath exhaled in a puff, and her body jumped.

There it was, the power and the exhilarating rush.

Shoving the material aside, he slipped her other hand in. He squeezed and tugged, scratched and rolled. Her bottom squiggled on the mattress, and that hungry heat filled her belly.

"My She-a! My lovely princess." He hummed inside her, luxuriating in her. They'd walk farther tonight. He'd loved the prickle of grass under her feet and the brush of wind against her skin. What would the rain feel like? He could only imagine that cold dampness splattering across her—

What was that?

He lifted her head off the pillow with a jerk.

Was that a noise? Downstairs? He curled her lips into a snarl.

Again? The creature growled. He thought they'd chased them away. Why couldn't the interlopers leave them alone?

He bounced her from the bed and looked around for something hard. He knew how to stop this now. He tore the plug for the bedside lamp out of the wall and stomped toward the door. He yanked it open and—

"Weaver!"

It was standing right in front of him with its mean eyes glaring.

Pain scorched the Somnambulist, too much to enjoy. That hand of death came at him, and he lurched back. He jumped right out of his She-a's body and dispersed, just pulled apart and disappeared.

Still, the fingers seared him, and he screamed.

Shea jolted. She came awake so fast, it felt as if sleep was being torn from her. She gasped for air and clenched at the doorjamb. A scream rang in her head.

Had she made that sound?

Footsteps pounded. Lightning lit up the room and, this time, she knew her scream was her own. It ripped through her vocal cords and hurt her ears. Someone was standing right in front of her!

"Shea!"

The figure caught her firmly by the shoulders. Her entire body shuddered when those strong hands gave her a hard shake.

"Shea! It's me. Wake up."

She blinked, confused. "Derek?"

He hit the light switch. Light flooded behind her, but that didn't make the picture any easier to bear. She found herself standing in her doorway, with no idea how she'd gotten there.

A weight pulled at her hand. She gasped when she looked down.

Her lamp clattered to the floor, smashing and sending sharp glass flying.

Derek jumped out of the way and pulled her out into the hallway. Shea pulled back worriedly. The light from the bedroom cast a misshapen rectangle on the far wall, but outside of that everything was pitch-black.

What had just happened?

"Are you all right?" he asked.

"Are you?"

They both glanced at the shards on the floor.

"I'm fine," he said. "You're the one who's shaking."

He pulled her closer, and she went to him instinctively. Her fingers bit into his waist. He felt strong and whole. She could see he wasn't hurt, but he could have been. If she'd hit him with that lamp—

"This means nothing," he said. "Don't read anything into this."

"Read anything into it? It's spelled out pretty clearly, don't you think?" She couldn't stop looking at the glass and metal on the floor. This was exactly what she'd been afraid would happen. This was why she'd wanted him anywhere but here.

"We've got to get you warmed up. Stay here."

Shivering, she watched as he carefully stepped around the hazard. She had to get him to leave. *She* needed to leave. The sleep clinic couldn't make her wait any longer. She'd go sit on their doorstep until they took her in.

"Here," Derek said, appearing in front of her again. "Put this on."

He had her robe. She stuck her arms into the sleeves as he tied the belt securely around her waist. Catching her by the lapels, he made her look at him. "Don't even think about it. I'm not going anywhere. If you had let me sleep with you, you never would have made it off the bed."

She wasn't so sure. The skin of her palms crawled, and she closed her fists, letting her fingernails dig in deep. What else had her hands done? Where else had her feet trod? Had she attacked Phillip?

She hated that Derek had seen her like that.

"I need a drink," she said hoarsely. She maneuvered past him and walked unsteadily down the hallway.

His footsteps followed close behind. "What about the sleeping pills?"

"I stopped taking them." They hadn't worked, had they?

Nothing was working!

She slapped the light switch at the top of the stairs. Her knees felt wobbly, and she took the steps one at a time. When she started to cross the living room, her steps slowed. "Did we leave a light on?"

Derek looked over her shoulder. "Not that I remember."

The kitchen light was wavering, flickering.

Shea's skin pulled tight. That wasn't a bad bulb. She knew what that was.

Lifting up the hem of her robe, she ran across the room. She spun into the kitchen, but stopped so fast, her knees nearly went out from under her.

"Oh, God," she said, fighting for air. "No!"

Derek skidded in behind her. "Shit!"

Everywhere Shea looked, candles were glowing. Candles on the counter. Candles on the chairs. Candles on the floor. The acrid smell of fire filled her nose and choked her throat.

She let out a cry and dove for the one nearest her. Blowing fiercely, she tried to put out the flame. Clapping her hand atop the bell jar next to it, she robbed that fire of oxygen. She whirled around to tackle the next.

"Careful," Derek snapped. He caught her arm and tried to pull her back.

She wouldn't go. She couldn't leave—not this time.

Fighting back her fear, she ventured deeper into the room. Fire jumped all around her. Her air was coming in and out of her lungs so fast, she didn't know if she had any to spare.

She started blowing anyway.

"Go back," he said. "I'll take care of it."

She spun. There were more on the table. Tea lights. Oil lamps. Candles in jars and pillars. Votives.

"It's all right. They're under control. Just let me put them out before—"

A taper candle was burning too closely to the paper towels under her cabinets. She turned fast, and her robe billowed.

Derek roared.

Everything happened in a blur. He caught her by the shoulders and started yanking her clothes off her. He was yelling at her, but she only caught pieces of what he was saying. "On fire," rang in her ears.

She knew the room was on fire. She tried to pull away from him to help, but his grip turned rough. She heard her robe tear, but then he was throwing it into the sink. Wide-eyed, she watched as he turned on the faucet and doused the material.

She'd been on fire.

"Get out," he ordered. He pushed her toward the living room. "Get out!"

She stumbled back, but she couldn't make herself leave. She watched, terrified, as Derek went back into the room.

She couldn't let him go back in there. Not him!

She reached out to pull him back, but even in her terror, she noticed how in control he was. And how smoke wasn't burning her eyes...

She drank in deep gulps of fresh air and, slowly, realized that it wasn't as bad as she'd thought. The sight of those sinuous flames made her want to recoil, but she made herself look closer. Each of them came from a wick. This wasn't a conflagration. The room wasn't engulfed.

A pinch here and a puff there, and soon the room was dark.

But the fear had already taken root. She couldn't contain it. She backed away and bumped into the back of the couch. She gripped it with both hands.

Her chest... it hurt. She couldn't breathe. She wanted to scream.

Derek came out of the kitchen, his eyes hard. His jaw was rigid, and his fists were clenched. The light from the stairs lit him jaggedly, emphasizing the shadows that surrounded them both. The shadows that liked to play with her...

Shea rubbed her breastbone with the ball of her hand. Her heart felt like it was going to burst from her chest. It had happened again. The unthinkable had happened again!

"It's out." He approached her carefully, as if she were a wild animal ready to run or lash out at him. "It's gone."

"It's not gone!" How could he say it was gone? "It's back. It's back, and it's inside me."

He stopped with his hand lifted toward her. "What's inside you?"

"The thing that did *that*."

He looked over his shoulder so fast, it was a wonder he didn't get whiplash. "You didn't do that."

She rocked back and forth. She couldn't take this. She couldn't. "Yes, I did. It likes fire. It's dangerous. *I'm* dangerous."

Derek looked confused and concerned. He must think she'd totally lost it.

Scary thing was, she just might have.

"Shea, somebody else did this. Somebody got into your house. We need to call the police."

She laughed, the sound humorless. "The same somebody who left the footprints? The somebody who hit Phillip over the head? Face it, I nearly attacked you!"

"You never made it out of your bedroom door. Somebody

got in, somebody who knows you're afraid of fire. Who has keys?"

She shook her head. He didn't understand. Couldn't.

"Check the cameras!" He pointed at the one in the living room, but he cursed when he realized it had been pointed at the stairs, not the kitchen. He moved up to her fast. Fingers biting, he caught her by the shoulders. "Listen to me. You didn't light those candles."

"Yes, I did. It's just like before."

"You don't even keep them in the house."

"It doesn't matter. I would have found a way."

"What are you talking about?"

"This isn't the first time this has happened. Derek, I started that fire in our trailer when I was little. *I was sleepwalking then, too.*"

There it was, the nasty, festering secret she'd been keeping for years.

Yet letting it out didn't make her feel any better. The words felt bitter against her tongue. It made her want to be sick.

"Curie," Derek said on an exhale. He was looking at her in horror.

She knew why. She could barely look at herself. Still, his reaction hurt.

Instead of pushing her away, though, he latched on to her more tightly. She tensed as he pulled her into his arms and buried his face in her hair. How could he touch her? How could he stand to be anywhere near her?

"What happened?" he asked against her ear.

She shuddered. She'd never wanted to relive this again, but here she was looking at wisps of smoke coming out of her kitchen and waiting for the smoke detectors to start wailing.

"Tell me."

She swallowed hard around the lump in her throat. "I... I woke up outside that night. I was lying in the ditch. The lights and sirens roused me."

Her eyes stung as if she'd really gone back in time.

"The flames were so big. They reached up so high into the night sky, and things started popping." She flinched as the ugly sounds echoed in her ears. "I couldn't find my dad. He wasn't anywhere I looked, but Mrs. Lupescu saw me. She... she crossed herself against me and ran. That's when I knew."

"No." Derek pulled back to look into her face. "I read about that fire. The results of the investigation were inconclusive. Nobody knows what started it."

"I know. The Somnambulist did it."

He stilled. "What did you say?"

She looked at him mournfully. He was going to think she was crazy—believing in spirits and monsters—but it was what she'd been told as a child. She was older now. She knew the laws of physics and the nature of science. Deep down, though, it didn't make a difference. She knew what was true. She knew it as well as she knew her own name.

"A Somnambulist," she said, daring him to challenge her. "Mrs. Lupescu told me I was hexed. She told me that an evil spirit lived within me at night, making me do bad things. She was right. I'm possessed."

She lurched away from him, unable to bear the way he was looking at her. "It lit the fire. I lit the fire. It makes no difference. My dad was almost killed because of me. He went back into that trailer to find me, and he'll bear the scars for the rest of his life."

Her words hung in the air as, suddenly, the room went quiet. Too quiet. The storm had moved on. It only made the sound of her breaths harsher. She and Derek stood apart, staring at each other. His look was laser-like and intense. Unreadable.

"You think I need help," she whispered.

"Yes, I do."

His words felt like a smack in the face. Still, she nodded. "It would probably be for the best. They'll have to take me there. I'll... I'll check myself in."

She looked down at the ice-blue nightie she wore. It was the same one she'd been wearing when he'd crashed in her front door and made love to her. "Just let me change."

"No."

"I can't go like this."

"You're not going anywhere."

"But Derek—"

"Mrs. Lupescu was right."

Silence pulsed in the air again. Even the wind was gone. Shea watched Derek warily, not sure she'd heard him correctly. "Right about what?"

"You are possessed. You have a Somnambulist. I saw it."

The moment the words left his lips, Derek knew he'd jumped into the deep end. He'd never confessed his abilities to anyone—no full-blooded human, at least. It just wasn't done. But she needed to know. He couldn't just stand here and let her think she was going crazy. He couldn't let her think she'd nearly killed her own father.

What must it have been like to live with that guilt?

He watched for her response, but she looked dumbstruck.

He raked a hand through his hair and felt his chest bunch with tension. He hadn't wanted to tell her like this. He'd been trying to work up to it and test different avenues of approach. Unfortunately, the opportunity for subtlety had passed.

"I can't believe how your neighbor played with your head, but she was right," he said, his voice like gravel. "You have a parasite, and it's called a Somnambulist."

Shea's lips trembled. "Please, Derek. Don't do this."

He took a step toward her. "They only stay with their hosts for short periods of time, long enough to gather strength. I nearly had yours just now, but it got away."

She took a step back. "I know you think you're helping, but this is cruel."

"I'm not trying to mollify you. I'm telling you I can stop it."

She hesitated. "How?"

"You know how. I've told you." His heart thudded. "I'm an Oneiros—in every sense of the word."

Her eyes widened, but then it was as if she dissolved from

the top down. Her eyelids closed, her shoulders slumped, and her hands fell limply at her sides. "Oh, Derek."

Desperation filled him. Going at her fast, he backed her up against the sofa. He had to convince her now. He had to get her to trust her heart over her mind or he would lose her. She tried to hold him off, but he pressed his body tightly against hers until heat coursed between them.

"I'm not trying to scare you. Just listen to me."

His heart was beating like a bass drum, but he kept his touch gentle as he laced their fingers together. "People need me to help them dream. They go through the other sleep stages naturally, but that only repairs their bodies. I deal with the mind. It's my job to bring the human consciousness into the dream realm—my world."

The empathy in her eyes nearly broke him. She thought he was as unstable as she was. *The Somnambulist*, he thought, his brain working fast. If she believed in it, why couldn't she believe in him?

"You've studied mythology. You know that most legends are born in truth."

She inhaled shakily, and her breasts rubbed against his chest. He kept the contact flush. He had to keep her close and off balance. It was the only way he was going to get through.

"My mother's name is Nyx. I have an army of brothers. You met only a few of them. I knew you were having sleep problems the moment you stepped into my office that day. Do you need me to go on?"

She licked her lips, and he could practically see the cogs in her brain turning. "What did I dream tonight?" she asked, challenging him.

"You didn't. It got to you first."

She went still. "Then last night."

She was analyzing things. She needed proof. He could give her that. "You finally found a place to put that carbon element on your magic molecule."

Her jaw went slack.

"I assume that had something to do with your research?"

She ignored the question. "The night before that," she said, her voice coming back strong.

A slow smile pulled at his lips. "Well, now that would be the night you dreamed of the two of us in your laboratory."

The color drained from her face.

"I believe I had you bent over your lab bench." Deliberately, he swung his hips toward her. "Your lab coat was thrown over your head as I—"

She pushed at his shoulders. "How do you know these things?"

"I'm your Dream Weaver." He looked at her steadily, wanting her to see into him. He needed her to take that leap of faith even when logic told her not to. "I can make it better, Shea. Somnambulists are my natural enemy. If anyone's going to get rid of that thing, it's going to be me."

She took a measured breath.

"I can help you."

She shook her head. "Just because I'm crazy doesn't mean you have to be."

"Neither of us is crazy."

"Why are you doing this?" she whispered. "Why are you telling me these things?"

"Because you need to know." Looking at her, though, he knew it went deeper than that. "And because I love you."

CHAPTER FIFTEEN

Derek held the door to the restaurant open for Shea. As she passed, his hand automatically settled at the small of her back. Although she didn't stiffen, she still somehow managed to pull away.

His fingers curled in toward his palms.

Things between them were strained and had been ever since last night.

It wasn't that they were fighting. Neither of them seemed to know what to say or how to act. In the heat of the moment, they'd both confessed to things that they weren't sure they wanted the other to know. Now it was too late to pull the secrets back.

Honestly, he didn't want to.

Shea paused ahead of him, uncertain which way to go. Wordlessly, he pointed to the back. She started moving in that direction, and he fell in step behind her. Unchecked, his gaze swept down her sleek body. She was wearing a tank top that showed off her velvety skin and a long, flowing skirt. With her blonde hair brushing against her shoulders, she looked fresh and feminine. Seductive as hell.

Damn, this had to work.

Her steps paused. She still couldn't quite meet his eyes. "Are we having breakfast with your brothers?"

"Yes."

"Who's that with them?"

"They're all my brothers."

That earned him a look. Then again, the full local family contingent was here—except for Mack, who was on day duty. Derek took a long, slow breath. If he was going to do this, he wanted to face them all at once.

Going through the buzz saw twice didn't appeal to him.

Taking the surprise in stride, Shea headed to the table. "Tony," she said in greeting. "Cael."

Zane pulled out a chair for her, and she slid into it gracefully. "Thank you. Good morning."

Introductions were made. As always, his brothers reverted to their best behavior with a beautiful woman around. Still, Derek could already feel the sidelong looks drilling into him.

"When did we start letting girls join?" Zane asked, a smile on his face.

"Today, apparently," came a smooth answer. "You have a problem with that?"

Zane's head snapped up, but his smile only broadened when he saw the woman standing over their table with one hand propped saucily on her hip. "Not at all. How you doin', Red?"

Cael glowered at their younger brother. "Her name is Devon."

He hooked an arm around his girlfriend's waist. Taking into account the family environment, he gave her a quick but heated kiss. "What are you doing here?"

"Derek invited me." Her eyes sparked with interest when she noticed Shea. "Hi, I'm Devon Bradshaw."

"Shea Caldwell. Nice to meet you."

Derek drummed his fingers against the tabletop as seats were switched and room was made for their latest arrival. He could feel Cael's curiosity and irritation cutting across the table like a knife, but his brother could grumble all he wanted. He'd asked Devon here for moral support: Shea's *and* his.

"Hi, guys," Sally said, hurrying up to their table. Looking rushed, she stuffed her order pad into her apron and passed out menus like a Vegas poker dealer. "What are you doing here on a Saturday? This is our busy morning. I won't be able to talk today."

"We're wounded," Zane said with a pout.

"Yeah, like you don't get enough female attention." She winked at the newcomers. "Can I take your drink orders?"

Derek looked around the restaurant uncertainly. Now that they were here, he didn't know if it really was the right place for this discussion. Saturday mornings were busier at this hour than Sundays, and IHOP was hopping. Having so many ears around made him edgy.

He didn't need the added strain.

As normal as his brothers were trying to act, they were exchanging looks. Chairs were shifting, and muscles were tensing. Shea wasn't immune to the mood. Her hands knotted in her lap as she sat quietly.

"Derek?" Sally said.

He almost jumped. "Uh, water. Water is fine."

He reached to straighten his tie. His hand fumbled when there wasn't one around his neck. Instead, he rubbed his palm against his jeans. He felt like he was getting ready to jump off a cliff here.

Sally shuffled away, but nobody at the table was thinking about food. All eyes were on him.

Finally, Shea asked the question that was on everyone's mind. "Why are we here, Derek?"

He braced himself, but then just let go. "We're here because I need you to know I was telling you the truth. There's a reason our last name is Oneiros."

Not one of his brothers moved. No one even blinked. If there was any reaction at all to the unexploded bombshell he'd dropped right onto the middle of their table, it was quickly covered.

That didn't mean he didn't feel the atmosphere in the restaurant building like a pressure cooker.

He swept his gaze over the stoic faces, and he knew he had to act fast. "She believes in Somnambulists, and she knows she has one."

"Derek." Reaching out, Shea caught his arm.

Her grip was tight, and she'd paled to the color of chalk. She looked like she wanted to flay him for revealing what she considered a humiliating secret, her belief in nighttime monsters.

He barreled ahead anyway.

"It's getting worse, and she needs to know we can help her. That *I* can help her."

Silence greeted him from all sides, and the tinkle of laughter from surrounding tables rubbed against his nerves.

Finally, Tony started fiddling with his silverware. It was the only movement at the table. "Did something else happen that we don't know about?"

"The Somnie took another walk with her."

"With you in the place?" Zane blurted. He caught a startled look from Shea and sank deeper into his seat.

"Yes, with me there." Derek's knee began to bounce under the table. Somebody needed to step up, or she was going to be through with him. The little parlor tricks with her dreams weren't going to be enough to hold her.

"She studied Greek mythology in college. I told her that the myths about us are true—that we are the real Oneiroi."

This time, the reactions couldn't be avoided. Tony dropped his fork, and it rang like a bell. Wes tilted onto the back legs of his chair, and AJ cursed.

Shea looked around the table uncertainly. Derek knew she thought he'd been trying to placate her with his stories and claims. Just one word, just the slightest bit of confirmation would help.

He searched his brothers' faces, waiting so intensely he was hardly breathing. He'd just committed their greatest sin. He'd exposed them, and right in the middle of a crowded restaurant. But she was important to him, too, more so every day. Couldn't just this one time somebody—

"He wasn't supposed to tell you that."

Derek's head snapped toward the voice. It was Cael, their

leader.

"But it's true," his older brother said. "We are Dream Weavers."

"Oh, thank God," Devon whispered. Reaching out, she caught her boyfriend's hand.

His brother's stern features softened as he turned to Shea. "What do you need to know, Dr. Caldwell?"

For a moment, Shea didn't respond. Dumbfounded, she looked around the table. Gazes were quickly diverted. Fingers thrummed, and a spoon twirled. Yet as she waited, nobody denied what had been said.

"Dream Weavers?" she said tentatively.

"It's what we call ourselves," Cael explained. "It's a loose translation of the Greek word, *Oneiroi*."

The pulse at her temple fluttered. Derek could see she was torn between disbelief and wanting to ask questions. His own heart began to pound a little faster.

"I thought you lived in a cave in Erebus," she teased. She wanted to laugh this all off, it was clear.

"We integrated into society a while ago." Cael's tone turned dry. "The commute was a bitch."

Her responding smile was nervous and unsure. "And the black wings?"

"Ugh. Those stinking black wings." Zane slung his arm over the back of his chair as he turned to face her. "I mean, really. Did those scribes have to go and make us ugly? At least Hermes only got tiny ones on his feet."

"Zane," Wes hissed.

Shea was staring at Zane with clear astonishment. His disdain was obvious. He didn't like the myth, but as counterintuitive as that was, it made it all the more believable.

"Sorry," he said, catching her look. "I just—"

"Can you read minds?" she blurted.

Derek shot her a surprised look. She *had* been trying to figure out how he could see into her dreams.

Zane blushed, actually blushed. "Only when the person is dreaming," he mumbled.

Giving in to her scientist's need for answers, Shea leaned forward. Instinctively, she seemed to know to lower her voice. "How do you do it? How do you manage sleepers' thoughts? How do you decide what dreams they'll have?"

Tony stopped twirling his knife between his fingers and pointed it at her. "That's another misconception."

He blinked, surprised at his own outburst. Uncomfortable, he set down the knife and aligned it precisely with the rest of his silverware. "Sorry, but that's one of my pet peeves. We can lead dreams, but we try not to. We just get you going. Prime the pump, so to say."

"But how?"

Everyone looked at each other.

Cael finally answered. "Suffice it to say we don't sleep like normal people."

"Oh, tell her," Devon said. She traced her boyfriend's knuckles and threw Shea a shrewd look. "They have magic hands, but you already know that."

Derek watched Shea flush red, yet her eyes turned bright as she zeroed in on the only other woman at the table.

"They can control brain waves with their fingertips," Devon said. "They lead sleepers out of the deepest stage of sleep and into REM."

"How do they get to people, though?" Shea asked.

"By astral-projecting. They split themselves in two."

Cael shifted uncomfortably when a busboy passed their table. "That's simplifying it quite a bit."

"It's the easiest way to describe it, and none of you have seen yourselves do it." Devon pushed her hair over her shoulder. "It's unnerving. Their spirit literally separates and goes into the dream realm."

Shea drew back slowly. "Leaving their bodies in a sleep that looks like a coma?"

"Yes." Devon fought off a shudder. "Just like that."

Derek suddenly felt Shea's touch. Glancing under the table, he watched as her fingers wrapped around his. His breath caught, but then the knot in his chest loosened.

Gripping her back tightly, he settled their joined hands on his thigh.

"And Somnambulists?" she asked.

Finally, she was looking at him. Finally, she was talking to him.

"They're real, too," he said.

"But you can get rid of them?"

"I can."

"How?"

He hesitated. "That's why we're here. I need to talk to my brothers and make a plan."

Devon got the message fast. She swept up her purse. "Let's go powder our noses, Shea."

"But I want to hear this. I want to help."

Derek gripped her hand a bit tighter. "This is something we have to do without you."

"But I know this thing better than any of you."

"And it knows you." He let his voice drop so it was only the two of them. "It can tap into your consciousness, Curie. How do you think it knew Phillip's phone number?"

"Oh," she breathed, understanding dawning. "Oh, God."

"It can't know when we're coming or how."

She swallowed hard, but then nodded. "We'll take our time."

Derek rose and helped her with her chair. More than one person glanced up as the two women headed toward the restroom. He didn't blame them—they were beautiful.

But they were taken.

A calm came over him. His brothers could do whatever they wanted to him. He didn't care. The risk had been worth it.

Still, the shots started coming before he even sat back down.

"What do you think you're doing?" Tony's arms bulged as he braced his elbows on the table. "We're not supposed to talk about things like that in front of people. She's a liability now."

"I had to," Derek said. "She won't say anything."

"You don't know that."

"Yes, I do. She's good at keeping secrets." Too good, in his opinion. If she'd told him earlier about the sleepwalking or that she believed in the supernatural, he might have been able to do something. "Besides, she's a well-respected scientist. It's not like talking about us would help her professional reputation."

"But did you have to tell her?" Without even realizing it, Tony picked up the saltshaker and knocked it against the table. "Why not work it from the other side like we usually do? Just cleave the Somnambulist from her and be done with it?"

"Because this thing is out of control, and so is her stalker."

Tony's face fell. "What happened now?"

Derek raked a hand across his face. "Somebody got into her condo last night and lit a bunch of candles. Shea lost it. She thought she'd set the kitchen on fire while she was sleepwalking." He sat back heavily in his chair. "She was talking about committing herself. I had to tell her so she wouldn't think she was crazy. It was the only way to settle her down."

"She's terrified of fire," Zane said. "Something like that would have messed her up big time."

The mood turned somber. Things got even quieter when Sally showed up with their drinks.

Cael waited until she was out of earshot before he leaned in close. "This person obviously knows her. How did they get in?"

"The door," Derek said, shaking his head. He'd already changed the locks. "Phillip had her backup key. He checked, and it's gone from his keychain."

"Any idea who it is?" Cael asked.

"I have concerns about some of her employees." Derek glanced at Zane. "Was Tamika sleeping around midnight last night?"

His brother grimaced. "She didn't call for me until almost

two o'clock. I swear, it's almost like she's not sleeping on purpose."

"Tamika Hendricks?" AJ's head snapped up. "I haven't seen her on the running trails, either."

"What about Lynette Fromm?" Derek asked. "Tony, don't you have her?"

"Lynette who?"

"Fromm."

"Oh, yeah. She's one of mine."

"How's she been sleeping?"

Tony scratched his chin. "She sleeps in patches. Her brain wave patterns have always been all over the place. I really couldn't tell you when she got to bed last night. Sorry, I've got a lot of charges."

"Right." Derek ran his thumb over the lip of his glass of water.

"What is it?" Cael asked.

"The Somnambulist. I don't like how deep it's gotten its claws into Shea."

"Did you see it last night?" Wes asked, his curiosity clear. Like Zane, he was young and hadn't had to deal with an adult of the species.

"I nearly had it." Derek watched as his thumb went round and round. "I singed it, but it's fast. Real fast."

"What do you want to do about it?" Cael asked. "I know you already have a plan."

Derek took a deep breath.

"I think we need to make some changes that we should have made a while ago." He glanced at his older brother, knowing that he would understand. "I need to be on Shea 24/7."

Zane snorted. "That's obvious."

Derek nailed him with a look. "She has threats coming at her from all angles. I can't constantly be leaving her to deal with other charges. If I'm going to protect her, I need to be there for her full-time."

He fisted his hand around his glass. He was worried about

the stalker. The Somnambulist was another thing. He knew how to combat it, how to bring it down.

And he wanted it bad.

"It's a lot to ask, I know, but I need all of you to cover my other charges until I get this thing. It's obsessed with her."

And not in a good way.

His skin crawled. The thing was maturing sexually. Shea hadn't wanted to see the pictures taken by the camera in her bedroom—at least not the ones where she'd been sleepwalking. It was a good thing she hadn't. The shots were still flashing through his head. He could see her arching as she fondled her breasts, her sleeping face flushing with pleasure, and her legs parting.

He swore underneath his breath. Any other time, the video would have made him hard. Knowing the Somnambulist controlled her, though, made him see red.

"Do you really think it will come back?" Cael asked. "Now that it knows you're close to her?"

"It'll be back." Without a doubt. "It might lay low for a while, but it will be back. And I'll be waiting."

"You can't." Cael insisted. "Not if you want to get rid of it for good."

"He's right." Tony sat back in his chair and crossed his arms over his chest. "You can't stand guard over her. If you do, it will stay just out of your reach, hounding you, and waiting for you to make a slip."

"I'll get it," Derek growled. There was no other option.

"This is not a game of tag that you want to play," Cael said. "The best way to catch it is to back off. You need to let the Somnie think that she's vulnerable, that you've left her to him."

"What are you saying?" Zane sat forward in his chair with his fists clenched nearly as tightly as Derek's. "He's supposed to let it get her?"

A muscle twitched in Cael's jaw. "That's exactly what I'm saying."

Tony nodded. "Let it overtake her."

Derek's neck began to ache. "I can't do that."

He couldn't take seeing her that way, a vacant shell. He knew how petrified she was of the thing. He'd just told her he could protect her!

"You have to," Cael said, "because as soon as it's distracted, you're going to go in for the kill."

The table fell silent once again.

"Don't miss this time," Tony warned. "You might not get another chance."

The ache in Derek's neck spread to his shoulders and down his arms. He had to get it. This thing had been terrorizing her for years. It had made her do unbearable things. She couldn't take much more. It was up to him to finish it.

But this particular Somnambulist was crafty. It had gotten by him too many times.

"I'll take on as many of your charges as you need," Zane said. "Save your girl."

Derek looked at him in surprise. As much of a pain as he could be, his little brother did care about Shea. "Thanks," he said gruffly.

"I'll take some off your hands," AJ offered.

"Don't worry, D-Man," Tony said. "Your charges will be covered."

As one, his brothers nodded in agreement.

Heads at surrounding tables started turning again. Derek saw two bombshells, one redhead and one blonde, making their way back across the room.

Cael's gaze homed in on Devon. "Are you sure you don't need any backup?"

Derek watched as Shea came toward him. "No. That Somnie is mine."

* * *

Breakfast had been memorable.

That was about as close as Shea could come to describing it. She still wondered what had gone on at the table when she and Devon had left, but she had a feeling she'd never find out the answer to that question.

At least things had calmed down when they'd returned, and she'd enjoyed meeting Derek's brothers and future sister-in-law immensely.

Yet as she watched him sliding a shiny key into the new lock on her front door, her agitation returned. Her gaze slid up from his sure hands to his muscled arms and shoulders. Nervously, she ground her sandal into the sidewalk beneath her. The last time she'd felt this edgy, she'd been standing outside another door—the door to his office.

That felt like so long ago.

Her home opened, welcoming them, and Derek stepped back. His gaze landed on her as it had so many times before, hot and searching. She stepped over the threshold and felt his hand touch the small of her back.

This time, she didn't shy away.

"Thank you for breakfast. I like your brothers." She heard the door close as she tossed her purse onto the couch.

Derek stood behind her, tense. "Do you believe me now? Do you understand what we are? What we—"

She kissed him—just walked up to him, laid her hands on his chest, and pressed her lips against his.

She understood a lot. He had a family that loved him.

"I missed you," she said as she slid her hands up around his neck.

His arms came around her. "I missed you, too."

She went up on her tiptoes, kissing him harder, but he pulled back. "Do you believe me?"

She chose her words carefully. "My mind is open."

The things she'd been told were so fantastical, but he and his brothers believed them. That much was clear. Either they were all in on the game or there had to be some truth hidden in there somewhere.

And who was she to point fingers? She had beliefs that couldn't be proven. Early scientists hadn't believed Copernicus when he'd claimed the earth was round—and none other than Einstein had postulated on the existence of parallel universes.

Derek's head dipped. "Good enough for me."

His arms enveloped her, and relief poured through her. Last night had been terrible. The distance between them had almost been worse than what had happened to create it. She'd missed being able to trust him.

"Make love to me," she whispered.

He started nudging her toward the sofa, but she dug in her heels.

"The kitchen."

His mouth stilled against her neck. "Are you sure?"

It had to be the kitchen. She didn't want to be thinking about flames every time she walked in there. She didn't want to think of him rushing back into that firestorm.

"Show me my dream, Oneiros," she said impulsively. "Pretend that table is my lab bench."

He took the dare without missing a beat.

They stumbled into the room together, with Shea tugging at his shirt and him crowding her against the table. His mouth was voracious, and so were his hands. Her tank top stretched as he yanked it over her head, but then he was kissing her again.

"I'll protect you," he said as he went for her bra.

"And I'll protect your secret." She wrestled his T-shirt higher until he pulled it over his head and caught her waist. It was so much easier to get him naked this way than with his suits. The room spun as he turned her around. The underwire of her bra bit into her ribs as he fought with the hooks at the back.

He peeled the straps down her arms, and her bra fell onto her foot, but then his hands were on her, taking possession. He cupped her breasts and massaged them hard, his fingers pinching at the tender tips. She moaned, and her head fell back against his shoulder. Their bodies swayed together, and she gripped his thighs. He ground against her, and she trembled as one of his hands left her breast and skimmed down her stomach. It slid purposefully between her legs and cupped her.

"Bend over," he whispered into her ear.

The delicious words made her thighs clench. Could he feel that?

"Bend. Over."

He nipped at her neck, and need exploded inside her. Obeying, she bent at the waist. Reaching in front of her, he recklessly pushed aside the centerpiece and a napkin holder.

The candles were long gone. She'd thrown them all into a garbage bag last night. Still…

"Lie flat."

The order kicked the memory right out of her head, as she suspected it was meant to do. She took her weight off her forearms where she'd been braced, and his fingers spread wide between her shoulder blades.

"Do you want it like in the dream?"

He really could see into her head.

"Yes," she whispered, going all the way down.

Her breasts pressed flat against the hard wood, and anticipation hummed inside her. Her muscles jumped when he gathered the voluminous material of her skirt out of his way. He dropped to his knees behind her, and she quickly looked over her shoulder. All she could see were his hands pulling at her bikini bottoms. That, and the top of his head…

Turning her face into the table, she pressed her forehead against the sturdy surface. He peeled her underwear down, and the air in the kitchen felt cool as it hit her exposed flesh. Her fingers left smudges against the tabletop when his hot breath puffed against her.

"Derek," she groaned.

His hands slid down the backs of her thighs, all the way to her feet. He caught her ankles. "Spread."

A cry left her lips as pressure started pushing her feet outward. Her sandals slipped on the slick floor, and her heel hooked her bra strap. He didn't stop. Wider and wider he took her, until her toes bumped into the legs of the table.

"All right?" he asked.

"Mmm." She was so turned on.

His breaths were right against her, yet he didn't touch. Instead, he slid his hands down to her feet. "Let's get these off of you."

Shea kicked at her shoes. Off or on, she didn't care. She just wanted—

"Ah!"

Her entire body jerked when his tongue stroked over her, all raspy and wet.

She just wanted *that*.

The pleasure was sharp and intense. His hands tightened on her ankles, denying the instinctive strain in her thighs. His mouth went at her more aggressively, and she let out a long groan.

"Ohhh. Oh, yes!"

He was licking at her, nipping at her sensitive folds. Just when she got used to the sensation, he switched it up and began sucking on her clit. His tongue suddenly plunged into her, and her body clenched.

Standing abruptly, he began tearing at his jeans. His belt came undone, but he just let the ends dangle as he unbuttoned the denim and yanked down his zipper.

Shea rocked back against him. She was so close.

He caught her hips, and her cry echoed off the walls of the kitchen when he thrust into her hard.

He bent over her, his chest hot against her back and his zipper digging into her thighs. "If you'll let me, I'll make all your dreams come true."

Shea moaned. He had her trapped, her breasts pressed flat, and his cock buried deep.

"Please," she pleaded. "Take me."

"One more detail to match your dream."

Her heart jumped when he caught her skirt again. The polished walnut tabletop beneath her suddenly clouded with condensation from her harsh breaths. She knew what he was going to do, but she didn't know if she really wanted…

Too late. He spread the material wide and tossed it over

her. It fluttered, catching the air, as it drifted relentlessly downward.

Covering her.

Bringing darkness.

Shea came. The orgasm just rushed through her.

She was climaxing as he began to thrust.

For the first time ever, the darkness called to her and unleashed its own wicked pleasure. Her skirt brushed against her cheek and nose. It fluttered against her face with every inhale she took. She couldn't see. All she could do was feel, and listen, and *ohhh*...

"Derek," she gasped.

His abs flexed against her butt as his cock worked deep. Her pussy grabbed him and held him tight.

"I—" Shea cried.

His shout rang in her ear, and then he was coming with her.

Pleasure rocked her. "I love you, too."

CHAPTER SIXTEEN

The Somnambulist was frantic. He needed to get to his beloved. He ached for her. Didn't she ache for him? His energy was so low, his particles were barely moving. Some had already drifted off. Bit by bit, he was detaching and dying.

"She-a," he hissed. "*She-a!*"

He flew to the next window, peering inside. He shouldn't be here. He knew it. The mean Weaver had almost gotten him last time he'd visited her. That had been nights and nights ago, and he was still out there somewhere. Dark eyes glowing, hot hands burning...

The creature winced. He still hurt. The spot where the Weaver had touched was gone, unfillable. The pain had been unlike any he'd experienced before. It had been too much to enjoy.

But he had to get to her. His She-a was in trouble.

The face in the window was back!

The Somnambulist floated outside her bedroom, willing her to wake up. She didn't move. She slept on peacefully, ignoring him, oblivious to his panic. His particles reverberated in annoyance, humming so badly he almost lost a few more. He should leave. If the reeking Weaver wanted her so badly, he could save her.

But where was he?

Flying around the second story of her building, the

Somnambulist double-checked the guest bedroom and the bathroom. He'd learned from his mistake. He'd felt the Weaver last time because he'd been hiding nearby. Tonight, though, the rooms were empty. Still, the creature was afraid to go inside. Even though he couldn't sense the Dream Weaver, it might be waiting again. This might be a trick.

Bad trick, if it was. Dangerous.

He scampered back to She-a's window and pressed his particles flat. Concentrating, he tried to get into her head from a distance. "Open eyes. Listen!"

He screeched when his lovely rolled on the bed, away from him.

"No!" His particles swirled, and he spun around in midair. The moon suddenly caught his eye, and fear filled him. Dark clouds floated over the glowing crescent. "Painted sky. Good time to die."

His particles shook until they were keening. What was he supposed to do? He couldn't leave her like this, not his beloved.

Down below, a flicker lit the darkness. The creature gasped when he saw oranges and yellows and reds. Fire! The evil human had brought fire!

Anger made the colors dance inside his head. He couldn't let it happen again—his beautiful girl could never stand it. With a scream, he dive-bombed the intruder.

Out of control, he tried to push the figure in black away. His particles just skimmed around the solid body. Wildly, he tried to penetrate the waking entity and take it over. None of it helped. His powers only worked in the land of sleep.

The oranges and yellows and reds got brighter, building like his temper... Twisting like his fear...

He couldn't wait any longer.

Barreling upward, the Somnambulist tumbled into She-a's room, sprawling at the foot of her bed. The move nearly splattered him apart. Gathering himself together, he crawled up onto the mattress with her. Not going slow like he was supposed to, he shoved his essence into her.

She moaned and pulled her knees into her chest.

"Sorry, sorry," he said, already unfurling her long legs and putting her feet on the floor. "We go walk now. Tonight, we *run*."

He moved too fast, not situated inside her correctly, and her body lurched sideways, almost falling down. The Somnambulist growled. He pulled her upright and pushed her toward the door at the same time. The footboard of the bed dug into the side of her leg. Pain shot through them both, nice and juicy.

He gobbled it up, letting the power help them both.

"Open door," he huffed. "Run down stairs. Skip down stairs. Fall down stairs."

He didn't care how. She had to move!

Down the stairs they went. She tripped once, and the creature clung to the railing with her hand to stop her from tumbling all the way down. "One step, two step. Please, my pretty!"

Finally, they made it to the first floor. The creature's nose scrunched. He could smell the bitterness in the air and feel the awful tickle in his beloved's throat.

"Flat floor. Easy now. Go fast."

Her legs moved at his orders. Still, she plodded as he pushed, yanked, and shoved her to the kitchen.

"Look," he panted. "Look. See the face—"

Pain suddenly ripped through him like a hot electric knife. It cut through him… Cut him off from her…

The creature screamed as he was wrenched backward. He twisted as the burn sizzled and scorched him. It was too much, excruciating. He tried to get away, but couldn't.

And he knew what that meant.

Reaching out with every cell in his being, he clung to She-a instead. Without her, he wouldn't survive. She whimpered and stumbled back.

"Shea!" a dark voice rumbled.

The Somnambulist lurched, coiled, and struggled. The pull was unbearable. Too much pain. It hurt. *It hurt.*

He held on tighter, the molecules of his toenails digging in. She-a screamed, and his palms turned slippery. Tears rolled down her cheeks. He tried to stretch out, but he was caught inside her. He tried to disperse, but couldn't. In this form, he was stuck.

Then with an agonizing heave, he was suddenly out of her.

Out of his home... Away from his playmate... Without his love... He reached for her, wanting her. *Needing her.* "She-a."

"Her name is *Shea.*"

Looking up through pain-filled eyes, the Somnambulist saw a tough, dark gaze.

He saw his death.

* * *

Shea was suddenly caught in that vague, hazy void somewhere between sleep and wakefulness. The world around her was somehow heavier. The shadows were deeper and the air sultrier. Even the feel of her skin was more erotic.

Yet it was the sound of a scuffle that made her turn.

Her breath caught when she saw Derek tangling in her living room with... with... A thing? A creature?

She couldn't take her eyes from it. Whatever it was, it was tall and wispy. She could practically see right through it, but as Derek's hand wrapped around its bony shoulder, she could make out a definite form. It wasn't easy to look at. It had long, spindly legs with knobby knees. Its fingers and toes were abnormally long, but its chest was small and sunken in. The face, though, captured her. Mostly snout, it had one of those faces that was so ugly, it was almost cute. Almost...

But its eyes.

Her heart squeezed.

Its eyes were unbearably lovely. Eyes that were soft as they held her gaze adoringly, longingly...

"Derek," she whispered, her throat working hard. She couldn't stand to see it in pain. Couldn't take—

"Look," the creature whined, ignoring its captor and the pain it was obviously in. Derek's hand moved toward its forehead, but it squirmed away. Concentrating only on her, it pointed one bony finger over her shoulder. "The face. *The face in the window.*"

Shea turned.

When she transitioned from sleep to wakefulness, she didn't know. Yet suddenly, she found herself alone in her kitchen with dampness on her cheeks.

And somebody staring in the window right at her.

Her scream lodged in her throat. Fear froze her.

The stare-down was silent and shocking—until clouds drifted away from the moon. In the dim light, Shea saw a wisp. A malicious, snakelike wisp curled upward from her watcher's hand.

Her fear morphed into fury, and she charged toward the sliding glass door. "You bitch!"

* * *

"The face in the window."

Derek's head snapped up, and two realizations hit him at once. Shea could see them, and someone was outside.

His stomach dropped.

Her stalker. His head snapped from the window to the Somnambulist. What was he supposed to do? He couldn't deal with them both at once, not even split as he was.

"You bitch!" Shea suddenly yelled, bringing his attention back fast.

She was awake and alert and moving so fast toward the sliding glass door, it scared him. She'd taken the decision out of his hands. He literally took a step to stop her before he remembered he was in Dream Weaver form.

And he had a wiry, nasty Somnambulist to deal with.

He turned, intending to take the thing out fast. He had it in his grip. Assembled as it was, this was the closest it could get to humanoid form. With all its particles bunched so tightly, it was at its most vulnerable. He reached for the creature's forehead, but it squirmed away, seemingly triple-jointed.

"Help her," the thing whined. "Let me help her."

"She can't stand any more of your help," Derek snapped. "She wants you gone."

"Liar!" The Somnambulist writhed like an eel, trying to get away from the burning touch at its shoulder. It saw the hand coming at his forehead, and it ducked. "I help her. She needs me. She always has."

"You scare her."

"I protect her."

Derek didn't have time to deal with this. He looked worriedly toward the door. Curtains flapped over the opening, and he couldn't see what was happening. He had to get back to his car where his body was sleeping. He'd moved further away from her to lure the Somnambulist in, but he hadn't expected this. He had to get out there, and help—

A screech pierced the air outside. "You crazy psycho!"

"She-a!" The Somnambulist bucked, nearly throwing him off.

Derek grabbed on with both hands and smelled the thing charring.

Still, it struggled and kept its eyes on the doorway. "Let me go. I showed it to her. Where were you?"

That jab hit too close to home. Unable to help himself, Derek gave the thing a shake. "Is that why you came back? Is that why you're here?"

"She's mine," the thing hissed. Its eyes turned beady, and pain contorted its mouth. "We've been together forever and ever."

"She's mine," Derek growled.

Using his weight, he pinned the thing down. It was stronger than it looked. It had taken more power from her than it should. So help him, if it left any long-lasting side effects on her...

The pictures from the motion-controlled camera suddenly flashed in Derek's head.

Enraged, he leaned down closer. "You make her do things she doesn't want to do. You take her places she doesn't want to go. *I saw you touch her.*"

The thing actually stilled. "She-a touches, not me. We're a team. Soul mates."

"Shut up!" Derek reached for its forehead again, but roared when the thing bit him.

His grip loosened, but instead of dispersing, the creature started crawling toward the sliding glass door. "My pretty girl. My beloved."

Derek caught it by its ankle. Flipping it on its back, he overpowered it.

The Somnambulist's eyes looked up at him, sad and heart-wrenching. "Painted sky. Time to die."

Its puny chest heaved up and down.

"Don't let She-a die, Weaver. You're mean, but don't you let her die!"

In its own way, the thing did love her. But Derek was a Dream Weaver, and he had a job to do. Even if he scared this thing off Shea, it would just take on another host. As mature as it was—and as sexually aware as it was becoming—he couldn't let that happen. He'd seen fear in his lover's eyes one too many times.

He cupped his palm over the creature's forehead.

It whimpered and caught his forearm. Instead of pushing him away, though, the Somnambulist pulled him closer. "She can't hear me. She doesn't listen. You have to tell her... Promise me you'll tell her..."

At first Derek thought it was another trick. When he saw the yearning in the thing's eyes, though, he leaned down. The creature whispered into his ear, and the words had him pulling up fast, his heart racing. He looked into the thing's eyes. It wasn't lying.

"Let her know I loved her."

All Derek could do was nod.

Then he made it fast and clean.

Merciful.

And the Somnambulist was no more.

* * *

Shea hit the lock on the sliding glass door and yanked on it.

The thing stuck solid. Letting out a frustrated cry, she kicked at the floor door lock Derek had installed.

The door rolled open, smooth as silk. It bounced hard against the bumper, but she was past it before it could hit her. Exploding out of the condo, she turned on the ball of her foot. Suddenly, she found herself face-to-face with the person who had been terrorizing her—the woman who had been breaking in to her home, messing with her things, and generally toying with her mind.

"Lynette!"

Caught in the middle of an empty backyard, the woman froze. "Stay away from me," she cried. "I'm warning you."

Light suddenly caught the corner of Shea's eye, and her head snapped toward the window. Her breath seized. A fire burnt on the windowsill where Lynette had been standing. It curled and danced, showing off in the darkness.

Instinctively, Shea stepped back. It was then that she spotted the newspaper. Crumpled newspaper was packed in wherever it would stay, in the nooks of her kitchen window and at the base of the building under the aluminum siding. Worse yet, expired matches lay on the ground.

"You crazy psycho!"

Fighting every instinct that told her to run, Shea instead rushed forward and knocked the burning paper onto the ground. Spinning around, she clenched her fists tight. "What's wrong with you?"

The angry expression on Lynette's face deepened to rage. "I'm not crazy. I know what you are."

Shea didn't move fast enough when a metal can came flying at her. It hit her in the side, splattering liquid all over the Mets jersey she was wearing as a nightshirt. She flinched at the unexpected pain, but it was the scent of lighter fluid that had her pulling up short.

Astonishment came over her just as surely as horror.

This wasn't some sick mind trick Lynette was trying to pull. The woman was set on killing her.

"You're out of your mind!"

"Me? You're the one who's possessed. I've seen it in you!" Lynette was desperately trying to light another match.

Footsteps suddenly pounded behind them.

"Shea!" Derek yelled.

The match hissed against the starter strip, and a flame sprang to life. Watching her defiantly, Lynette tossed it toward the newspaper she'd bunched up on the ground. The tiny flame danced atop the tip of the match, but then caught. It licked its way quickly across the paper, doubling in size, tripling in an instant.

Shea stiffened, terrified beyond measure.

And incensed beyond thought.

With a fierce growl, she struck back. If Lynette thought she'd go for the fire first, she was wrong. The woman's eyes widened in surprise, and she lifted her hands. It was too late. Shea was on her. Her fist flew out, and her weight was behind it. Her knuckles crunched against Lynette's chin, and the woman went down hard, yelping.

The sound turned into a scream when she fell onto the burning newspaper.

Fire quickly ate its way up her sleeve. Spatters of the lighter fluid fed it, making it more voracious. Shea watched in horror as flames exploded across the black sweatshirt.

Lynette's scream ripped through the still night.

"Shea!" Suddenly, Derek was there, pulling her out of the way. "You've got starter fluid on you. Stay back."

She struggled in his arms. "Roll," she yelled at Lynette. "Put it out."

Her would-be arsonist just sat there screaming and slapping at the fire that was quickly nearing her shoulder.

All the terror and fright of that night so long ago built up in Shea's chest. She couldn't watch this happen again. When Derek ran to get the garden hose, she hurried back to Lynette. Taking care not to get too close, she shoved her bare foot against the woman's hip. "Roll, Lynette. Drop and roll!"

The woman finally got the message. Flopping like an oxygen-starved fish, she ground her shoulder into the grass.

She sputtered when a stream of water hit her full-on.

"You crazy fucking bitch." Derek doused their assailant before turning the stream of water onto the building. "Shea, are you okay?"

She looked herself over. She didn't see anything smoldering. "I'm fine."

"Are you sure?"

She looked around. No flames leapt into the night sky. Nothing popped or snapped. Smoke still trailed upward, but she could smell fresh air. "I'm okay."

People started to appear, coming out of doorways and leaning out of windows. Her next-door neighbor took over on hose duty, and Derek strode back to her fast.

Shea actually took a step back when she saw the look on his face. He'd told her once that he didn't let his feelings loose very often—but his anger had escaped, and it was hard-boiled. He looked big and tough and out of control.

All for her sake.

When that anger turned toward the woman sitting on the ground, though, she instinctively stepped between them. This was her fight.

She rounded on her attacker. "Why?"

When she got no answer, she dropped down to a crouch so she could look into Lynette's face. "What did I ever do to you?"

This maniac had terrorized her while hiding in the shadows like a coward. She'd made her doubt her rationality, made her think something was wrong with her.

"Why would you do something like this?" Shea asked.

"I have to stop you. You poisoned her. You're poisoning everybody!" Spittle flew from Lynette's lips. She wiped her face where Derek had drenched her and reached to cradle her arm.

Shea's brow furrowed. "Poisoned who? What are you talking about?"

"She was fine until she saw you interviewed on TV. By then it was too late. Your lotion had sunk into her pores. She couldn't get it off no matter how many times she washed."

"What are you talking about?"

A fire truck had arrived, but Lynette shoved away the medic who was trying to look at the burns on her arm. The pain flared, and she doubled over. When he tried to help, she kicked at him instead.

"She knew what you did as a child. She saw how evil controlled you." Lynette tucked her legs underneath her and tried to get to her feet. The grass was slick, though, and she went back down. "She tried to ward you off then, but you came back."

Another whimper left the woman's lips, and she leaned over her arm. Shea looked at it, so red and bright, and her stomach turned. She knew better than most what fire could do to human skin. She reached out. "Here, let me see that."

Lynette lurched back. "Stay away from me."

"I can help."

"No!" Reaching into her pocket, Lynette pulled out a piece of bread. "Begone, demon! Begone."

Shea froze. Everything stopped in that moment. Even the wailing of the sirens faded into the background. "Mrs. Lupescu?"

"The stepmother," Derek said, stepping closer.

Shea swallowed hard. "Is your stepmother Lorna Lupescu?"

"Fromm. Her name was Fromm!"

Shea folded her hands over her face. *Oh, dear God!*

"I saw it with you just now," Lynette hissed. "That Somnambulist was inside you. You've kept it with you all this time."

The fireman pulled back with a strange look on his face.

Shea cleared her throat. "Derek, would you get my briefcase?"

His eyes narrowed.

"Please? I'll be all right."

Shea sat back on her heels and wrapped her arms around her knees. It was like two worlds colliding. She'd done so much to separate her past from her present, but her past wouldn't stay there.

She pressed her lips together. She and Lynette had been fighting the same battle. They'd both been trying to get rid of the parasite inside her, only Lynette hadn't cared if she'd taken her down with it.

Shea's fingers bit into her knees. She'd seen the Somnambulist with Derek. In that split-second between sleep and wakefulness, she'd seen the two of them fighting. After all these years, she'd finally come face to face with it.

An exterior light came on, and she winced. The bulb was bright, and she reached up to dry her eyes.

More firefighting equipment had arrived, as had the police. Officials were checking the condo to make sure the fire was completely out while others talked to witnesses. The fireman who was trying to treat Lynette finally managed to cut off the remains of her sleeve.

Derek's gaze met Shea's as he approached. She couldn't believe she was going to do this.

"Thank you," she said as she took the case.

Her hands shook. Adrenaline was still pumping through her veins. She took a deep breath and focused. "Do you give me permission to treat that burn?"

"What? No!" Lynette pulled back and hugged her arm to her chest. "Keep your evil potions away from me."

"You know it will help." Shea spoke with a calm she really didn't feel. "You've got a degree in chemistry, and you read my lab book."

Lynette's mouth flattened even as tears coursed down her face. Her arm was fiery red. The pain had to be hot.

Shea picked out two vials. "It's a silver ion solution that has antimicrobial, pro-healing, and anti-inflammatory properties for burn wounds. It's not evil. I'm trying to help people, not hurt them. Do you want it or not?"

"You're trying to trick me." Lynette looked away. The throbbing in her arm was so intense, she was rocking back and forth. "Make her go away," she said to the fireman.

"She's trying to poison me."

The fireman pushed his helmet back on his head. The look he shot Shea was sympathetic.

"I should inform you it doesn't yet have FDA approval." Shea waited. When she still didn't get a response, she closed her eyes. "It's the antidote, Lynette."

"What?" Her secretary's head snapped back, and her eyes narrowed.

Shea pushed away all her feelings: her shock, her outrage, and her hurt. "You're right," she whispered. "A Somnambulist has been possessing me all these years. He's made me do evil things, but this is the antidote to all that lotion my company has been selling. If you'll agree not to tell anyone about me, I'll give it to you."

"Liar!" Lynette said. Still, there was a look of hope in her eyes.

Derek dropped down on his haunches beside her. "Mind giving me some of that stuff, Curie? I singed my fingers a bit back there."

His fingers were perfectly fine, but Shea nodded and concentrated on measuring out the correct amounts and mixing the active ingredients.

"You're a bigger person than I am," he said softly.

She glanced toward Lynette. "I hate that the first person I'm helping is the one who tried to burn down my home."

He looked down at the solution in her hands. "That's quite the advancement, Curie."

She swallowed hard. "The wrinkle cream was just an interesting side product. This was what I've been working towards ever since I got my PhD."

She looked into his eyes, needing to share the moment with someone.

He gave her a soft smile. "You're going to help so many people. Your dad will be so proud."

The emotions finally got to her. Leaning closer, Derek wrapped an arm around her shoulder and kissed her temple. For a moment, she pressed her face into the crook of his neck.

Then, gathering herself, she finished the preparatory work she'd done so many times in the lab. She dabbed a bit onto Derek's knuckles. He flexed his fingers and stood.

She looked to Lynette.

The woman's mouth worked.

"Fine," Shea said, turning away.

"Give it to me." Lynette looked ready to cry.

Shea handed the finished product to the fireman. "An occlusive dressing works best, but treat the burn with this first. Sorry, it's a bit messy."

She watched as he did first aid.

Her goal was to aid those who suffered worse burns, those unfortunate victims who now ended up scarred and in pain. She hadn't yet figured out the best delivery method for the treatment, but she was working on it. If only something like this had been available the night of the trailer fire...

She blinked as the wetness came back to her eyes. That was just too much to think about right now.

She focused on putting everything away, but by the time she was done, her whole body was trembling. She pushed herself to her feet and instinctively turned into Derek's arms. He gathered her up close and moved them back into the shadows, away from the crowd.

"She's out of her mind," Shea whispered. It was only hitting her now what had happened. She pressed her face against his chest. "She didn't even think of the other people in the building."

She heard his heart beating under her ear. It was racing fast, just like hers. They both knew the woman had been intent on just one target.

"I should have made the connection," he said.

"How?" Shea dug her fingers into the muscles of his back, and he pressed his cheek against the top of her head. His embrace was tight and protective. "I never knew what happened to Mrs. Lupescu after we moved away."

"I should have spent more time on the background

search."

"You were looking into Lynette's background, not her stepmother's."

"It doesn't matter. I should have been the one to stop her." His fingers tangled in her hair. "I was sleeping in my car. It took me forever to get here."

"No, I needed to be the one to stop her." This had been the fear Shea could face. She'd been fighting against the unseeable for so long. "I just didn't mean to hurt her."

"She meant to hurt you." Derek's voice turned hard. "It was self-defense—and one hell of a punch, by the way."

"When you grow up as the possessed freak of the North Solstice Trailer Park, you learn to defend yourself."

They both looked at the woman sitting and rocking back and forth on the ground.

"She's been watching me sleepwalk. She knew the Somnambulist was back."

Derek rubbed her back gently. "It's over, baby. It's really over."

She glanced up at him. "All of it?"

The night fell silent. Somewhere nearby, a cricket chirped.

"You saw it, didn't you?"

"Yes." If she'd had any doubts left, they were gone. She'd only been in his world for seconds, but she knew all the stories were true. Dream Weavers. Somnambulists...

Her heart squeezed. Those soft, loving eyes. Oh, she didn't want to ask. "Is it... gone?"

"It won't be bothering you anymore. *Neither* of them will."

"But... how will we ever know what really happened?" She watched as the fireman finished up Lynette's dressing. "How will we figure out who did what? Or why?"

"It doesn't matter." Derek hooked a finger under her chin and looked into her eyes. "All I care about is that I've got you to myself, safe and whole."

"Are we really alone?"

"Yes, Curie. It's finally just the two of us." His eyes darkened. "And you won't believe how I'm going to take

212

advantage of that tonight."

CHAPTER SEVENTEEN

"This is all my fault."

Shea looked at Phillip sharply. He was sprawled out in the chair in her living room with his arms hanging limply off the sides. At Derek's insistence, she'd stayed home from work. She hadn't realized that would make everyone at Biodermatics even more concerned. Her partner and her assistant had shown up on her doorstep not long ago.

Phillip, in particular, was not handling things well.

"How can you say that?" she asked. "You were attacked just like me. Worse, in fact. Lynette confessed to it."

"Yes, but you had concerns about hiring her. I was in too much of a hurry to listen." He looked at his shoes morosely. "Next time I question your woman's intuition, just slap me upside the head."

Everyone stared at him in disbelief.

That shook him out of his gloomy mood a bit. Reaching up, he rubbed the knot on the back of his head. "Well, maybe you could make that a gentle nudge."

"Or maybe you should just put me in charge of hiring the office staff," Tamika said.

She crossed her legs, and her foot bumped the stack of cards on the coffee table. The piece of furniture was laden with candy, flowers, and even a teddy bear. Well-wishers and curious neighbors had been dropping by all day.

"Now that's an idea," Phillip said, sounding serious.

Shea snuggled into the corner of the couch and tucked her legs underneath her. She was glad her friends had come. There was still a sense of disconnect about everything. The quicker things got back to normal, the better she would feel.

"If we're taking blame, my name needs to go on the list."

She looked over her shoulder to the kitchen. Derek stood in the doorway. The suit was gone; maybe for good. He looked tough, fit, and thoroughly pissed off with himself.

"I should have dug deeper into that two-year break in Lynette's work history."

"But she did take a break to care for Lorna."

"Right. Lorna Lupescu Fromm, who scared the crap out of you as a child." He clapped his hand against the doorjamb. "I should have caught that there was a connection there."

"How?" Phillip leaned his head back against the plump cushions of the chair. "She changed names, and medical records are sealed."

"Thank goodness," Shea muttered. She knew she didn't want anyone poking around in *her* medical history.

Leaning down, Tamika tore open the bag of Baby Ruths that she'd brought over with her. "I think it's time we broke into these."

Shea sighed, looking at the bag with envy. "Oh, you guys. You know how guilty I feel when I eat those things. If my dad caught me, he'd never watch a Mets game with me again."

Tamika wasn't shy. She picked a snack-sized candy bar out of the bag. "We won't tell. Besides, you deserve a cheat day after what you've been through. Hell, we all do. I wouldn't have gone toe-to-toe with the woman if I'd thought she was capable of burning me out of my home."

Derek came over for a candy bar. He dropped two in her lap, and Shea drifted her fingers across his hand as he walked by. He was still too wound up to sit. "She was the primary caregiver for Mrs. Lupescu—Lorna—for a long time. After a while, sanity must have blurred with superstition."

Phillip rubbed his hands over his face. "Bruce showed me that production schedule. She was trying to shut us down any way she could."

Derek stared hard at a burnt spot on the ground in the backyard, and Shea watched him closely. His face was smooth and emotionless, but she could see the stiffness in the set of his shoulders. He'd told her that his brothers called him "The Machine." He held a lot in sometimes, but there were signs of the emotions going on under the surface. Signs that she was beginning to understand he only let her see...

"She got in once using Phillip's keys," he said. "She must have seen the havoc it caused, but when she came back, we'd changed the locks on the doors." He shook his head. "I think that threw her. When she wasn't able to get inside, she had to improvise. The lighter fluid came from the next-door neighbor's barbecue."

Shea cleared her throat. "Can we all agree that none of this is our fault?"

"I'm all for that." Pulling over the hassock, Tamika propped up her feet. With the short skirt she was wearing, her legs just seemed to go on and on. It was her shoes, though, that caught Shea's attention. She was wearing the zebra stripes.

Sometime shoes were just shoes.

"I didn't like her from the start," her assistant said matter-of-factly.

"Really?" Phillip said. "We couldn't tell."

Derek looked at Tamika. "Why have you stopped running?" he asked.

Her chin jerked up. "I haven't stopped. I've just been too busy to train regularly."

"Doing what?" Shea asked. "Why all the late nights?"

Tamika's eyebrows rose. "Has somebody been watching me, too?"

"Come on," Phillip said dryly. "You've got to admit you've been a little testy."

Their assistant's gaze bounced around, meeting all their

looks. "Have I really been that bad?"

Shea shrugged.

"I'm sorry. I've just been tired." Tamika slumped back against the cushions. "I didn't want to tell you yet, but I've been going to night school."

Shea blinked. "But that's great."

"I might have loaded up too heavily on classes."

Phillip dropped his feet to the floor and sat forward. "What are you taking?"

"Business management." She played with the fringe on the pillow tucked up against her side. "I didn't like it when you hired that twit in at the same level as me. I know she had a background in chemistry, but I've been working at that job for three years. I'm good at it."

She twisted in her seat, obviously emotional. "I know a good thing when I see it. Biodermatics is going places, and I want to be a part of that. I know I can do more. I want to be the office manager."

Shea caught her friend's hand. "I think that's a great idea. You should have let us know. We might be able to work out a more flexible schedule for you."

"Or help with buying books or part of the tuition," Phillip offered.

"Really?" Tamika looked honestly surprised and more than a little touched. "That would be fantastic."

"You deserve it." Shea could have kicked herself for not coming up with the idea on her own. "I'm sorry we've taken you for granted."

"No more of that," Phillip agreed. Gingerly, he rose from his chair. "Why don't we go grab a cup of coffee and talk about it?"

Shea felt Tamika's speculative look sweep over her and Derek. "Yeah, I think it's time we left these two alone."

Shea blushed, but she wrapped her arms around her friend's shoulders when she leaned over to give her a hug.

"I'm so happy you're all right," Tamika whispered. She gave Derek's hand a squeeze, too. "Both of you."

Shea lifted her cheek for Phillip's kiss. Derek escorted their guests to the front door and shook Phillip's hand. When he closed the door and turned, though, that purposeful look was back in his eyes.

Shea let out a long breath. She loved the way he looked at her.

He started to slowly stride back across the room. "Nice people, but I thought they'd never leave."

She stretched out more fully on the sofa. Eyelids heavy, she lay back against the armrest. When he crawled up over her, her hands went naturally to his waist. He kissed her neck, and his weight settled on her more fully.

"Feeling better?" His lips brushed against the lobe of her ear.

"Mm hm," she said. "Those loose threads were bothering me. I'm glad we know everything now."

Pulling up slightly, he looked down into her face. The intensity in his gaze had shifted, and it made her uneasy.

"What is it?" she asked.

"Actually, there's one more thing I have to tell you. Your Somnambulist shared something with me before he... left."

Shea's chest squeezed. "Do I really want to hear this?"

"You do. It's about the fire when you were twelve."

Shea stiffened. It was as if a cool breeze had just blown across the room. It made goosebumps pop up on her skin, and a shiver trickle down her spine. "I don't—"

"You *didn't*."

She went still.

"You didn't set the fire. Neither did your Somnambulist."

Her lips parted. Breathing was suddenly difficult. "I don't understand. How can you be sure?"

"It was an electrical fire. The wall went 'snap, crackle, pop.'"

"What?"

"That's what the Somnie said. Sparks came out of an outlet in your bedroom. You were sleeping and didn't realize what was happening."

Her fingers bit into his waist. "But *it* did?"

Derek closed his eyes and dropped his forehead against hers. "It got you out of that fire, Shea. It wasn't your fault. Somnambulists aren't good for much, but that thing got you out of there."

Her breath caught. "It took me down the stairs to show me what Lynette was doing, too."

"It was trying to look out for you. It was... fond of you."

Tears suddenly pressed at her eyes. "What did we do, Derek? Look at how we repaid it."

He shook his head firmly. "It lived a full life for a Somnambulist. It was ready to go. It knew it was time to give your nights back to you."

The band of tension around her ribs loosened, and then disappeared entirely. He was the one giving her nights back to her. Her nights, her days, her self-confidence, and her love.

She wanted to give him something in return, and she knew what he wanted most.

"Will you sleep with me tonight, my Oneiros?"

The darkness in his eyes intensified. She could feel his muscles tensing and his heart pounding.

She smiled up at him. They hadn't slept all night, and he'd waited such a long time.

"Sleep," she whispered. Gently, she stroked her hands along his back. "All night long, in my bed and at my side? Will you watch over me from the dream realm?"

With a groan, he leaned down and kissed her.

"Curie, I thought you'd never ask."

THE DREAM WEAVERS

They are the Oneiroi, Greek daemons of dreams. As dream weavers, their mission is to watch over sleeping humans—for without dreams, chaos can reign. So the Oneiros brothers blend in with the waking world by day and watch over their charges by night, protecting humans from the creatures who would prey upon their sleep. But what happens when the Oneiroi have dreams of their own? And what if they fall in love with those they're duty-bound to protect—or the enemies they've sworn to fight?

DREAM RIDER
Dream Weavers, Book 3

As a Dream Weaver, Zane Oneiros isn't supposed to hitch rides on the dreams of his charges, but he can't help himself when the dreamer is Emily Hutchins. Beautiful Emily is his work friend, but in her dreams, Zane wonders if he can find more. When they share a kiss, everything changes. In her dreams, and in the waking world. Cautious Emily becomes more daring, and Zane worries that meddling with her dreams may be the cause. Soon he's battling to get the old Emily back and make their dreams turn real, not the nightmares.

EXCERPT FROM DREAM RIDER

Emily sat at the picnic table looking girl-next-door pretty in her sneakers, jeans, and High Score T-shirt. So pretty, it made Zane ache. She had her chestnut-colored hair half up in a clip, with the rest tumbling down her back. It wasn't long, and it wasn't short. It was just the right length to swing around her shoulders as she moved.

And when it came to the way she moved—

Her brown gaze landed on him, catching him mid-fantasy, and he rubbed the back of his neck. Sighing, he headed back to the table.

She started to climb off the bench, but he wasn't ready to go yet. He so rarely got her out of the office. Yeah, he took her to lunch all the time, but she was always on such a set schedule. A salesman and a project manager? The two didn't mix well.

But damn, how he wanted to mix.

Climbing up on the picnic table, he sat atop it and watched a kid obviously new to motocross attempt the baby jump in front of the bleachers. The afterschool crowd was starting to show up. The kid made it, even though he had to put his foot out on the landing to balance himself. That was how you learned—by falling down and getting back up, not by stopping yourself from trying in the first place.

But he'd already tried so many times with her.

"You think Larimer's still interested?" she asked. "Even after all the liability stuff?"

The guy was interested, all right. Zane did his best not to snarl.

"He owns a company. He knows about lawyers and HR, and all that comes with it." Zane rolled his head on his neck. "I know I went around the system, and I shouldn't have. I just ran across this biking thing in his bio. It was something we have in common, and yeah, it was a way in. But more so, it sounded like a good time."

"I know." Climbing up onto the table, Emily took a seat

next to him. "Sitting in the office at a desk isn't your thing, and it shouldn't be. Kevin doesn't like it when his salespeople spend too much time in the office."

Kevin was their CEO and, fortunately, his biggest supporter. The guy knew that deals were made where the clients were.

Zane shook his head. "I'm sorry they sent you out here to rein me in. It's not your job."

"*I'm* sorry I have the crossing-guard personality that lets them use me like that." She watched a chipmunk as it discovered a tortilla chip that had fallen off their table. "I wish I could be more fun."

"You're fun."

She let out a laugh that disagreed.

He nudged her with his shoulder. "Stick with me, kid."

She gave him a weak smile. "I'm serious."

"So am I."

The newbie appeared again as he finished his first lap around the track, only the kid wasn't being aggressive enough on his half-sized bike. He went up for the jump at about half the speed he needed to, and... *splat.*

"Oh, no." Emily flinched. "Not the mud."

"It will cool him down." Before the stuff dried out and got all itchy. Zane knew from experience.

They both sat there, primed to go help, but the kid waved off a park employee. He pulled his bike off the course, scraped the mud off his goggles, and climbed right back on.

"Are you really going to go riding with Larimer again?" she asked as the kid zipped up the incline with more determination.

"Sure." Zane loved to ride, and he wasn't going to let his employer, of all things, stop him. So maybe he couldn't do it as a replacement for a sales meeting. They couldn't dictate what he did in his free time.

"He acted like Comet Tail was something different."

"It is." Zane nodded to the track. "This is motocross. It's a race on a closed route with planned obstacles. Trail riding is just like it sounds, riding on trails out in the countryside where it's allowed, like Comet Tail Park. The bikes are different, too, but you probably don't care about that."

"Out in the country? What if you have an accident? There's nobody around like here." She pointed at the park attendant who was now handing a towel to another racer who'd come off the track.

She sighed. "Sorry. There I go again." She eyed him up and down. "At least you're wearing more protective gear than I expected."

Zane liked having her gaze on him, but he was surprised when it got stuck on his riding boots. His boots? Really? Excitement lit in his gut. "Do you want to try it out?"

"What?" she squeaked.

Oh yeah. She'd slipped with that look, and he'd caught her. "Take a ride around the track? I could teach you."

"Me? Out there?" She laughed nervously. "In my dreams."

And, just like that, his excitement centered in his crotch. "I can make that happen."

Her eyebrows lifted. "Well, that's bold, but you can't get inside my head as easily as you do with other people, Zane Oneiros."

She had no idea what he could do once night fell, and people drifted off to sleep. "How much do you want to bet? Lunch?"

"On what?"

"That I'll get you on a dirt bike tonight in your dreams."

The look she gave him was flabbergasted. "Why would you make that bet? You won't know if it happened or not. All I'd have to do is tell you I didn't dream. You'd never know."

"I'd know."

Time slowed in that moment, and her breath hitched.

"Come on, Em. That's what dreams are for, trying new things and working through your fears."

"I'm not scared. I'm... I'm thinking through all the angles. Why are we even talking about this?"

His gaze dropped to her lips. Because they never talked

223

about this... and sometimes you had to stop thinking and jump.

ABOUT THE AUTHOR

When taking the Myers-Briggs personality test in high school, Kimberly was rated as an INFJ (Introverted-Intuitive-Feeling-Judging). This result sent her into a panic, because there were no career paths recommended for the type. Fortunately, it turned out to be well-suited to a writing career. Since receiving that dismal outlook, Kimberly has become an award-winning author of romance and erotica. She has written for seven publishing houses, both domestic and international, and has recently focused her efforts on the exciting world of self-publishing. When not writing, she enjoys movies, sports, traveling, music, and sunshine.

Learn more about Kimberly's books and sign up for her newsletter at https://kimberlydean.com.

www.ingramcontent.com/pod-product-compliance
Lightning Source LLC
Chambersburg PA
CBHW050520260626
47157CB00004B/1397

* 9 7 8 0 9 8 4 6 5 1 1 9 1 *